MERCY

BY

GENE HALE

Order this book online at www.trafford.com
or email orders@trafford.com

Most Trafford titles are also available at major online book retailers.

Printed in the United States of America.

ISBN: 978-1-4669-6816-5 (sc)
ISBN: 978-1-4669-6817-2 (e)

Library of Congress Control Number: 2012921376

Trafford rev. 11/08/2012

 www.trafford.com

North America & international
toll-free: 1 888 232 4444 (USA & Canada)
phone: 250 383 6864 ♦ fax: 812 355 4082

1

Chapter 1

It was a cool, sunny morning in the forest located in the Upper Peninsula of Michigan.   Shafts of sunlight pierced the tall, sturdy trees, casting dark shadows on the ground. A soft warming breeze would soon turn the chill air into a beautiful, summer day.

A timber wolf rambled out of the woods, looked around and continued on his way. The birds chirped in the quiet, cool air. A raccoon sat in the dewy grass, washing his glossy fur with his front paws. Suddenly, the timber wolf stopped in his tracks, the birds stopped chirping and the raccoon ceased his ablutions and lifted his head. They had heard the noise of a Jeep coming up a small path entering the forest.

Inside the Jeep sat three sturdy looking men wearing red, white and blue sweatbands around their foreheads. It was Gil Aller and his two uncles, Dan and Eric, three lumberjacks on their way to work.

"Hi, Ho, Hi, Ho," sang Uncle Dan, tapping the steering wheel.

Gil and his Uncle Eric joined in with, "Hi, Ho, Hi, Ho. Off to work we go." They were letting the animals know that soon the forest would be bristling with the sound of saws and shouts of "Timber," as the big trees were felled and cut into different sizes.

The Aller men, experienced lumberjacks like their fathers and grandfathers before them, were the first to arrive on the job. Old Harry Clemens pulled up five minutes later, clutching his trusty harmonica. The four men sat around drinking coffee and talking about the latest sports results. Their favorite baseball team, the Detroit Tigers, had lost again.

Old Harry pulled out his harmonica and started playing a lively, peppy song. The Aller men loved to dance. Uncle Dan started hopping and jumping to the beat of the music; soon he was joined by Gil and Eric. Forming a line, they kicked their legs high like the Radio City Music Hall Rockettes. Then they broke away from each other, leaping on tree stumps and fallen trees, dancing in step to the music. A wooden table stood nearby. Jumping on top of it, Gil and Uncle Dan grabbed each other by the arms and danced in a circle.

"There's nothing like a good kicking time to get your body moving in the morning," shouted Uncle Dan.

"Yes, sirree," yelled Gil, moving his body in rhythm to the music.

A few moments later, Mike Carter, the foreman, drove up and jumped out of his truck, clapping his hands. "I want you to save some of that strength for the job," he said with a chuckle. Mike walked over to Gil and put his arm around his shoulder. "So today's your last day with us," he said. "We're sure gonna miss you, but if things don't work out in New York, you'll always have a job here." Gil smiled. "Your mother was telling me that you're hoping to get a job dancing in a Broadway show," continued Mike. "I'm not much into dancing myself, but you Aller boys can sure move and dance. I hear there's gonna be a big going-away party for you back by the pond on Sunday."

Gil and his family lived on a 300-acre farm, where they grew wheat and corn. A long, circular dirt path led to a pond on the back of the property. Gil enjoyed spending time at the pond on hot summer days, where he could cool off and enjoy the tranquil environment.

"That's right," Gil replied, "and you better show up with your wife and kids. It's going to be a pig roast and everyone's invited. Some of my uncle's friends are camping out back by the pond already getting the area cleaned up. There'll be plenty to eat and drink, so make sure you come."

Mike nodded. "We'll be there,' he said as they all piled into the back of a big, blue pickup truck, belonging to their employers, Dennis & Dale Co., and headed back into the forest. They would be working "Section Fourteen," today. Small, wooden signs marked the trees to be cut down. For each tree felled, one would be planted. The company knew how important trees were to the environment; so they donated money to an organization called Save the Environment.

The day had now turned hot and humid, with little breeze. Stripping to the waist, the Allers grabbed the chainsaws and set about felling the towering trees, one after the other. Sweat glistened on their strong, muscular frames – all three were powerfully built men. Gil stood six feet tall, with broad shoulders and slim hips, and rock hard arms like steel rods. A shock of short, blond hair framed his finely chiseled face and his piercing blue eyes crinkled when he smiled, revealing perfect white teeth.

The day finally came to an end and Gil walked up to the rest of the workers; he shook hands with all twenty, and wished them the best. Some of the men had tears in their eyes; Gil was popular among his co-workers, and a good friend – they would miss him.

"Take care of yourself in the Big Apple," they cautioned, "it's a far cry from the good old Iron Mountain region. Just watch your back." They had heard some bad things about New York, and hoped Gil wasn't making a big mistake in going there. "See you at the pig roast on Sunday."

On Saturday, Gil and his family started preparing for the party. They set up tables, chairs, horseshoes and a volleyball net. Guests could go swimming or fishing in the pond. Or, if they wanted to sun themselves, they could lie on a float, out in the middle of the pond. For shade, they could sit under the three tall maple and oak trees. A wide variety of foods would be served, including pasta, sauerbraten, chili, hamburgers, hot dogs and homemade pies and cakes. And for liquid refreshment, the Allers had secured four kegs of beer on tap, along with a selection of wine, soda, iced tea and refreshing lemonade.

Early Sunday morning, after a hearty breakfast of bacon and eggs and home fries, the Allers set off for church. Father Wenz would be saying Mass this morning. Gil liked the priest for his devotion to the church, and for his keen sense of humor. He could still hear Father Wenz's first Mass; "I have an easy name to remember. W for west, E for east, N for north and Z for 'zouth.' "

At 5'7", with a medium build and thin graying hair, Father Wenz exuded warmth and compassion. Just looking at his soft brown eyes, the parishioners knew that they could trust him, that he cared about them. His sunny smile and outgoing personality made him a favorite of all, especially Gil. "We'll see you at the pig roast, Father," said Gil, shaking Father Wenz's hand as he left the church after the service.

"I'll be there, Gil," replied the priest, his brown eyes twinkling.

After Mass, Gil and his family stood outside the church and talked to their friends. At nineteen, Gil was the youngest of five. He had one brother, Ray, who was thirty years old, and three sisters: Violet, twenty-eight, Florence, twenty-six and Elaine, twenty-two. Elaine was away at college and wouldn't be coming to the party. Gil made sure that everyone had been invited to the pig roast. If they couldn't make it, then Gil shook their hand and told them, "I will see you when I come home." The Aller family was well liked in the community.

On returning home, Gil and Ray strolled down to the pond and put the beer kegs and soda on ice. Although still early, the temperature had already soared into the seventies.

"It's gonna be a scorcher," said Ray, squinting up at the sun, blazing down from a cloudless sky. "Everyone's gonna be dry and thirsty."

Gil nodded his head in agreement. "Yep, and most of our friends are coming straight from church, so we better make sure everything is ready," said Gil. He peered down the driveway and saw three cars heading toward the pond. "In fact, some of them are here now! Let's party!"

An hour later the pond area was packed with guests. Kids were swimming in the pond under the watchful eye of two adults. Some people were playing horseshoes, others, volleyball; a few went fishing. Later in the afternoon there would be a softball game.

The shade trees provided welcome cover from the hot sun. The beer was going fast, so fast, in fact, that Ray had to go into town and buy another keg. Fortunately, there was plenty of soda and wine back at the house. Gil was carving the pig. "Can't you go any faster?" his friends joked. We're starving!"

Gil laughed, a twinkle in his blue eyes. "Hey, there's plenty of cake and pie over there," he said, pointing to a picnic table set up by the pond.

Despite the festivities, nobody knew how sad Gil was feeling. As he looked at his mother and his siblings, an aching emptiness filled his heart. He thought about his father who had died in a car accident when Gil was one. Except for some faded photos that his mother kept in a music box, Gil never really knew his father. But he often found himself wondering about him.

How can I leave them? he thought to himself. *I'll tell them I've changed my mind about going to New York.* But deep down, Gil knew that he had to go; he had to try to make it as a dancer, even if it meant failing. He knew that if he didn't go now, he never would. Shaking his head sadly, he looked around at all his friends, at his beloved family, and realized that he might never see them again.

Eleven o'clock. The party was slowly starting to break up. As Gil bid farewell to his final guests, a part of him silently wished that the party could go on forever. "I will carry this night in my heart always," he murmured softly.

Chapter 2

Monday was cleaning up day. The party had been a huge success -- everyone had had a marvelous time. Ray took a few days off from work to help clean up and to spend some time with Gil, before he left for New York. Down by the pond, Ray found a couple of bottles of wine, and the two brothers settled down to enjoy the afternoon and polish off the wine. They brought their three dogs with them: Ginger, a collie, Adam, a German shepherd, and McGiver, a golden Labrador retriever. The dogs frolicked in the pond, while Gil and Ray relaxed nearby, in two chairs.

They talked about Gil's imminent departure for New York. Gil would be leaving early on Tuesday morning. He planned on taking his time and spending the first night at a motel, before heading into New York. Ray and his family were worried about Gil's going off to a strange city, where he didn't know anybody, and especially about the crime. They had heard horror stories about muggings, robberies and shootings, and they didn't want Gil to become another statistic.

"Take care of yourself, little brother," said Ray. "New York is a big city and you don't know a soul. Are you sure you won't change your mind about going? We're sure gonna miss you."

Gil patted his brother on the shoulder. "Don't worry about me, Ray," he said reassuringly. "I'll be fine. This is something I have to do, otherwise I'll be wondering all my life, 'if only...if only...'"

Ray nodded. He understood. Ever since they were small boys, his brother had always had a wandering spirit.

Tuesday morning came quickly and Gil had everything packed and ready to go. His closest friends and family members gathered around his car, a Ford Galaxy. Gil shook hands with all the men and hugged and kissed all the women as they wished him good luck and Godspeed. Gil's mother was worried about her beloved son, but she knew he had to go so he could pursue his dream.

"May God watch over you and keep you safe, until we meet again," she said, her eyes filling with tears. She handed him two red, white and blue sweatbands. "Wear them for luck."

Gil threw his arms around her and held her close, brushing the tears from her eyes. "Don't worry, Mother, I'll be fine," he whispered. "I'll call as soon as I'm settled, and I'll be back to visit before you know it."

Gil's grandmother walked out of the house and handed him two cherry

pies, his favorite. They were fresh out of the oven, and still warm.

"You'll have to come back home to get more," she said. "And watch out

for the pits," she chuckled as Gil placed the pies in the back of his car.

Gil was ready to leave. Bidding everyone a last farewell, he jumped into

his car, started the engine and drove slowly down the driveway. With his left hand

on the steering wheel, he waved goodbye with his right hand. A little boy ran

after the car and Gil stopped so the boy could hand him a red, white and blue

sweatband. Then, with a final wave, Gil made a right turn out of the driveway.

He was on his way to the Big Apple.

As he stepped on the gas pedal, Gil wondered what New York City would

be like. He decided to take Interstate 75, which circled Detroit, in order to avoid

all the traffic. Although it was after rush hour, there were still plenty of cars and

trucks on the road. From the Interstate, he drove onto Route 80, in Ohio, and

headed toward New York City.

Gil spent the night in Pennsylvania Dutch country. It was his first

encounter with the Amish, and he found them to be a warm and friendly people.

After thanking them for their hospitality, Gil waved goodbye and continued on his

journey.

He followed the signs pointing toward New York, finally arriving about

noon. Gil's eyes widened in amazement at all the traffic clogging the streets, at the sea of yellow taxis weaving in out, the drivers frantically beeping their horns, and at the crowds of people bustling along the sidewalks. This was a whole new world to Gil. He looked up at the tall buildings and thanked God for cement. *There wouldn't be enough trees in the whole United States to build these big boys,* he thought to himself.

Gil noticed that most of the streets went one-way. He wasn't used to that, nor was he used to all the traffic lights, and the people and taxicabs swarming around him like bees. In his state of confusion and bewilderment, he almost ran a red light. Taxicab drivers were yelling and cursing at him. And when two taxicabs cut him off, Gil had no choice but to turn down a one-way street. Luckily for him, no cars were approaching. He had driven halfway down the street, when a police officer walked off the sidewalk and put his hand up for Gil to stop.

The police officer, a jolly-looking man, with a round face and a ruddy complexion, walked over to the driver's side of the car and said, "Do you have a problem with one-way streets, because you just happen to be going the wrong way on one?"

"I'm sorry, officer, I didn't realize it was a one-way street until it was too late. I was looking for a driveway so I could turn around."

The policeman asked for Gil's driver license. Then he pointed to the sweatband around Gil's head and said, "What's with the red, white and blue thing on your head?"

"Well, I used to be a lumberjack. My mother and grandmother made it for me, to keep the sweat out of my eyes. And my whole family is very patriotic."

"A lumberjack from Michigan," the officer said as he walked to the back of Gil's car to check the license plate. "How long have you been in New York?"

"About fifteen minutes, officer," replied Gil.

The police officer chuckled and said, "I have to give you a ticket."

I only have so much money with me, Gil thought to himself. He had two hundred dollars in his wallet. "How much is this going to cost me?" he asked.

The officer turned toward Gil and said, "They will probably drop a dime on you."

"A dime? How much is a dime?" asked Gil.

"You don't know how much a dime is?" replied the police officer.

"Never heard of it," said Gil.

The police officer looked dumbfounded. "If you don't know what a dime is, then forget about the ticket."

Gil was incredulous. He walked over to the policeman and thanked him.

"All right," said the cop, "now get this car turned around and enjoy the rest of your stay in New York."

As Gil drove back down the street he thought about his worried family back home in Michigan. "Gee, I've only been in New York half an hour and I already met a nice person."

For the next few hours, Gil drove around the city, looking for a place to stay. He spotted a big Catholic Church, and decided to stop and talk with the monsignor. Parking his car a block away, Gil walked to the church and rang the rectory bell and waited for someone to answer. The door opened and a tiny gray-haired lady asked Gil if she could help him.

"I've just arrived in New York," he said, "would it be possible to see the monsignor for a few minutes?"

"Please come in and sit down, " she said with a kindly smile." I will check to see if the monsignor is available."

Gil took a seat. A few minutes later, the lady returned and beckoned for Gil to follow her to the monsignor's office. Once inside, she pointed to a hard back seat by the window. "Please be seated, the monsignor will be with you shortly." And she left the office, closing the door behind her.

Gil sat, and glanced around the monsignor's office. In the corner stood a fish tank with brightly-colored fish – black angelfish, goldfish, sunfish – swimming around. Bookshelves lined the walls filled with a myriad of books. Gil noticed that most of them were bibles, and books on theology. A large crucifix hung on the wall by a big redwood desk, with a red leather chair.

The door opened and in walked the monsignor, a balding middle-aged man with a friendly smile. "Good afternoon, young man, I'm Father O'Leary, how may I help you?" he said. The two men shook hands, and Father O'Leary sat down opposite Gil.

"Good afternoon, Father," Gil replied. "My name is Gil Aller, and I have a little problem."

"What could that be?" the monsignor asked. "You look to be in perfect health."

"I've just arrived in New York. I came here to be a dancer, and I'm hoping to get a job in a Broadway show," Gil told him.

"Do you have any friends or relatives in New York?" asked Father O'Leary.

"No, I don't know a single person in New York - my whole family is back in Michigan."

"Well, you came to the right place as far as dancing is concerned. But New York can be a rough and sometimes dangerous place for a stranger. I would suggest that you go back home to your family in Michigan, where you'll be safe."

"I'm sorry, Father, but all my life, I've wanted to be a dancer. I have to try and make my dream come true."

Father O'Leary noted the look of determination in Gil's piercing blue eyes, and smiled.

"I like your spirit, my son, and I can see your mind is set. Now, is there any other way I can help you? Do you have a place to stay?"

Gil shook his head. "No, Father."

The priest walked over to his desk and picked up a copy of *the New York Daily News*. Turning the pages, until he came to the classified section, he scribbled down a few names on a piece of paper. "Here," he said, handing the paper to Gil, "you're going to need a place to stay, so I have written down a few places that I know. One place had a room available the other day. The owners, Mary and Bob Keely, come to my church; they have clean rooms, and are decent, hard-working people. Go straight down the street to the stop sign and then make a right onto Twenty-fourth Street and Second Avenue and go to the middle of the block," said the monsignor, pointing in the direction that Gil should go.

Gil stood and grasped the priest's hand. "Father, thank you for your help, I really appreciate what you have done for me."

"You are more than welcome, my son" replied Father O'Leary. "By the way, are you Catholic?"

"Yes, Father, I'm Catholic and I will see you on Sunday for Mass," he said.

Father O'Leary smiled, and made the sign of the cross. " May God be with you," he said.

"And with you, Father," said Gil as he turned to leave.

"Oh, and Gil…" said the monsignor, a twinkle in his green eyes.

"Yes, Father?"

"I like your red, white and blue sweatband."

Gil reached his car before the time on the meter expired and headed for the Keelys' rooming house. Father O'Leary had written down two other places, but Gil was hoping that the Keelys still had a room available. He liked what the monsignor had told him about them. Gil found the rooming house easily. After circling around the block a few times, looking for a parking spot, he parked the car, then walked up to the front door and rang the bell.

A thin lady with black hair swept up in a bun answered the door. "Hello," she said with the hint of an Irish brogue. "And what can I be doing for you, young man?"

Gil introduced himself and told her about his visit with Father O'Leary. "He told me that you might still have a room available," he said. "I just got into New York this morning and I need a place to stay. I came all the way from Michigan and I want to become a dancer in a Broadway show."

Mrs. Keely smiled. She liked the look of Gil, with his shock of blond hair and eyes as blue as the ocean; the way he stood, so tall and straight, which belied the fact that he was shy and trusting. She surveyed his long, thin face with the solid square jaw, his warm smile, revealing teeth as white as pearls. "Do you have a job?" she asked.

"I've only been in New York for about six hours…" Gil paused, "but I do have money," he said, patting his wallet. "My savings," he added quietly.

"Well, I usually don't take people without a job, but you look like a decent lad," she said, smiling, "so I'll make an exception. The florist down the street is looking for a driver," Mrs. Keely suggested.

"I will be down there at 9:00 tomorrow morning. Besides, I also need money for dancing lessons. Gil shook her hand warmly. "Thank you very much, Mrs. Keely. This will save me from looking all over New York City for a job."

"You're very welcome, and I am quite sure that the owner, Mr. Gree, will be glad to have you for a driver. You do a have a driver's license?" asked Mrs. Keely.

"Yes I do, Mrs. Keely, and I have driven trucks and vans, so there should be no problem."

"Good, I am glad to hear that. Now, let me show you to your room."

The room was about the size of a child's room. A twin bed stood near the window, next to a night table with a three-way glass lamp. Opposite sat a sturdy oak desk and matching chair and dresser. *This will do nicely*, thought Gil to himself. Mrs. Keely then showed Gil the bathroom, which he would share with the other boarders. Small but clean, it had a bathtub and shower, and a large wooden framed mirror hung on one of the walls, over the sink. Gil chuckled at the signs placed over the toilet: "Please Flush After Every Occasion," and over the bathtub: Leave it Clean Like You Found it."

Next, Mrs. Keely led Gil to a small kitchen, which all the boarders shared. Clean and compact, it contained a table with two chairs, a refrigerator and a stove. Opening the refrigerator door, she pointed to the bottom shelf. "This will be your shelf," she said. "And.," she added, rummaging around in her pocket, "here is your key. Why don't you fetch your things and get settled."

Gil smiled as he took the key. He decided that he liked Mrs. Keely. *We will have a good relationship,* he thought as he bounded down the steps of the rooming house. *I hope my luck holds and the florist hires me tomorrow.*

It took Gil about one hour to put away his clothing and to set up a few personal items, such as a toothbrush, toothpaste, a razor and after shave lotion. Gil heard a knock on his door. It was Mrs. Keely. "My husband gets home at five o'clock. I want you to join us for a cup of tea and a piece of pie about six o'clock."

At 6:00, after Gil had eaten his dinner at a diner down the block, he had tea with Bob and Mary Keely. Mr. Keely had wisps of gray hair around his temples and the back of his head, but the top of his head was bald. Bob was a self-employed carpenter, so it was up to his wife, Mary, to run the boarding house. Gil considered himself lucky: the boarding house was clean, the Keelys were decent folk, and he appreciated the fact that Mrs. Keely ran the place with an iron fist. He was happy that he had taken the monsignor's advice and made the Keelys' place his first stop.

That evening, Gil took a stroll down the street to locate the florist shop, and to check out the surrounding neighborhood. He found a laundromat, a grocery store, a dry cleaners, a pizza parlor, a luncheonette, a hardware store and a couple of bars. The night air felt cool and refreshing. Gil spotted the florist shop, with the sign "Driver Wanted," in the window. Timing his walk back to the rooming house, he raced upstairs to his room and set his alarm clock for 7:30 am. He would be ready and waiting by the florist shop when it opened.

Chapter 3

Gil awoke to the ringing sound of the alarm. Wiping the sleep from his eyes, he snapped off the alarm and jumped out of bed, eager to start the day. After showering and shaving, he dressed for the interview, opting to wear a pair of blue jeans and a blue and white striped shirt. On his way to the florist, he stopped at the luncheonette for a cup of coffee and a bagel with cream cheese. Gil thought that it might be a good idea if he was a little late, to give the florist time to open up for the day. After finishing his coffee, he walked briskly down the street to the florist shop. A bright, red neon sign displayed the name *Green's Florist,* in green lettering.

Gil entered the shop and greeted the pretty, young woman standing behind the counter. "Good morning," he said.

"Good morning," she replied, "can I help you?"

"Yes, I'm here for the driver's job. I hope it's still open."

"Yes, it's still open. Let me get the boss."

A stately man with a mustache walked out. "I'm Bob Green, the owner," he said, offering his hand. "You're here for the driving position?"

"Yes, sir," Gil answered, stepping up to the counter to introduce himself. He liked the florist's strong handshake. Bob Green looked Gil straight in the eyes and asked, "Do you have a driver's license and can you read a *Hagstrom's* map?"

Gil nodded. "Yes, sir."

"Well, then, you got the job."

Gil was taken aback by the florist's quick decision. "I just arrived from Michigan yesterday," Gil replied, "and I don't know much about flowers."

The florist looked at Gil and said, "Do you want the job or don't you?"

"Yessir," he replied quickly. "When do you want me to start?"

"Let's say in about fifteen minutes. I'm working on a couple of arrangements and they will be ready in half an hour. Go have yourself a cup of coffee. But first, come into the back and we'll talk about your wages."

Gil was satisfied with the salary that the florist offered him. Ten dollars an hour would cover his rent and food, and he'd have a little money left over for himself. Gil couldn't believe his luck - he'd been in the city less than 24 hours and already he had a job, a place to stay, and he had met some interesting people. *After all,* Gil thought, *I really don't know how to arrange flowers and I really don't know the streets, yet. I am happy just to have a job.*

Gil soon settled into a comfortable routine. He enjoyed working for the florist, and on his days off, he started looking for a job as a dancer. On some evenings, Gil would stop at one of the neighborhood pubs and have a few drinks. His favorite place was aptly named *Your Favorite Place*. Gil liked it the best because it had a dance floor and he could dance to keep in shape. He had no problem getting girls to dance with him, once they saw how he moved on the dance floor. Gil put on quite a show, dancing the salsa and the tango. His long, muscular arms and legs allowed him to move gracefully and smoothly around the dance floor.

Most of the men, however, didn't care for him too much. They considered Gil to be a show off, and were jealous of him and his dancing acumen. Yet one look at his strong, muscular body and piercing blue eyes told them that he wasn't a man to mess with, especially when it came to women and fighting.

Gil respected women. After all, he had a mother, a grandmother and three sisters. He had gotten into many fights at school when some of the bullies had disrespected his sisters, calling them "whores and bitches." Gil felt that every man should respect women.

He had been working at the florist for a few months now, and had become very friendly with Corinne, the pretty girl who worked behind the counter. Slim and petite, with shoulder length brown hair and green eyes, Corinne also liked to dance. Gil had told her about *Your Favorite Place*, and they would meet there at the weekend and dance the night away, gliding across the dance floor together like two birds in flight. Gil had told her about his desire to be dancer in a Broadway Show and she prayed that his dream would come true.

One Friday night Gil arrived at the club a little late. Taking a seat at the bar, he ordered a beer and looked around for Corinne. The place was packed; couples swept across the dance floor, their bodies swaying rhythmically as the band belted out a lively tune. As Gil sipped his beer, he noticed two men at the end of the bar, one white, the other Hispanic. They were cursing loudly, but Gil paid no attention to them - Mike, the bartender, would take care of any problems that arose at the club. Gil didn't know that the white man had asked Corinne to dance earlier and she had turned him down. He wasn't too happy about her answer.

The man's name was Lenny, and he had just been released from prison, after serving five years for assault and battery. Carlos, his Hispanic friend, was also an ex-con, who had served time for stabbing another man with an ice pick. The two men had been cellmates.

"The bitch wouldn't dance with me," Lenny told Carlos, grabbing his glass and taking a swig of beer.

"Did you really think she would dance with you, bra?" said Carlos. "You're not good enough for her, and besides that, you got no class, bra."

"Shut the hell up," said Lenny, slamming his glass on the countertop. "And I suppose you do? You have the class of a moron, but I'll tell you one thing I got that you don't."

"Yeah, what's that, bra?" asked Carlos.

"I got guts, and I'm gonna have a dance with that bitch before the night is over, or my name's not Lenny."

Carlos started laughing and coughing on his drink.

"What the hell are ya laughing at?" Lenny demanded to know.

"I'm trying to think of your new name," Carlos said, still laughing.

Lenny leapt to his feet, his face bright red with anger. "One more smart remark from you," he said, shaking his fist angrily, "and I'm gonna knock your teeth out."

"All right, all right, bra, calm down," said Carlos. He pulled on Lenny's arm. "Sit down and I'll buy you a drink."

Lenny pointed his finger at Carlos. "And I'm damn tired of you calling me 'bra.' Learn how to speak English and start calling me 'bro' not 'bra.' Ya hear me, Carlos, I'm tired of it."

"All right, bra," said Carlos, still tugging on Lenny's arm, "let's have that drink and forget everything."

Exasperated, Lenny threw up his hands in the air and plunked down on the stool. "I give up, he'll never learn how to say 'bro.' Hey, bartender, give me a double shot," he shouted.

Mike sauntered down the bar toward them. "Hey, guys, keep the noise down," he said. "I think both of you should go in the men's room and loosen up your bras," he chuckled. Hearing Mike's joke, the people seated nearby started laughing.

Lenny stood and turned toward them. "Very funny, very funny, the laugh's on us," he said, his face unsmiling. Then he turned back to Mike. "Okay, funny guy, give us a drink, and make mine a double. And take the money from him," he said, looking at Carlos.

Mike nodded. "Just keep it down, okay?"

"We're cool, man," said Carlos. "We're cool, just give us the drinks."

Gil watched the exchange from his seat at the bar and ordered another drink. "Another beer, please, Mike," he said, raising his glass. "Looks as if you've got your hands full with those two." He nodded toward Lenny and Carlos who were still arguing loudly.

"Yeah, you got that right," agreed Mike. "I'm gonna keep a close eye on them. Any trouble and they're out the door."

As Gil sipped his beer, Corinne tapped his shoulder and sat down next to him. "Hi," she said brightly. "I was beginning to wonder what happened to you. Have you found a job as a dancer?"

"Sorry I'm late," he replied. "I've found a small job dancing for a band that plays at Dandy's, that big place on the corner. I'll be dancing there next Friday and Saturday, just to get the crowd in the mood to dance."

"Oh, that's wonderful, Gil. I'll make sure I'm there. And I'll bring along a few friends," Corinne said.

Gil smiled. "I appreciate that, Corinne. I need all the help I can get." The two friends chatted for a while, then Gil asked Corinne to dance. And linking arms, they strolled out into the middle of the dance floor and danced the salsa.

Carlos noticed the couple as they glided across the floor. He nudged Lenny. "Hey, bra, look, your girlfriend is dancing with that guy with the red, white and blue sweatband."

Lenny swiveled around and glared at Gil and Corinne. "Can I help it if I'm not a fag?" he said.

"It's like I told you, you're not good enough for her, bra," taunted Carlos. "And you got no class."

Lenny's face turned deep red. "Shut the hell up, asshole! I don't see you asking anyone to dance, gutless one!" he barked. "Like I said, I'll be dancing with that broad before the night is over."

The song ended and Gil and Corinne walked back to the bar. They continued their conversation about Gil's new dancing job. "I have to wear a costume, and they're gonna call me *The Maskette*," Gil said. They both laughed.

"Sounds really exciting, Gil," Corinne said. "I can't wait until Friday night. What time do you go on?"

"About ten or a little…" Gil stopped in mid-sentence when he saw Lenny standing behind Corinne, a wild look in his eyes.

Lenny asked Corinne to dance. "I'm sorry, but I'm busy right now," she said.

"Oh, yeah, I can see you're busy talking and dancing with this fag with the sissy sweatband on his head," he sneered, pointing at Gil. "Betcha don't know what it's like to dance with a real man."

Mike walked out from behind the bar. "Hey, pal, I won't tell you again, keep it down or you're outta here," he said to Lenny.

Lenny threw Mike a nasty look and stomped back to his seat.

"That's the smallest amount of guts I've seen all day, bra," said Carlos.

"Will you shut the fuck up? And stop calling me 'bra.' You're starting to piss me off, bigtime."

Sitting at the far end of the bar were a short, stocky man called Louie Costello, and his friend, Huey Shorter, a tall, black man. Partners in the nearby L&H Gym, they trained and promoted boxers. Louie, streetwise and savvy, was the promoter and manager; Huey, an ex-boxer and former contender for the heavyweight championship of the world, was the trainer. Financially, the two friends were down on their luck, barely hanging on by a shoestring. Artie Garcia was their best fighter, and he was only rated in the top ten. They needed a big break, and they needed it soon.

Louie and Huey often frequented the pub. They had known Mike, a good friend and a big fan of boxing, for years. They also knew most of the patrons. The two men had heard Mike's exchange with Lenny; they had also heard Carlos egging his friend on. "I smell trouble," said Louie, turning to his friend. "This ain't over yet." Huey nodded in agreement.

Gil and Corinne continued talking. Something was bothering Gil. "What's a fag?"he whispered to Corinne. "Some kind of cigarette?"

Corinne laughed. "You really don't know what it means?"

Gil shook his head.

"It means you're gay, Gil," Corinne told him.

Upon hearing this, Gil could feel the hairs on the back of his neck stand up straight. *I'm the farthest thing from being gay,* he thought. He had nothing against gay people, but this was a new word to him. For the first time that evening, Lenny and Jose had Gil's attention. *Stupid morons,* he muttered to himself.

The music started playing again and Lenny jumped up and marched over to Corinne.

"Let's dance, bitch," he said, grabbing her roughly by the arm. "This time I ain't taking no for an answer."

"Let me go," Corinne screamed at him, "you're hurting me."

Gil leapt to his feet. Stepping in front of Lenny, he pried his hands off Corinne, causing Lenny to lose his step and stumble backward. "Leave her alone, you jerk. You owe this lady and me an apology," Gil said as he stood between Corinne and Lenny.

"Apologize for what, asshole? I ain't done nothing," Lenny said, scowling.

"For pulling her onto the dance floor without her consent, and for calling me a fag," Gil said.

Lenny laughed. "I don't apologize to bitches and I don't apologize to fags," he said, taking a swing at Gil. Gil blocked the blow with his forearm and let go with his right, hitting Lenny above his left temple and knocking him out cold. Then Gil felt a hard punch to his kidney. Turning around, he saw Carlos and blocked his next punch by ducking and backing away from his shot. Carlos threw another shot. Gil blocked it again, then landed another right hand shot, just above Carlos's right eye. Knocked out cold, Carlos fell on top of his friend.

Mike ran over to Corinne and Gil. "Are you all right?" he asked

Gil and Corinne answered in unison, "We're fine."

"I should have cut them off when they first started up," Mike said as he threw cold water on Lenny and Carlos and told them to get out of the bar.

The two men cursed and swore at Gil. "We'll get you one day, you faggot."

Louie and Huey, still sitting at the other end of the bar, were astonished at what they had just witnessed. Huey whispered to Louie, "Did you see that? This kid has some punch. Did you see how fast he is?"

Louie leaned back in his chair, lost for words. That was amazing," he finally said. And to himself, he said, *This could be the big break we've been waiting for.*

"Louie, do something. You gotta do something," Huey urged.

"Lemme think, lemme think; something will come up," Louie whispered. "It takes a while. I ain't as young as I used to be. It takes more than a while sometimes. It's just like God up and blessed us," he said.

"Louie, you gotta come up with one of your brainstorms. I know you get a headache when this happens, but please come up with something," Huey begged.

Louie placed both hands on his head. "Mike, bring me a couple of aspirins, and give the young man and his lady friend a drink," Louie yelled. "It's on me."

Mike looked at Louie in amazement. "Did I hear right?" he asked Huey. "Is this the Louie I know? The Louie I know never buys a drink for anybody. "

Huey chuckled. "I think he's having a brainstorm and you know how dangerous he can be when he has a brainstorm. If I were you, I'd give them a drink."

Mike nodded his head in agreement. "I think you're right," he said as he walked back to the other end of the bar where Gil and Corinne were sitting. "The little guy at the end of the bar would like to buy you a drink," he said.

Gil and Corinne accepted, and raised their glasses to thank Louie. Louie nodded, then got up from his barstool and walked over to the couple. He shook Gil's hand and said, "My name is Louie. And that's my good friend and business partner, Huey, at the other end of the bar," he added, pointing to Huey.

Huey raised his hand and said, "Nice to meet you."

"I'm Gil, and this is Corinne," Gil said. "Thanks again for the drinks."

"Well, after that unbelievable performance I thought maybe you could use a drink," Louie said. "What kinda work are you doing?"

"Well, right now I'm driving a delivery truck for a florist down the street to make some money."

Corinne cut in and said, "Gil used to be a lumberjack in Michigan. He came all the way to New York to be a dancer. He's hoping to get a job in a Broadway show." She paused, and before Gil could stop her, proceeded to tell Louie all about Gil's new dancing job.

"Where is this place?" Louie asked Gil. "What time do you start?"

"It's Dandy's, on Twenty-fourth Street," Gil replied, feeling a little embarrassed. "I start dancing around ten. They're paying me thirty-five bucks a night. I need the money so I can take dancing lessons from this retired dancer from Las Vegas. He's very expensive."

"Me and Huey'll be there, kid," Louie said. "You can count on it." He started walking back to his seat, then turned and said, "By the way, kid, what's with the red, white and blue sweatband?" Gil told him that his mother and grandmother made them for all the lumberjacks.

"Hmm," muttered Louie, an idea already forming in his mind. He waved at Gil and Corinne. "See you on Friday." *Yessirree, I can feel it in my bones,* mused Louie. *Our big break has finally arrived, and he's sitting on that barstool!*

....

The next day at the gym, Huey said to Louie, "Between you and me, I think this kid Gil, with a few lessons, could be one helluva boxer. In fact, with his knockout power and his fast hands and feet, he could go right to the top."

"I love the way you talk, Huey," Louie said. "And I love myself, I love myself." Louie danced around the gym, kissing his arms and saying, "I'm a genius, I'm a goddamned genius." He paused and looked over at Louie. "I'll pick you up around nine o'clock on Friday night. We have a date at Dandy's -- our big

break is dancing there at ten sharp."

Chapter 4

Friday night found Gil hurrying along to Dandy's, eager to prepare for his big debut. It was a balmy summer's evening, with a full saucer-shaped moon, and a sprinkling of stars dotting the inky sky. When Gil arrived at the club, Jim, the leader of the band, handed him a costume and told him to wait behind the curtain until he was called on-stage. Heavyset, with wavy black hair and thick bushy eyebrows, Jim smiled as he shook Gil's hand. His rock and roll band, *The Good Boys*, had a huge following – people came from all over the tristate area to hear them play. Gil's job was to get the crowd in a happy, dancing mood.

Gil peered out from behind the curtain. He felt nervous. People were crowding into the club. *Would he be able to get them moving?* He spotted Corinne and a few of her girlfriends sitting at the bar, near Louie and Huey. They had arrived early to get a seat with a good view of the stage. Huey noticed that Louie was nervous because he was trying to figure out how to persuade Gil to become a fighter.

The band played for thirty minutes, beginning with a fast number called *The Rock and Roll Blues,* and finishing with a slow song called *Rock.* The crowd, mainly comprised of young singles, stood on the dance floor swaying to the music. After each number,

they applauded enthusiastically. They loved this band.

But Jim was unhappy - the people weren't dancing. So he walked up to the microphone

and announced, "Ladies and gentlemen, tonight we have a pleasant surprise

for you. All the way from the West Coast, just to get you in the mood, I give you *The Maskette*."

The curtain opened and there stood Gil. He wore a black hat, a tight-fitting black,

silk shirt, a pair of snug, black leather pants and black, patent leather dancing shoes. A red

sparkly mask covered both his eyes.

Corinne screamed when she saw him. Louie and Huey stood up in amazement,

their eyes and mouths wide open. *Could this be the plucky fighter they had seen the other*

night? Some of the girls in the crowd were clapping and screaming, "Woo, woo, woo."

Gil remembered what Jim had told him. "Get everyone in the mood by making

sure they have fun. Because the more fun they have, the more people we will get on

our mailing list and that's very important. This is first time we've tried this and we're

hoping it will be successful."

Gil wanted to be sure that he danced his best. He stood on-stage for about ten

seconds, while the crowd yelled and screamed for him to dance. The band played a

fast, sexy number. Gil's hips swayed and swiveled in sync with the music. The crowd

was clapping in unison and yelling, "Take it off. Take it off. Take it off." Gil danced

to two songs before Jim walked up to the microphone and said, "Wasn't that great?

Let's give *The Maskette* a big round of applause. He'll return later."

The girls in the crowd kept screaming, "Take if off. Take if off. Take it off." Gil thought they were talking about his mask. The band played a few more songs before taking a break. Gil was backstage drinking a soda when Jim walked up to him and said, "I don't know if it's your dancing, the mask, or the way you're dressed or maybe it's just the crowd. Whatever it is, everyone seems to be having a good time. If this keeps up, I may want you to work with the band all the time."

Gil was thrilled. A second job would give him enough money to take dancing lessons.

Corinne and her friends were having a good time, dancing and talking. Louie and Huey sat at the bar waiting for Gil to return to the stage. "The crowd is really getting into the music," Louie said, slurring his words. Huey could tell that Louie was waiting for another brainstorm. *But there'll be no brainstorm tonight*, thought Huey. Louie was drunk. And when he was drunk, he couldn't think.

Jim returned to the stage. "Once again, I give you *The Maskette*," he announced. The crowd resumed their chanting, "Woo, woo, woo." Gil came out on-stage, swaying and moving to the beat of the music. He looked like a professional dancer, with his long legs and arms, his wide shoulders and thin waist. After facing the crowd, Gil decided to turn around and put his back to the crowd. He wiggled his tight ass. The women screamed. "Take it off. Take it off. Shake it, baby, shake it."

Gil turned around to face the crowd again, as a heavyset woman pushed her way through the crowd, saying, "He's mine. He's mine. He's all mine." She looked like a center for the Dallas Cowboys.

Another woman, tall and thin, and a deadringer for Popeye's girlfriend, Olive Oil, said, "Like hell he is," and pushed the heavyset woman into the middle of the crowd, knocking drinks and people flying. Then some of the women from the audience rushed on-stage and lunged toward Gil and the band. Louie and Huey watched the incident unfold from their seats at the bar. Louie's eyes widened in horror. He turned toward to Huey. "We gotta do something, Huey," he said, "they're gonna kill him. We gotta do something, and we gotta do it fast."

"You're right, Louie," Huey said. "This could get a little messy. I got an idea. Louie, bring your car around to the back door and make sure you keep the rear door of the car wide open and the engine running so we can jump right in and take off. I'll get Gil."

Louie rushed out the front door as Huey pushed and shoved his way through the crowd, trying to reach the stage. On stage, a gaggle of panting women was piled on top of Gil, tearing and pulling at his clothes. One woman grabbed Gil's hat; another snatched it from her, and all hell broke loose. When Huey finally reached Gil, he was lying on the floor, crushed underneath all those women, bleeding and half-naked. "Come on, Gil," said Huey, grabbing Gil's arm and pushing the women off him. "We gotta get outta here, fast!" Gil groaned. Huey helped him to his feet, and half-dragged him to the back door, fending off two women who were holding onto Gil's legs. Huey pushed Gil out the door and into Louie's waiting automobile, a 1965 Cadillac, nicknamed *Betsy* after Louie's high school sweetheart.

Thank God, Louie left the back door open, Huey thought to himself. Jumping in beside Gil, he closed the door and yelled to Louie, "Get the hell out of here." Louie stepped hard on the gas pedal. Betsy hesitated for a minute, then took off with the wheels squealing, and a pillar of black smoke and an orange flame shooting from the exhaust pipe. The car sped away from the club. Police sirens sounded in the distance. "We made it," said Louie.

"But only just," said Huey. They all sighed in relief.

Louie maneuvered the dark blue Cadillac through the traffic. The paint was peeling and smoke still flowed from the exhaust pipe. The inside was a different story; Louie had put in new, light blue vinyl seat covers.

"What happened back there?" Louie asked Gil.

"To tell you the truth, I really don't know," Gil said.

"Louie, drive to the gym so Gil can get cleaned up," Huey said. "And so I can take care of some of those scratches."

"I think all this happened because it's a full moon tonight," Louie said.

"Well, I think it was a toss up between Gil dancing and that crazy looking costume," Huey said, grinning.

On reaching the gym, Louie parked the car in front and jumped out. He walked over to the front door of the gym and unlocked it. Huey opened the back door of the car and helped Gil to get out. The gym was located in downtown Manhattan, on Twenty-seventh Street. Built in the early 1900s, from the outside, the old brick building looked worn and shabby. But inside it was beautiful: clean and well maintained, with polished oak floors. Iron weights, punching bags, training bags and treadmills were scattered throughout. Louie and Huey needed good equipment to train a champion fighter. All they longed for was a big break.

"Welcome to paradise!" Louie said as he turned on the lights.

Huey handed Gil a towel and a bar of soap and directed him to the shower. "Here you go," he said, " clean up and then I'll take a look at those scratches."

Before stepping in the shower, Gil paused and looked back at the sign on the door; it read *Men's Room and Office*. It struck him as odd that Louie and Huey would have their office in a men's room. He shook his head and turned toward the two men. "I want to thank you both for saving me from a very embarrassing situation," he said.

"Don't mention it, kid, we were happy to help," said Louie, patting Gil on the shoulder.

When Gil emerged from the shower he wrapped a towel around his waist and glanced around the gym. L &H Gym was a combination health club and training center for boxers. The boxing ring in the middle of the floor caught his eye. This was the first time that Gil had seen a boxing ring, let alone the inside of boxing gym. *Impressive*, he thought to himself. Yet, he had no desire to be a boxer, his heart was set on dancing in a Broadway show.

Louie looked at Gil, alarmed at the scratches on his arm and chest. "My God!" he exclaimed, "you're bleeding."

"They're only fingernail scratches," said Huey. "Nothing to worry about. They'll heal in a couple of days."

Louie and Huey were both impressed by Gil's big shoulders, his pistonlike arms and his strong legs. Although not muscle-bound, in the light, his muscles glistened. *So this is what happens when you cut down trees*, thought Louie. He handed Gil a sweatsuit. "Here you go, kid, take this. You can change in my office."

"Thanks, Louie," said Gil. He decided that he liked Louie and Huey. From what he had observed, Louie was the funny one who didn't take life seriously, while Huey was more serious and practical.

After dressing, Gil walked out of the office to find Louie sitting behind a desk and Huey sitting on top of it. The desk was medium sized and painted black – Louie had bought it at a going-out-of-business sale. "So, kid, where do you practice your dancing?" Louie asked him.

"In my room," Gil replied.

"How big is your room?" Louie asked.

"Not very big. I don't have that much room to practice."

"Me and Huey have been talking," Louie said, exchanging glances with Huey, "and you're welcome to practice here. You can workout at any time. We open at eight in the morning and close at ten at night. One of the boxers has a key and he opens up in the morning. Me and Huey are in and out of the gym all hours of the day and night." They each took turns opening up the gym - one of them arriving early and the other closing up at night.

"You mean I can come here any time I want to?" Gil asked.

"Yep, that's right," Huey said. "Besides, Louie is having an extra key cut, so you can come here any time you want to. Just make sure you lock the door behind you."

Gil was incredulous. "How can I ever repay you?" he asked.

"Don't worry about it," Huey said. "We know you're an honest person. You want to get ahead. You have a dream. Maybe we can make your dream come true." Huey and Louie had met all types of people through their work and they knew instinctively that they could trust Gil by the way he talked and the way he behaved.

Louie and Huey took Gil back to his room at the boarding house, before heading back to their own apartments. Louie lived on Twenty-fifth Street, Huey, one street away on Twenty-sixth. Besides working together, the two partners hung out after work at *Your Favorite Place*. Sometimes they would disagree about minor things, like paying the bills on time, but they usually worked out their differences over a few drinks. They both agreed that Gil was *one helluva dancer*, and prayed that he would be *one helluva boxer.* But the big question on their minds: *Would Gil give them their big break?*

Chapter 5

Gil woke up at 7:00 the next morning, relatively pain-free. After last night's little escapade, he had expected to be feeling sore, but apart from the scratches, he felt fine. Before breakfast, he completed his usual exercise routine – deep knee bends and arm stretches, sit-ups and push-ups - to keep himself in shape for dancing. Gil was reluctant to work out at the gym, as Louie and Huey had suggested. He liked the two men, but didn't know them well enough yet to feel comfortable about accepting their offer. For the time being his small room would have to do.

It was Louie's turn to open the gym for the day. Artie Garcia, their top boxer, usually opened the gym about eight and watched the place until Louie or Huey arrived. After opening up, Louie dropped by Hungry Man's Luncheonette to eat a hearty breakfast of fried eggs, bacon, home fries and two slices of buttered toast.   When finished, he headed to the locksmith's shop to get two keys made for Gil. He planned on dropping by the florist shop, on the pretext of needing a rose for his aunt, and to give the keys to Gil.

Gil was busy delivering flowers all morning and had no idea that Louie would be stopping by the shop, while he was gone.

When Louie arrived at the florist's, Corinne was standing behind the counter. "Can I help you?" she asked.

"Don't I know you from some place?" Louie asked.

"Yes," Corinne said, recognizing Louie. "I was responsible for starting that fight the other night at *Your Favorite Place*. I recognize you. Your name is Louie, and you and your partner own a gym."

"That's right," Louie said. "That was some fight. You sure know how to start trouble," he chuckled, glancing around the shop. "Look, is Gil around? I wanted to give him these keys, and I need a rose for my aunt."

"Gil won't be back until noon, but I'll gladly give these keys to him when he returns," Corinne said.

Louie handed over the keys, which dangled from a chain along with two black boxing gloves. Louie had ordered a box of 500 key chains and handed them out to the patrons of the gym.

"It's very important that he gets these keys because they're for the gym. We're letting him use the place so he can have room to practice dancing," Louie said.

"That's very kind of you, " Corinne said. "I never saw him practice, but he's a real nice person and everyone here likes him." Three other people worked at the floral shop aside from Gil and Corinne: Keith and Debbie, two floral designers, and Jay, who cleaned the flowers, and kept the shop clean. "He's very helpful and he does his job," Corinne continued. "We consider ourselves lucky to have him work with us." Corinne took a red rose, some baby's breath, a sprig of Baker's fern and a sheet of colored paper. She wrapped a piece of red ribbon around the paper and tied a bow. "Here you are," she said, passing the rose to Louie. "I hope your aunt likes it."

"Yeah, sure, thank you," said Louie sheepishly. He handed Corinne four dollars. "It's nice seeing you again," he said as he walked out of the shop. *Mission accomplished*, he thought to himself. Louie figured that by giving a key to Gil, he would lure him to the gym, and Huey could show him how to box. As Louie walked down the sidewalk he muttered to himself, "You're the greatest."

On returning to the gym, Louie sat down behind his desk and waited for Huey to arrive. When Huey walked in, he saw the rose and said, "Louie, I know you love yourself, but don't you think this is going a little too far?"

Louie touched the rose, his face flushed with excitement. "Huey, you're gonna love me when I tell you what I did this morning."

"All right, I'm listening..."

"I stopped by the locksmith's shop and had two keys made for Gil. Then I went to the florist's shop... And do you remember that girl who was with Gil at *Your Favorite Place*? Her name was Corinne?"

"Yeah, I remember her," Huey replied.

"Well, I left the keys with her and she said that she'd make sure that Gil got them."

"Louie, you're the greatest. Once we get him into the gym, I'll start giving him some boxing lessons. Hopefully he will stop down here tonight after work."

"I know. I know. I know." Louie jumped up and danced around the desk.

After work, Gil dropped by the gym to thank Louie and Huey for the keys. The two friends could barely contain their excitement. They gave Gil a guided tour of the gym, pointing out the light switches, and showing him how to use the exercise machines and equipment, as well as the equipment not to use when he was alone, like the heavy weights.

"No charge, Gil," said Louie. You can come here any time to exercise or practice your dancing." Louie hoped that Huey would eventually get Gil interested in boxing. All Gil had to do was keep the *Men's Room and Office* clean. Louie walked over to his desk to make some telephone calls. "I'll see you later, kid," he said.

Huey motioned for Gil to come over to the boxing ring. "Have you ever been inside a boxing ring before?" he asked.

"No," Gil replied. "Never."

Huey stretched the ropes and said, "Get in. Get the feel of the ring." The ropes were made of plastic and covered with red cloth.

Gil was surprised at the small size of the ring – it was about twelve square feet – and at the firmness of the padding on the floor.

"Bounce off the ropes and get the feel of them," Huey told Gil. The ropes were firm and Gil found himself being propelled into the center of the ring. In his mind, Huey was picturing Gil wearing a pair of red, white and blue trunks, and matching sweatband, fighting for the light heavyweight championship title of the world. Once Gil climbed out of the ring, Huey showed him how to use the punching bag, the training bag and the jump rope. "Dancing and boxing are pretty much alike," Huey said. "You won't be dancing with a lady and you won't be dancing on stage in front of other people. You'll be dancing to keep the other fighter away so he doesn't knock your block off. May the best man win."

"Hmm, I never made the connection between dancing and boxing before," said Gil. "But now that you mention it, I guess they are alike."

Gil and Huey walked over to Louie, who was sitting at his desk. "Are you still dancing at that club?" asked Louie.

Gil shook his head. "Nah, the bandleader called me at the florist's shop and told me that he couldn't use me anymore because of the fighting that broke out the night before," Gil said. "He said that things were going good up until that point. So, I'm out of a job, except for the florist. I was hoping to save that money for dancing lessons. Guess that will have to wait."

"That's too bad," Louie said, glancing over at Huey, a look of mischief in his eyes. "If we hear of anything, we'll let you know, won't we, Huey?"

Huey nodded. "Definitely," he said. Even if a job were available next door, Louie and Huey would never tell him.

Gil headed for the door. Before leaving, he turned and said, "Thanks for showing me around the gym. I really appreciate it. If it's okay with you, I'll come in early tomorrow morning, about seven, and work out before I go to work."

Louie and Huey beamed. "You got it, kid," they said in unison. As soon as Gil left, the two friends square danced around the gym. Their *big break* might be just around the corner.

Chapter 6

Early the next morning, Gil headed to the gym to work out. He was working up a sweat, stretching and exercising before practicing his dancing, when the telephone rang. Gil didn't know what to do. Should he answer the phone or let it ring? *It could be Louie or Huey*, he thought, picking up the phone.

A man's voice, raspy and mean, rang in his ear. "Is asshole Louie or that other asshole, Huey, there?" the man yelled into the receiver.

"No, they're not here," Gil said. "Can I take a message?"

"Yes, you can, asshole. If you're smart enough to write, asshole," the man said. "Make sure you get it right, asshole. Tell the two assholes that Sparkey Morrison called. My telephone number is 555-6884. By the way, what's your name, asshole?"

"My name's Gil and I'll make sure they get the message, asshole," Gil said as he wrote down Sparkey's phone number on a pad of paper, which was lying on Louie's desk.

Sparkey slammed down the receiver, leaving a ringing in Gil's ear. "What an asshole," muttered Gil.

Just then, Gil heard a key being turned in the lock on the front door of the gym. A man walked in and said, "Are you Gil, the lumberjack from Michigan? You wanna be a dancer in a Broadway show?"

"That's right," Gil answered. "And what's your name?"

"My name is Artie Garcia," Garcia shook Gil's hand, "I'm one of the fighters who Louie and Huey are training." Artie was muscular to the point of being muscle-bound. About five foot seven and weighing 140 pounds, he had short black hair and a friendly grin. Whenever he smiled, his white teeth sparkled like lights again his tan complexion.

"Nice to meet you, Artie." Gil glanced at the clock; it was eight o'clock. "Time goes fast when you are having fun," Gil said. "Somebody by the name of Sparkey Morrison called. I left a message on the desk. He wants Louie and Huey to call him back."

"Don't tell me that you talked to that asshole."

"You know him?"

"Yeah, I do. Louie and Sparkey have been bitter enemies for years. Sparkey used to be Huey's manager; Huey hates him too. He screwed Huey big time; screwed him out of money, and wanted Huey to throw fights. One day Huey decided that he'd had enough and punched Sparkey, knocking him down. That was it. Huey stopped fighting for Sparkey and teamed up with Louie."

Artie took a deep breath, then continued with his story. "When Huey first started boxing, he won a lot of fights, and was in line to fight for the heavyweight championship of the world. But after the fallout with Sparkey, he decided to quit fighting altogether. He was nearing forty – it was time to hang up his gloves. So when Louie asked him to be his partner in the gym, to train the boxers, Huey jumped at the chance. The rest is history."

"That's quite a story," said Gil, smiling. He decided that he liked Garcia. He seemed friendly, and he looked forward to seeing him again, at the gym. Now it was time for him to go to work. After taking a quick shower in the *Men's Room and Office*, he hurried to the exit. "It was nice meeting you," he called to Garcia. "I'm sure I'll see you again soon."

Garcia smiled and waved. "Likewise," he said. " See you later."

Louie arrived at the gym at ten. Noticing the scribbled message from Gil, he walked over to Garcia and asked, "What's this?"

"It's a message that Gil took from Sparkey Morrison," Garcia replied. "Gil said that it's important that you call Sparkey back. That's his telephone number," Garcia said, pointing to the piece of paper.

"What does that asshole want with me?" Louie said. He hadn't spoken to Sparkey in nearly a year. "He's only got the best light heavyweight champion of the world, Percy "Mean" Williams. Sparkey makes all kinds of money. What could he possibly want from me?" Louie picked up the receiver and dialed Sparkey's number. Louie had an old black, rotary dial telephone. He didn't want to spend the money to have a new line put in for a push button phone.

Sparkey's phone rang twice before his secretary answered. "Good morning," she sounded sweet and polite, "can I help you?"

"Good morning. This is Louie from L&H Gym. I'm returning Sparkey's call."

"Oh yes, he's been waiting for your call," the secretary said as she transferred the call to Sparkey's office.

Sparkey's raspy voice echoed down the line. "Hello, asshole. You still in business?"

"Yeah, but not thanks to you," Louie answered.

"Well, I have a deal for you," Sparkey said. "I hope you can help me out."

"What? You have a deal for me," Louie said. "Thanks, but no thanks."

"Don't you dare hang up the phone, asshole. This is a damn good deal and it might be worth your time to listen."

"All right, you have my attention," Louie said. "What's the deal?"

"I'm looking for a fighter to fight Percy in an exhibition fight for the Developmentally Disabled Children's Fund, and I was hoping that you might let Artie Garcia take on Percy for three rounds. It's worth five grand. Think about it, asshole, and let me know in two days." Sparkey slammed down the receiver. It left a ringing sensation in Louie's left ear.

Louie thought to himself, *What a bastard he is.*

Huey walked in five minutes later. "Good morning, everyone," he called out in a cheery voice, addressing all the customers who worked out at the gym, as well as Louie and Garcia.

Louie waved to Huey to come over to his desk. "We gotta have a meeting in the *office*," he said. Huey nodded, and the two men walked into the men's room, where nobody could hear them. "Sparkey Morrison called to say that he has a deal for us," Louie said.

"That bastard has a deal for us?" Huey said. "What the hell does that crook want? Our blood?"

Louie told him. "Just think, Huey, five grand for three rounds. I know how much you dislike him. But we need the money. I just want you to think about it."

"Well, who could we possibly put up against Percy?" Huey asked.

"Sparkey mentioned Artie Garcia," Louie said.

"No way in hell will I let Garcia go up against Williams," Huey said in a loud voice, almost yelling. "Garcia's the best fighter we have. If we lose him, we might have to close the gym. You know that Williams will try to kill him; Sparkey taught him well."

Percy would try to kill anyone who got into the ring with him. As his nickname suggested, "Mean" was a nasty individual.

"You're right, we can't put Garcia up against Percy," Louie agreed. "He'll kill him. We have a few more fighters who might be able to go three rounds. Anyway, we have a few days to think it over."

Louie had trouble sleeping that night. He tossed and turned, unable to stop thinking about Sparkey and the five thousand dollars that was waiting for him and Huey. Louie had no other fighters in mind who could spar with Williams because he feared they might get killed or seriously injured by him. But how could he turn his back on $5,000? If he and Huey accepted Sparkey's offer, they could finally pay off their bills. Louie tried counting sheep, but that didn't work. He tried praying. Then he thought about the night the women ripped off Gil's clothes at the club. He laughed and turned onto his back from his side. Then, as if a bolt of lightning had suddenly struck him, Louie sat up straight and jumped out of bed. Dressing in a white T-shirt and blue pants, he slipped his feet into a pair of black slippers and dashed out of his apartment. He was so excited that he forgot to put his shoes on.

Louie ran to his Cadillac, and stepping on the gas, he drove one block to Huey's apartment. After he parked and stepped out of the car one of his slippers fell off. "Damn," he said out loud, "I forgot to put my shoes on." He placed the slipper back on his foot and walked quickly to the front door of Huey's apartment building. Taking two steps at a time, he raced up the flight of stairs to the second floor.

Huey lived in apartment A-2. Louie banged on the door with his fist and pushed the buzzer. "It's me, Huey," he yelled. "Open the door."

Huey opened the door and said groggily, "What the hell is going on, Louie?" He was still half-asleep.

"Huey," Louie said, grabbing Huey's arm. "I got it! I got it! I got it!"

"Is it curable?" Huey asked, letting Louie inside his apartment.

"No, no, no, it's nothing like that," Louie said, excited, dancing around the kitchen. "I love myself. I love myself. I love myself." The kitchen was small, with barely enough room for a table and two chairs. Huey lived in a two-room apartment. He had a kitchen and a living room, with a pullout sofa bed in the middle of the room. An overstuffed chair, draped with a brown slipcover, sat to the right of the sofa bed. Huey kept his boxing trophies locked in a glass cabinet, which stood across from his sofa bed, by the wall. A television set sat on top of a small wooden table, near the end of his bed.

Huey watched in amazement as Louie danced the twist at four o'clock in the morning. *What the hell is wrong with him?* Huey thought. As Louie continued to dance in a frenzy, Huey heated some water in a pot on top of the stove and made instant coffee. Turning to Louie, he said, "Louie, take it easy, before you have a heart attack."

As soon as the coffee was ready, the two friends sat down at the kitchen table. Louie started kissing himself: the back of his hand, his arm, working his way up to his shoulder. "I love myself. I love myself more today, than ever before. I'm a damn genius!" he exclaimed.

"Please tell me what this is all about before you forget," Huey said.

"Huey, you need money. I need money. You're poor. I'm poor. We're poor, poor, poor."

"I'm so poor," Huey said, "that the coffee you're drinking is yesterday's coffee."

"We need that five grand," Louie screamed. "I need money. We need money. Who else needs money that you know? I'll give you a hint: Think, Gene Kelly or Fred Astaire, you know, dancers?"

Huey stood up so fast that he spilled his coffee on the table. "Gil," he yelled.

Now both men were dancing around the kitchen. And Huey was yelling, "Louie, Louie, Louie."

- - - - - - - - - - - - - - - - - -

When Gil arrived at the gym the next morning the door was already open and all the lights were on. Louie and Huey were there to greet him. "Gil, how would you like to make a thousand dollars in nine minutes?" Louie asked.

"One thousand dollars in nine minutes?" Gil said incredulously." Are you guys serious? Of course I would, but I'm not doing anything that's crooked."

"No, this is on the up-and-up," Huey said.

"We know this promoter, he's the manager of Percy "Mean" Williams, the light heavyweight champion of the world," Louie told Gil. "And he's putting on an exhibition fight for the Developmentally Disabled Children's Fund. He wants somebody to take on his fighter for three 3-minute rounds, a total of nine minutes for the entire fight."

"That must be the guy who calls everyone asshole," Gil said.

"That's the guy," Louie said, "and he has plenty of money."

"You mean, if you have plenty of money, you can treat people like dirt?" Gil said.

"That's it, kid. That's the way Sparkey sees things," Louie said.

"I don't know much about fighting. Just what my uncle taught me," Gil said.

"Don't worry about it, kid," Louie said. "Huey was a contender for the heavyweight championship title of the world and he'll teach you everything he knows. You only have one month to train."

Gil was silent for a few moments. Finally, he said, "Okay, you're on, I'll give it a shot."

"Attaboy," said Louie, patting him on the back.

Louie called Sparkey right away. "I have a fighter by the name of Gil, who is willing to take on Percy for three rounds."

"Gil? Gil? That name sounds familiar. Have I ever met this Gil?" Sparkey asked.

"He's the one who took your message the other day," Louie said.

"That asshole? Do you know that he had the nerve to call me an asshole and slammed the receiver down in my ear?" Sparkey said.

"He did that to you?" Louie asked, acting surprised.

"Damn right, he did," Sparkey yelled into the receiver. "And I'm going to make sure that Percy gives him a good beating. You can tell that Gil that he's a real big asshole."

"Well, just wait until Gil comes in," Louie said, feigning anger, "I'll get on his case about it." He knew that Sparkey was blowing steam and he didn't intend to reprimand Gil.

"That no-good nobody don't have the right to call Sparkey Morrison an asshole," Sparkey said. "I have some other things I want to talk to you about, but it can wait." Sparkey slammed down the receiver. Louie sat in his chair, dumbfounded. *What an asshole*, he thought to himself.

Chapter 7

From then on, whenever Gil walked into the gym, he was treated like a hero. Louie told everyone, "This is the man who had the nerve to call Sparkey Morrison an asshole." Boxers and customers alike lined up to shake Gil's hand and congratulate him.

Gil took the fight seriously, and was determined to train hard for it. Arriving at the gym at 6:00 every morning and returning after work, he undertook a grueling exercise regime. Huey was an exacting taskmaster, but under his guidance and expertise, Gil was developing into a formidable fighting machine

Louie and Huey were proud of their young protégé. Gil's dancing background was excellent training, segueing perfectly into the boxing arena, and making their job that much easier. They wanted Gil to become a boxer, rather than a dancer, but they knew that Gil would use the $1,000 for dancing lessons.

"How's Gil coming along with his training?" Louie asked Huey a week into Gil's training.

"Very nicely" Huey said. "He's a fast learner."

The phone rang, interrupting their conversation, and Louie answered it. Huey strained to hear what Louie was saying, but Louie's voice was barely a whisper, his hand cupping the mouthpiece of the receiver. It was a departure from Louie's usual loudness when he talked. Usually he could be heard from one end of the gym to the other. *He must be talking to Sparkey*, Louie thought. If Sparkey did someone a favor, he usually wanted something in return. Nothing came free with Sparkey.

Louie hung up the phone and walked back over to Huey, who was standing next to the ring watching Garcia spar against another fighter.

"Huey," he said, "from now on could you give me weekly updates on Gil's progress."

"Sure," Huey began. "I can tell you right now that Gil has power in both his right and left hands. I can feel the power coming from his big shoulders and his long, pistonlike arms. He also has good hand speed and he's very fast on his feet."

"I can't believe what you're telling me, Huey," Louie said. "He don't look muscle-bound to me."

"No, he's not muscle-bound. But if you get too muscle-bound you can sometimes lose your arm speed, which is bad," Huey explained. "Working in the woods, cutting down trees and lifting and carrying all those heavy logs has given him rippling muscles, which you can't see. But when you put pressure on them, holy cow! In Gil's case, he has pressure at the end of his fist, and if he connects, *boom!* down you go."

"You're scaring the hell out of me, Huey," Louie screamed. "Meeting, meeting, meeting," he said, grabbing Huey's arm and pulling him toward the men's room.

"What the hell's going on, Louie?" asked Huey, once they were safely ensconced in the men's room.

Louie frowned. "Well, when I talked to Sparkey, he told me that the check was in the mail if Gil loses big time, and goes down in the second round."

"Louie, are you saying that Gil has to throw this fight?" Huey asked. "I hope you made sure that we get the money before the fight. A check could take several days to clear. If it clears?"

"That's right," Louie said, pounding on the desk a couple of times. "You know, Sparkey was the main suspect in the killing of that fighter, Bill "Rocky" Simmons and his manager, Jimmy Smith, a few years back. Remember? The suspects set fire to the car to cover up the crime scene?"
Huey nodded.

"I'm a dead man. I'm a dead man. I'm a dead man," chanted Louie.

"Damn it, Louie," Huey cried, "you're always getting yourself into trouble. And this sounds like big trouble."

"I have to take a piss," Louie said, unbuttoning his pants. "What are the chances of Gil making me a dead man?"

"Well, I can tell you this, if Gil connects with his right or left hand, Percy will go down," Huey said.

"I'm a dead man. I'm a dead man. I'm a dead man," Louie repeated. "And I'm so young and handsome. Forty-five and in my prime. Now I'm not going to live to see forty-six," Louie whined as he stood in front of the urinal. "Make sure I'm cremated and my ashes are spread around Las Vegas. I can't picture myself six feet under. Now that I'm so nervous and scared I have to take a dump."

"I'm outta here," Huey said. As he walked out of the men's room, he could hear Louie saying, "I'm a dead man. But I still love myself."

Huey was worried. He knew that Sparkey was capable of killing Louie if the fight went beyond the second round. *Perhaps we should let Garcia fight instead*, he thought to himself. Sparkey was notorious in the boxing world for his crooked deals and violent temper. And Huey had borne the brunt of his ex-manager's temper tantrums many times. Sparkey's motto was 'payback is a bitch,' meaning that if someone crossed him, he would get even.

Gil was the type of fighter every trainer dreamed of. He trained and exercised rigorously, he didn't do drugs, he didn't smoke, and he never drank to excess. Sometimes Huey held the training bag to keep it from swaying back and forth, and so that he could feel the impact of Gil's punches. Gil soon became used to the bulkiness of the boxing gloves and the uncomfortable headgear, which he wore during practice. Once he entered the ring and fought a professional fight, no headgear would be worn. Huey was pleased with Gil's left jab; it was quick and direct. Since Gil was right handed he jabbed with his left hand.

"It's important to have a quick and powerful jab," Huey explained, as he demonstrated the move. "This will keep your opponent back and off balance, allowing you to work your way in and throw the combination, one, two, three, and step back," Huey puffed as he stepped toward Gil and threw a fake combination, then stepped back. "See, nothing to it," he said, wiping his brow. "Now, you try it."

Gil stepped forward and executed the perfect jab combination. "Nice work, kiddo,' said Huey, patting him on the back. "You're a quick learner. Now let's work on your upper cut."

Gil's upper cut was still weak because he was a beginner. Huey knew that it would take time for Gil to perfect his boxing skills. As an ex-fighter, Huey showed a lot of patience in training Gil as he had gone through the same training. He showed Gil how to cover up his face and block punches if he was in trouble, especially if he were pinned against the ropes.

Gil was now in his third week of training. As he sparred with Garcia, under the watchful eye of Huey, Louie walked over to the ring.

"How are things coming along?" Louie asked Huey, who was standing outside the ring. "Will I be around for my next birthday?"

"Right now it's up in the air, but Percy could be in for a big surprise," Huey said. "Maybe you should tell Gil that he has to throw the fight."

Gil, who had climbed out of the ring to take a break, walked over to the two men.

"Since this is a charity fight, will this Percy guy give me any mercy?" he asked.

Hearing Gil's words, Louie started to gag, his face turning crimson. He turned his back to Gil, because he didn't want Gil to know that he was laughing at him. He especially didn't want Gil to know that Percy would be out to kill him as soon he stepped into the ring. Percy "Mean" Williams never showed mercy to any fighter. A vicious fighter, he fought dirty to win. Sometimes, he would throw his elbow into his opponent's face, he would hit below the belt, he would rabbit punch the fighter. Depending on the referee, sometimes he would get away with these machinations; other times, the referee would give a warning.

Huey started laughing along with Louie.

"What's so funny?" asked Gil, staring at the two men in puzzlement.

Huey grabbed hold of Louie and started dragging him toward exit door. "Oh, it's nothing, Gil, just a private joke between me and Louie," Huey said, stifling a laugh. "Will you excuse us a second, I've just remembered that I have to talk to Louie privately." Gil watched as the two friends hurried out the front door of the gym. He shook his head. *They sure are a couple of funny characters,* he thought to himself.

"Gil probably can't understand why we're laughing," Huey said to Louie, as they fell into Louie's car, and drove the four blocks to *Your Favorite Place,* to have a few drinks.

Louie was now helpless with laughter. "Will Percy give me any mercy? Will Percy give me any mercy?" he kept chanting over and over again.

The two friends were still laughing when they arrived at the bar.

"What's so funny?" asked Mike the bartender as he walked over to take their order. "Can I hear the joke?"

"It's personal," Huey said. He didn't think Mike would understand and he didn't want to insult Gil. Huey and Louie liked Mike; they had known him since opening the gym and had been frequenting the bar ever since.

Louie and Huey sipped their drinks slowly – vodka and orange for Louie and a gin and tonic for Huey – then ordered another round. They took their time, still laughing and talking about the upcoming fight. The bar was quiet. With the exception of Mike and a couple of punters at the far end of the bar, they practically had the place to themselves.

After finishing their drinks, they headed back to Louie's car, which was parked in a nearby parking lot. Turning left at the exit, Louie drove down the block and stopped at a red light. He and Huey were still laughing. "Maybe we should have had a couple more drinks," Louie said, thinking that if he had a few more drinks his stomach wouldn't hurt. "My gut hurts so much that I think I'm having a baby."

While they were stopped at the light, Louie took his foot off the brake, without realizing it, and the car lurched forward a few inches. Then Louie slammed his foot on the brake and stopped the car. He took his foot off the brake again and the car lurched forward. Louie repeated this action about six times.

Patrol officer Ernie Wells was standing on the corner. Ernie had always been a fair-minded police officer, until his divorce six months ago. He and his wife had broken up over financial woes. Ernie's wife, Anne, was dissatisfied with his salary. As a patrolman, Ernie only made $25,000 a year. His wife got the house and custody of their two children. To make matters worse, she started dating Ernie's best friend. The entire situation had left Ernie feeling angry and bitter.

Ernie noticed that Louie and Huey were laughing and that the car was jerking forward and stopping abruptly, so he walked over to Louie's car and asked, "Are you laughing at me?" Ernie was six feet tall, with short, black hair shaped in a crew cut. Sensitive to what others thought of him, especially now because of the divorce, he took everyone's comments personally.

"Of course not. This is a private joke," Louie said, laughing.

"Oh, a private joke. Could I see your driver's license and your insurance card?"

. Louie put his hand inside his back pocket to reach for his wallet. Ernie reacted by pulling his gun out and pointing it at Louie. "Pull your hand out of your pocket very slowly," he said. "Take out your driver's license and hand it to me."

"Easy, Officer," said Louie as he handed his driver's license to Ernie. Louie's wallet was made of black leather, a present from Huey on Louie's forty-fifth birthday. The two friends were still laughing. "I hope you guys aren't laughing at me?" Ernie repeated.

Huey told Ernie, "No, we're not laughing at you. It's a personal joke."

"Now I have to see your insurance card," said Ernie.

In order to get his insurance card, Louie had to reach over, placing his arm across Huey's lap, to open the glove compartment.

"Reach over toward the glove compartment slowly," said Ernie.

Louie opened the glove compartment and took out an envelope, containing his insurance card. He handed it to Officer Wells.

Wells checked both documents and was about to hand them back to Louie, when he smelled alcohol on Louie's breath. "Get out of the car," he ordered. Louie was laughing so hard that instead of turning and placing his feet on the ground, he turned and rolled out of the car, landing at the policeman's feet. "Oh, a private joke? Or too much to drink?" Wells said. "I'm taking you both to jail."

Gil was alone at the gym, waiting for Louie and Huey to return so he could lock up, when the phone rang. Hesitant to answer it after what happened the last time, he let the phone ring ten times before picking up the receiver. "Hello," he said cautiously.

Gil was glad to hear Louie's voice. "Huey and I are in jail and we need bail money," Louie said. "How much money do you have on you?"

"Only twenty dollars," Gil said. "Is that enough?"

"No, that's not enough," Louie said. "We need two hundred dollars to post bail. Look under the desk and in the right hand corner you'll find an envelope taped to the bottom of the desk with three hundred dollars in it. Take the envelope, hail a cab and get the hell down to the police station. This is a hellhole and me and Huey don't like it. Hurry."

Louie and Huey were locked in a holding cell with fifteen other men. Four were being held for drunken behavior, one for rape, six for illegally selling drugs and four for attempted robbery. One of the drunks was passed out on the floor. The man accused of rape was talking to a priest, telling him that the rape was the woman's fault. The drug dealers were huddled in a group in one corner, casting dirty looks at Louie and Huey, and whispering about them. Louie was the shortest man in the cell, so he was thankful that Huey was there to protect him.

Gil followed Louie's instructions. Pushing the chair away from the desk, he dropped to his knees and felt around on the bottom of the desk. The envelope was right where Louie said it would be. Gil opened it and found $300 inside. Tucking the money safely inside his pocket, he rushed outside and hailed a cab. "I want to go downtown to the 33rd precinct police station," Gil told the driver. "Please hurry." On the way there, Gil wondered why Louie and Huey were in jail. He was worried. Over the past few weeks, they had taken him under their wing and become like uncles to him. *I hope it's nothing serious*, he thought to himself.

When Gil arrived at the police station, he walked briskly inside, his brow wrinkled with worry. A burly desk sergeant was sitting at the front desk, an Irish fellow with thinning brown hair and and twinkling blue eyes. His name was Sergeant O'Malley.

"Hello, young man," he said to Gil. "Can I help you?"

"I'm here to pick up Louie and Huey. One of them's white. He's kind of short and stocky and the other is a big black fellow."

"Oh yeah, those two guys," the sergeant said, shaking his head and smiling. He thought Louie and Huey were acting goofy because they were laughing so hard when they were brought in. "Did somebody give them laughing gas? The two of them can't stop laughing."

"Gas?" Gil said. "The only gas I know Louie to have is when he eats too many tacos, and that's no laughing matter," Gil said with a rueful look on his face, not realizing that he had told a joke. He thought he was telling the truth. Gil wasn't the type of person to laugh at his own jokes.

"They'll be right out. Do you have the bail money?" Sergeant O'Malley said, laughing, "They were given a Breathalyzer test after they were brought in. Our patrolman didn't have his kit with him, so he brought your friends in because he smelled liquor on their breath, and he conducted the test here at the station. We were so backed up tonight that we had to put them in a holding cell before we could do the test. Don't look so upset, they passed."

"Yes, I have the bail money," Gil replied. He waited in the lobby, pacing back and forth in front of the sergeant's desk and glancing every few minutes at the clock hanging on the wall.

When Louie and Huey were finally released, Officer Wells escorted them into the lobby. He walked the two men over to the front desk, so they could each sign a release form. Ernie appeared to be in a better mood now because he realized that Louie and Huey weren't making fun of him. "I'm sorry," he apologized.

Louie and Huey stared at Ernie in disbelief, surprised at his sudden change in attitude.

Gil walked up to the front desk and handed the money to the desk sergeant. Then Ernie walked over to Gil and introduced himself. "I'm Officer Ernie Wells," he said, shaking Gil's hand. "I'm sorry to put you through all this trouble." Then he turned on his heel and walked quickly back to the door leading to the holding cells. Officer O'Malley reached under his desk and pressed a buzzer, unlocking the door, and Ernie disappeared inside.

Louie and Huey walked over to Gil and stood on either side of him. "Huey has something to tell you," Louie told Gil, smiling. Since Huey was the trainer it was his job to explain any problems or policies to the fighters.

"What's that?" Gil said, looking puzzled.

"Well, first, to answer your question from before: no, Percy "Mean" Williams will not show you any mercy. And second, we have picked out your fighting name," Huey said. "We had plenty of time to think while we were sitting in jail and this is what we came up with…"

"What's that?" Gil said, interrupting.

"Your fighting name will be Gil "Mercy" Ailer."

"Hey, I like it," Gil said, smiling, "How did you guys come up with that name?"

"Oh, it just came to us," said Huey, winking at Louie.

Chapter 8

The next morning Mercy arrived at the gym bright and early. He liked his new nickname, but he was scared about the upcoming fight. This would be his first fight, his first time in the ring. And his opponent was none other than Percy "Mean" Williams, the light heavyweight champion of the world. This scared him most of all.

Mercy pummeled the training bag, working hard to banish his nervous jitters. Sweat glistened on his forehead. He wore grey sweatpants and a white tee shirt, and his trademark red, white and blue sweatband was wrapped tightly around his head.

Louie and Huey arrived at eight o'clock and chimed in together, "Good morning, Mercy."

"Good morning," Mercy said, hesitating before he greeted them. He wasn't used to his new nickname yet. And he was still wondering how they came up with the name.

Louie walked over to his desk and dialed Sparkey's number. "I have a fighter called Mercy, who will be fighting Percy," he barked into the phone.

"What kind of an asshole is this Mercy with a name like that?" Sparkey asked.

"Just another asshole like Huey and me," Louie said. "Make sure you put the check in the mail."

"Well, tell this Mercy asshole to go down gracefully in the second round," Sparkey said. "And I'll put the check in the mail," he added, slamming down the receiver.

Louie motioned to Huey to meet him in the *Men's Room and Office.*

"What is it?" asked Huey, once they were settled in the men's room.

"We only have five days left before the fight and I have to tell Mercy to go down gracefully in the second round or I'm a dead man," said Louie.

"I'll go and get him," said Huey, shaking his head. He walked out of the men's room and asked Mercy to join them.

"What's up?" Mercy asked.

"We're having a meeting in the office about the fight," Huey said.

"Mercy, there's no easy way to say this," Louie said, "you're gonna have to go down in the second round or my life will be in danger. Look at this way, it's only an exhibition."

Mercy stared at Louie in astonishment, then turned to Huey. "Is this true?" he asked.

"Yeah, kid, it's true," Huey said, with a sympathetic look in his eyes. He didn't like the idea of throwing the fight. He hated Sparkey and his shady underhand deals.

"Well, to hell with both of you. I'm outta this. Find yourselves another fighter," Mercy said as he stormed out of the men's room, disgusted. Mercy was usually even tempered, but when somebody asked him to do something that went against his morals, his anger flared.

Huey shook his head as he watched Mercy's retreating form. "You know, Louie, that slimeball, Sparkey, is always pulling this shit?" he said. " I feel bad for Mercy."

Louie nodded in agreement. "Me, too," he said.

"I mean, look at it this way," Huey continued. "It's Mercy's first fight. He'll be going up against one of the best fighters in the world and he has no prior experience in the ring. What are the chances of Mercy knocking out Percy? Slim and none I'd say."

"You're right," Louie said. "I'm probably getting myself worked up over nothing."

Huey walked to the door and called out to Mercy who was furiously punching the training bag, his face suffused with anger. "Hey, Mercy, we're sorry," he yelled. "Come back here, will ya."

Mercy stopped punching the bag and walked slowly back to the men's room. He was still feeling hurt and angry. *How could Louie and Huey ask him to do such a thing?*

"Look, we're sorry that we asked you to throw the fight," Louie began as Mercy entered the room. "We talked it over and you're right, Mercy, you don't have to throw the fight. Just go out there and do your best."

Mercy stared at him, and said nothing.

"I want you go out there and kick ass," Louie continued.

"But, Louie, I thought you said your life is in danger?" Mercy said. He looked relieved, but inside he was worried about Louie.

"Don't worry about it, kid," Louie reassured him. "Sparkey can be a big bullshit artist sometimes."

Mercy was smiling as he shook hands with Louie and Huey, confident that he would hold his own in the fight. "Thanks, guys," he said as he walked out of the men's room. "I won't let you down."

Once Mercy had left, Huey said to Louie, "You know that Williams has a powerful right hand, so I'll tell Mercy to circle the wrong way, right into Williams' right hand. And you know how Percy likes to charge across the ring at the sound of the bell. Well, I won't tell Mercy about it."

"Thanks, Huey," Louie said. "I'll never do this again, as long as I live; which may not be that long!"

Mercy continued to train rigorously for the fight. He undertook a punishing regime of sit ups and push ups, jumped rope, punched the training bag and ran laps around the gym to build up his strength and stamina.

The night of the fight finally arrived. It was a clear autumn evening, crisp and sharp with a shimmering full moon. Louie had told Mercy that they would leave the gym at six to go to Nelson College in Queens, New York. Louie and Huey wanted to get there a little early so they could familiarize themselves with the setting and get ready for the fight.

The fight was scheduled to begin at 8:00 p.m., and would be held in the school's basketball stadium. Chairs and bleachers were set up around the outside of the ring. Ringside seats cost $25, the bleachers $15. Louie had asked Mercy to bring three red, white and blue sweatbands so they could each wear one as they walked into the stadium, a sign of solidarity and patriotism.

When they arrived Mercy was surprised to see that people were already crowding into the brightly-lit gym. *This Percy "Mean" Williams must be a very popular fighter*, he thought to himself. While making his way to the locker room, Mercy spotted a handsome black man and couldn't help staring at him. The man was strong, with muscular arms and mean penetrating eyes that seemed to look straight through Mercy. Mercy shuddered. He had a strong feeling that he had just locked eyes with Percy "Mean" Williams.

Fifteen minutes before the fight Louie noticed that Mercy seemed nervous. "Gee, Huey, Mercy looks jittery. I hope he'll be all right for the fight. I hope he makes it to the ring."

"Don't worry, it's his first fight," Huey said. "I was the same way before my first fight. The nervousness goes away at the sound of the bell."

There was a knock on the door, and in walked the referee. He wore a white button down shirt and a black bow tie and black pants. He explained the rules and told Mercy that he would repeat them before the fight began. "A custodian will let you know when it's time to come to the gym," he added as he left the locker room. A few minutes passed, it seemed like a few hours to Mercy, then someone knocked on the door and said, "It's time."

"Mercy, I want you to shadow box and do a slow jog on the way to the ring," said Huey. "Now, go get'em, kid," he encouraged, slapping Mercy on the back.

Mercy swallowed hard. *You can do this*, he said to himself.

Donning their red, white and blue sweatbands, the three men paraded into the gym. Louie led the way followed by Mercy, whose red, white and blue boxing trunks matched his sweatband. Huey brought up the rear.

Huey separated the ropes and Mercy climbed into the ring, continuing to shadow box and dance around the ring. Huey called Mercy over to their corner and rubbed him down. Mercy was stationed in the blue corner, Percy "Mean" Williams in the red corner.

"Relax, Mercy," said Huey. "You can beat this guy. Make sure you circle to your left."

Suddenly the lights dimmed. Rap music played, and Williams and his entourage entered the stadium. Sparkey led the way. The light heavyweight champion shadow boxed and danced down the aisle, while his friends and family twirled sparklers in the air. Sparkey held up the championship belt.

"Percy, Percy, Percy," the crowd chanted, caught up in the excitement. "We love you."

"I didn't know that Sparkey would put on such a performance," Louie whispered to Huey.

The sparklers stopped and the lights clicked back on. Sparkey spread the ropes and Percy jumped into the ring. He stared menacingly at Mercy as if to say, "I'm gonna kill you."

Mercy shivered. He turned to Louie and Huey. "I think we'll be lucky if we get out of this alive," he said.

An announcer spoke into a microphone. He wore a dark blue suit with a matching blue tie, a light blue shirt and black shoes. "Ladies and gentlemen," he said in a booming voice, "we are proud to announce our nontitled, three-round, exhibition light heavyweight championship fight, sponsored by Morrison Boxing, Inc. Standing next to me is the sponsor himself. Ladies and gentlemen, I give you Sparkey Morrison. Let's give him a nice round of applause." The crowd obediently obliged.

Sparkey stepped up to the microphone. "Thanks for coming to this exhibition fight. All donations go to the Developmentally Disabled Children's Fund," he said, looking over at Louie and giving him a sarcastic smile. He was confident that Louie had talked to Mercy and that he would go down in the second round. Sparkey handed the microphone back to the announcer.

"Before I introduce the fighters, I would like to hold a moment of silent for all our men and women serving in the armed forces, protecting us all over the world so we can have this fight tonight, in safety. Ladies and gentlemen, please bow your heads." The crowd bowed their heads and stood in silence for the next minute.

The referee in charge is Joe Cucci," the announcer continued. "And in the blue corner, all the way from the Upper Peninsula of Michigan, weighing in at one hundred and sixty eight pounds and wearing red, white and blue trunks, with a record of no wins, no losses and no draws; this is his first fight, I give you Gil "Mercy" Aller."

The crowd yelled and booed, "No Mercy! No Mercy! No Mercy!"

As Louie listened to their cries, he thought to himself, *Did I make a big mistake by taking on this fight?*

"In the red corner," the announcer continued, "all the way from Atlantic City, New Jersey, weighing in at one hundred and seventy pounds, wearing black trunks with gold stripes, with a record of thirty-eight wins, one loss and no draws; with thirty-five wins by knockouts, I give you the light heavyweight champion of the world, Percy "Mean" Williams."

The crowd started chanting, "Percy! Percy! Percy!" followed by "No Mercy! No Mercy! No Mercy!"

Percy raised his arms high above his head. "No Mercy! No Mercy! No Mercy!" he bellowed. The crowd went wild, cheering and yelling his name. Percy slowly lowered his arms and the crowd quieted. He shot Mercy another nasty look, curling his lip like a mad dog.

The referee called Mercy and Percy to the center of the ring. "Obey the rules and touch gloves," he told them. "Let's get it on."

Percy hit the top of Mercy's gloves with venom, then the two boxers returned to their corners and waited for the bell to ring. The fight was about to start.

Mercy sat nervously in his corner, tapping his feet against the padded floor. "What have I gotten myself into?" he muttered under his breath.

"Relax, kid," said Huey. "Don't be nervous. You're gonna do great." Mercy nodded, and Huey thought to himself, *Should I tell Mercy that Williams comes charging across the ring when the bell rings?* But before he could say anything, the bell rang and Percy came charging across the ring like a mad bull, pinning Mercy against the ropes in his corner. Percy was hitting Mercy with such force in the chest, the stomach and the rib cage that his only option was to cover up his face and try to protect his head, as Huey had taught him. Mercy knew he couldn't stay against the ropes. Williams was relentless and sooner or later one of his shots would connect. The rapid-fire punches continued to rain down on Mercy. It was Percy's goal to knock Mercy out in the first round.

Pangs of guilt assailed Louie. He had told Huey not to warn Mercy about Percy's mad charge across the ring at the sound of the bell. And because of his advice, Mercy was taking one *helluva* beating.

Mercy took two quick side steps to the left, escaping from the corner. Now he had Percy pinned against the ropes, and managed to deliver a few hard punches to Williams' rib cage just before the bell rang. Mercy returned to his corner. He had a cut above his left eye. Huey smeared a Q-tip with rosin and gently applied it to the cut. "It's nothing serious, kid," he said. This'll fix it."

Meanwhile Louie gave Mercy some water out of a plastic bottle and wiped the sweat off him with a towel. "Don't drink too much," he cautioned. "I don't want you to get stomach cramps."

"In the next round," Huey told Mercy, "move to the left." Huey knew that he was giving Mercy the wrong advice, but he had promised Louie.

Mercy looked up at Louie and Huey and said, "Now I know why they call him "Mean." He's trying to kill me out there."

The crowd was chanting, "Percy! Percy! Percy!" and "No Mercy! No Mercy! No Mercy!" Sparkey was delighted. He looked over toward Louie and Huey, a huge smirk on his face. The bell rang for the start of the second round, and once again William repeated his rapid charge across the ring, pinning Mercy against the ropes. He punched Mercy with force, striking him in the rib cage. An observant fighter, Mercy noticed that when Percy threw a right hand punch his left hand would drop, leaving his jaw vulnerable.

Mercy's thoughts drifted to high school. He remembered when Billy Bonds, the school bully, had challenged him to fight. Gil always turned him down because his mother told him not to get into any fights. But one day Gil had had enough. He told Bonds that he would meet him in the auditorium during lunch and fight him. When lunch period came around, the two boys stepped onstage and circled each other. Gil took a beating from this boy. Bonds punched Gil in the nose so hard that tears ran down Gil's cheeks. "Damn," Gil said to himself, "I'm getting the shit kicked out of me. I'd better do something about it." He noticed that when Bonds hit him with his right hand, his left hand dropped, exposing his head. So Gil decided to let Bonds give him another right hand punch, and waited for him drop his left hand. Then, Gil hit Bonds in the nose and mouth with such force that Bonds went down. "Do you want to continue?" Gil asked his opponent. Bonds lay on the floor, raised his right hand and said, "That's enough." Three days after the fight, Bonds walked up to Gil, in school, and said, "I still have a headache from the fight." After that Gil and Bonds became good friends.

Repeating the same maneuver from the last round, Mercy quickly sidestepped to the left and pinned Williams against the ropes. In his mind Mercy was telling himself, "You're getting the shit kicked out of you. So you better do something about it."

Mercy and Percy met in the middle of the ring. Percy was thinking that Mercy couldn't really hurt him. However, Percy was getting a little cocky and careless. He was dropping his left guard and sticking his face in front of Mercy, daring him to hit him. This was the opportunity that Mercy had been waiting for. As Williams dropped his left guard again, Mercy let go with a powerful straight right hand, catching Percy squarely on the cheekbone. Percy's knees buckled as the bell rang to signal the end of the second round, but he didn't fall down. Back in his corner, Percy told Sparkey, "I'm not hurt. I was just playing around."

"Percy isn't hurt," Sparkey told his attendants. "He's faking it," he said, casting a menacing look in the direction of Louie and Huey, and wondering why Mercy didn't go down in the second round. Sparkey felt as if he had been double-crossed.

Louie whispered in Huey's ear, "I'm a dead man. I'm a dead man. Did you see the look on Sparkey's face?"

Huey nodded. "You really caught him with a good shot," he told Mercy. "Percy was lucky that the bell rang."

Louie was yelling, "Mercy! Mercy! Mercy!" to the crowd.

The crowd shouted back, "No Mercy! No Mercy! No Mercy!"

The bell rang for the third and final round. This time Mercy was ready for his opponent. When Williams charged across the ring, Mercy stepped quickly to the left side as Percy swung his right arm and missed. Mercy pinned Percy against the ropes. But Williams punched his way out and the two boxers found themselves in the middle of the ring. They circled each other like Indians circling a wagon train. Only this time Mercy was circling in the correct direction; he was circling to the right, away from Williams' powerful right arm. They wound up in a clinch and the referee walked over and broke them up.

86

Once the fight resumed, Mercy was waiting in the middle of the ring for Williams to showboat again, as he did in the last round. The crowd was shouting and booing, "No Mercy! No Mercy! No Mercy! " Percy stuck his head out like a chicken, and with his arms straight down at his sides, he begged Mercy to hit him.

Mercy moved in with the quickness of a cat and threw three quick punches: a hard right to the stomach, a left to the chest and a hard right to the jaw. Once again Percy's knees buckled, but he didn't go down. Instead he stepped forward and began throwing jabs to keep Mercy away; all the while, shaking his head and muttering to Mercy, "You didn't hurt me." The bell rang and the fight was over. Before going back to their respective corners, Williams shook his head and said to Mercy, "Your punches didn't hurt me."

When Percy returned to his corner, Sparkey was waiting for him. He raised Percy's left arm and declared him the winner. Then he turned and glared across the ring at Louie and Huey.

Louie and Huey were pleased with the way Mercy had ended the fight, despite the fact that in the last round he had ignored their order, and circled to the right. "I'm proud of the way you handled yourself, Mercy," said Huey, unfastening Mercy's boxing gloves and handing him his red, white and blue sweatband. Mercy put it around his forehead.

The bell rang and the announcer declared Percy "Mean" Williams the winner. Mercy and Huey walked over to Williams' corner to congratulate him.

"I was just joking around," Percy said. "I was only pretending to be hurt. I didn't even train for this fight because it was unconditional and it didn't mean anything in the standings."

Sparkey, who had finished talking to some reporters, saw Mercy and Huey congratulating Percy, so he decided to walk over and join them. "That's right. Percy was just joking around. This asshole here didn't even hurt him," Sparkey said, turning toward Mercy and giving him a sarcastic look.

Two sports reporters walked over to Sparkey and asked, "Sparkey, is it true that Percy was just pretending to be hurt?"

"That's right," Sparkey answered. "We had this all planned just to get the crowd worked up. And I have to say, it worked."

Huey and Sparkey looked at each other. *What a line of bullshit*, thought Huey. *I know that Percy was hurt, and his knees buckled from the force of Mercy's punch.* "Maybe we'll meet again," he told Sparkey.

"I don't think so," Sparkey said. "Unless hell freezes over. Especially not with an asshole like him. He can't fight. It's a good thing Percy was just joking around."

"Let's get the hell out of here," Huey said, grabbing Mercy, "before there's another unconditional fight."

Mercy, Louie and Huey walked back to the locker room, wearing the red, white and blue sweatbands, as the crowd shouted, "No Mercy! No Mercy! No Mercy!"

Two wrestlers climbed into the ring to entertain the spectators. Later, two women would box.

Louie lagged behind Mercy and Huey. He was scared. Mercy had not gone down in the second round, and now Louie's ass was on the line. He heard a few people shout, "Mercy! Mercy! Mercy!"

Would Sparkey show him any mercy?

Chapter 9

The day after his fight with Percy, Mercy worked out at the gym, even

though his body ached.   He felt good knowing he had lasted three rounds with the

light heavyweight champion of the world. Garcia was already there, training for his

next fight. The telephone rang, and Garcia answered it. "It's for you, Mercy. It's

Louie. He wants to talk to you." Mercy stopped punching the training bag and

walked over to phone.

"Yeah, Louie, what do you want?" Mercy said.

"Do you remember when I was in jail and I told you to look under the desk

and get an envelope?" said Louie.

"Yeah, I remember," Mercy replied.

"Well, there's another envelope under the desk and it's for you," Louie said.

"See ya later."

Mercy crawled underneath the desk and found the envelope. He grabbed it

and carefully opened the seal, expecting to find $1,000 inside. Instead he counted

$1,200. Mercy laughed, thinking to himself, *Crazy Louie can't even count right. I'll give him back the two hundred dollars when I see him.*

The following morning Mercy arrived at the gym at seven. Louie and Huey were already there. Mercy walked over to Louie and handed him the extra $200.

"What's this?" Louie said, looking at the money. Surprise etched his face.

"You gave me too much money," Mercy said.

Louie yelled for Huey to come over. "Hey, Huey, tell Mercy why he has two hundred dollars extra," he said.

"Well," Huey said, "we both gave you a hundred dollars extra because of the aggressive way you handled yourself against Williams."

"Damn!" Mercy exclaimed. "You guys are the greatest."

"Yeah, yeah," said Louie, brushing off the compliment. "Now Huey wants to take a look at those cuts and bruises and make sure everything is OK." The telephone rang. Louie walked over to his desk and picked up the receiver. "Can I help you?"

"Louie, you asshole." It was Sparkey. "Where the hell did you get the balls to try and make a fool out of me, with that asshole, Mercy. Nobody makes a fool out of Sparkey Morrison. Where did you get this asshole anyway? Did you ship him in from Canada? Where was the asshole working, on a pig farm? Percy wants a piece of your ass, a piece of Huey's ass and a piece of Mercy's ass. How come that asshole didn't go down in the second round? That was the deal and now you owe me, Louie, you asshole." Sparkey slammed down the receiver.

"Yes, yes, yes," Louie shouted as he hung up the receiver. Although alarmed by Sparkey's outburst, he was thrilled that Mercy had actually hurt Percy. He danced around his desk.

"Louie, who was on the phone?" Huey asked.

"Sparkey, and he's pissed off," Louie said. "Mercy did hurt Percy in the fight and Sparkey and Percy were trying to cover it up." Louie grabbed Huey by the arm and they both danced around the desk. "I love myself. I love myself," sang Louie. Then he stopped abruptly and said, "Huey, discussion in the *Men's Room and Office.*"

The two partners walked into the men's room. "Louie, what the hell's going on?" asked Huey.

"We have to get Mercy more interested in boxing," Louie said. "I can feel it in my bones; Mercy could become a champion. During the fight, the crowd was yelling, 'No Mercy!' but when the fight was over a lot of people were yelling, 'Mercy! Mercy! Mercy!' The people will love him, with his red, white and blue sweatband and his easygoing manner."

"Well, he's not that easygoing once he gets inside the ring," Huey said.

"That's it," Louie said. "Mercy has an aggressive attitude once he gets inside the ring. Tomorrow, I'm going to make a few phone calls to see if I can set up another fight for him. If Mercy agrees, we'll take him to the New York State Boxing Commission and have him checked out for drugs. He'll have to get a physical and then we'll pay for his boxing license. Mercy will become a professional fighter."

"Make the phone calls after Mercy leaves tomorrow and see what you can come up with," Huey said. "I'll try to convince him to become a professional fighter.

"Hopefully, Mercy will think, sleep, dream, eat and sweat like a real fighter," Louie said.

"You guys have more meetings than the president of the United States," Mercy said as Louie and Huey walked out of the men's room.

"That's right," Louie said, grinning, "but there's one difference. We accomplish something." They all laughed.

Mercy woke up at 6:00 the next morning, shaved and jogged to the gym. The gym was about six blocks from his apartment, and jogging every day would build up his stamina. It was a brisk, sunny morning, with a slight chill in the air. As Mercy ran, he passed apartment houses, a gas station, a car rental shop, a few restaurants and *Your Favorite Place*. Except for a man delivering newspapers, the sidewalks were empty.

Arriving at the gym, Mercy was surprised to see Louie there so early. An open telephone book lay on his desk, and Louie was scribbling furiously on a piece of plain, white paper. "Good morning, Louie," Mercy said as he passed his desk.

Louie glanced up briefly and said, "Morning, Mercy."

Mercy paid no attention to what Louie was doing as he started his workout.

Once Mercy had left for work, Louie began calling other promoters to see if he could set Mercy's first professional fight. To his surprise, several promoters were interested in staging a boxing match between Mercy and one of their fighters. Word had spread about the fight between Mercy and Percy "Mean" Williams. Reporters at the exhibition match had written that Mercy gave Percy *one hell of a fight.*

When Huey arrived at the gym at about ten, Louie told him about the progress he had made trying to line up fights for Mercy. Huey was as excited as Louie was about the news. They both hoped that Mercy would agree to become a professional boxer.

"As soon as Mercy comes in for his nightly workout we should talk to him and found out what he wants to do," said Huey. Louie nodded in agreement.

When Mercy walked into the gym later that day, Louie greeted him at the door. "There's a meeting in the *Men's Room and Office,*" he said.

Mercy nodded. "OK," he said, following Louie to the men's room.

"We have two four-round fights lined up," Louie said. "Would you be interested in fighting in one of them? One fight is in two weeks, the other in five weeks." Louie paused to take a breath. " We want you to fight, but only if you're interested. Once you get your boxing license you can make lots of money, if you win. The fight, in two weeks, pays a thousand dollars if you win. And the other fight pays fifteen hundred dollars if you win."

"What do you mean, which one do I want? Mercy said. "I want both of them."

Louie and Huey exchanged glances, barely able to conceal their excitement.

"If you take these fights, you'll have to become a professional fighter," Huey explained. "That means, you'll have to go in front of the boxing commission and get a license."

"What do you have to do to get a boxing license?" Mercy asked.

Huey told him. "Let's go for it," Mercy said. "Now, tell me about these two fights."

Louie and Huey were both pleased and surprised by Mercy's enthusiasm. They had not expected him to agree to participate in a fight, much less two of them!

Back at his apartment later that night, Mercy called a retired dancer, whose name he had found in a newspaper called "Showbiz,"and asked him about his fee. The dancer's rates were high: $200 for a one-hour lesson. *Expensive*, Mercy thought, but the man had an excellent reputation and he probably had a slew of contacts. Mercy knew that the money he made from the fights would not last long, but he was excited that he would have enough money to pay for his dancing lessons.

95

The first fight would be held in upstate New York. Mercy would be fighting John "Albany" McGill, a hometown fighter from Albany, who had two wins by knockout.

Huey had Mercy working out every minute that he was at the gym. He kept reminding Mercy to "Jab, jab, jab," and "Combinations, combinations, combinations." And, " Move, move, move." It sounded like a chant. Mercy relished the strenuous training – he knew that if didn't train hard he wouldn't win. He enjoyed learning new things. He was brought up with the idea that learning was important no matter how unimportant it seemed; because one day it might help him to make something of himself and fulfill his dreams.

On certain days, when Louie, Huey and Mercy closed up the gym together, they would go to *Your Favorite Place* for drinks, wearing their red, white and blue sweatbands. Mercy would order Seagram's with seven-up, while Louie and Huey both ordered Dewar's Scotch. Some of the patrons would ask why they wore the headbands. Louie explained that it was now their trademark for Mercy, as a fighter.

The night before the fight, as they were sipping drinks at the bar, Louie told Huey and Mercy that they would leaving for Albany at seven the next morning. "I wanna leave early just in case *Betsey* breaks down," he said. Louie's Cadillac was twelve years old and needed some mechanical repairs.

Time passed quickly as the three men drove to Albany. Mercy was in top form, and ready for his first professional fight. Physically, he was in good shape, but mentally, he was nervous. To pass the time, they talked about other fighters, and about Sparkey. Louie was still worried that Sparkey was going to kill him because Mercy had not gone down in the second round. Despite the fact that Louie had to change a flat tire, stop for two tanks of gasoline and add three quarts of oil, they arrived in Albany at about 4 p.m. Mercy was scheduled to fight at ten o'clock.

They found a motel close to the sports arena, where the fight would take place. The rooms were clean, but the outside of the building needed to be painted. After grabbing a quick snack, the three men retired to their rooms. Mercy needed to relax for a couple of hours, to ease his nerves before the big fight.

This fight would be different from his fight with Percy. Ten other fights were also scheduled, as opposed to the one fight that Mercy and Percy fought for charity. Mercy's would be the sixth fight of the night. Huey and Louie tried to find out all they could about McGill, by talking to other promoters and boxers. They wanted to familiarize themselves with the opponent's boxing style and his weaknesses. They learned that he had a powerful right hand, but that he wasn't too fast with his hands.

The fight was scheduled to start in fifteen minutes. Clad in his in his red, white and blue boxing trunks, Mercy waited in the locker room with Louie and Huey. He practiced his punches and jabs by shadow boxing and by punching a big boxing mitten that Huey was wearing on his hands. Mercy was too busy warming up to think about being nervous, much less about fighting in his first professional boxing match.

A knock sounded on the door. The referee entered the locker room and introduced himself. His name was Fritz Martin. A former boxer, Martin had a solid, wiry frame, the muscles bulging beneath his black and white striped shirt. He explained the rules to Mercy, telling him to follow his commands. As he turned to leave, a security guard knocked on the door and said, "It's time to go out to the ring."

Wearing their trademark sweatbands, the trio made their way out to the ring, Mercy jogging along in the middle of his two friends. Mercy was surprised at the large number of people sitting in the bleachers, and in the chairs placed around the ring. The arena was sold out to capacity with cheering, yelling and waving fans. On reaching the ring, Huey separated the ropes and Mercy climbed into the ring amid shouts of "No Mercy! No Mercy! No Mercy!" Shocked to hear the fans booing him, Mercy surveyed the crowd. A thrill of excitement surged through his body as it suddenly hit him that this was his first professional fight. There was no turning back.

The shouting increased when John "Albany" McGill, the hometown fighter, entered the arena and jumped into the ring. McGill raised his arms over his head and the fans cheered wildly as they shouted, "Albany! Albany! Albany!" The hometown favorite stood about 5'9" tall. He had a strong, muscular frame, his dark, craggy face topped by a mop of curly black hair.

The announcer stepped up to the microphone in the center of the ring and asked the crowd to bow their heads in the moment of silence for all the men and women serving in the armed forces. "Thank you," he said, breaking the silence. "And now, ladies and gentlemen, we are proud to announce a four-round, light heavyweight fight." His deep booming voice echoed throughout the arena. "In the blue corner, wearing the red, white and blue trunks, and coming all the way from Michigan's, Upper Peninsula, is the challenger. Weighing in at one hundred and sixty-eight pounds, with no record, this is his first professional fight, I give you Gil "Mercy" Aller." The crowd booed and yelled, "No Mercy! No Mercy! No Mercy!" Louie and Huey could hardly hear themselves think – the noise was deafening. Nervously chewing their fingernails, they were praying that Mercy would win his first fight. A loss would be a terrible way to begin his boxing career.

"In the red corner," the announcer continued, "wearing the gold trunks with the white stripes, hailing from Albany, New York, weighing in at one hundred and seventy pounds, with a record of two wins by knockout, no losses and no draws, I give you, John "Albany" McGill." The crowd roared, "Albany! Albany! Albany!" followed by "No Mercy! No Mercy! No Mercy!" They were going wild, stamping their feet, clapping their hands, shouting and screaming. "The doctor at ringside is Chad Valentine; the timekeeper is John O'Conner and the referee is Fritz Martin," shouted the announcer, struggling to make himself heard above the raucous crowd.

The referee was already in the ring. He called Mercy and Albany to the center, and said, "Follow my commands. Remember to protect yourselves at all times." Huey had told Mercy, "Protect yourself at all times, even after the bell rings. Because sometimes if you get a hotheaded boxer, he will try to hit you after the bell. And there's always a chance that your opponent may not hear the bell."

Martin concluded by saying, "I want you to touch gloves, and may the best man win." Touching gloves is a mark of respect for the opponent, in professional boxing. Martin stayed in the middle of the ring, as the two boxers returned to their corners. Louie and Huey took their seats at ringside. Huey was thinking back to the night he and Louie first saw Mercy at *Your Favorite Place*, when Mercy knocked out the two men, Lenny and Jose.

The bell rang for the start of the fight. The two boxers met in the middle of the ring, jabbing and circling, trying to feel each other out. Mercy noticed that Albany was dancing around on his toes. They each threw a couple of sharp punches, then fell into a clinch. "Break it up," said Martin, walking over to them. The bell rang to signal the end of the first round.

Mercy returned to his corner, where Louie and Huey were waiting for him. "When you're fighting a hometown fighter, try to knock him out, if you can," Huey said as he wiped Mercy down with a towel. "If you leave it up to the judges, they will sometimes vote for the hometown fighter." Mercy nodded.

When the bell rang for the second round, Mercy and Albany met again in the center of the ring. Using his jab, Mercy worked his way in and landed a solid punch on McGill's jaw. McGill rocked back on his heels, then punched Mercy's nose with such force that the blood flowed out of his right nostril and ran down his cheek. Mercy retaliated by driving Albany into the ropes, and delivering two hard punches to his body. The bell rang and the round was over.

Back in his corner, Mercy took a sip of water from the water bottle, as Huey wiped the blood from his face with a towel. "You're doing good, kid," said Louie. " Just keep doing what you're doing."

"Albany is very slow with his punches," said Huey, continuing to wipe the blood from Mercy's face. "You should take advantage of that and start throwing some combinations. Try punching him with both hands."

The bell rang for the start of the third round. Albany pinned Mercy against the ropes by punching him and forcing Mercy to step backward as Albany stepped forward. Mercy covered up his face and waited for an opening. Using his strong arms and quick feet, Mercy threw a couple of punches to Albany's body, fighting his way off the ropes. Albany pinned Mercy against the ropes again, and Mercy's nose began to bleed again after Albany punched him in the nose a second time. Mercy pushed Albany off him and started jabbing his way in. He stepped back, then stepped in quickly. Albany dropped his guard, and Mercy hit him with a three-shot combination: left, right, left. Albany dropped to the mat.

The referee stepped in and told Mercy to go to the far corner. Martin started counting, "One, two, three, four, five, six, seven…" On the count of seven, Albany tried to stand up, but he was wobbling back and forth. The referee stopped the fight.

Huey and Louie ran over to Mercy. Huey lifted him up by his thighs, and Mercy raised his arms in victory. Louie was so excited that he tripped and fell down, landing on his stomach, in the middle of the ring. Embarrassed, he quickly rose to his feet and put his arms around Mercy, hugging him tightly. The crowd booed, but a few were chanting, "Mercy! Mercy! Mercy!

Mercy was jubilant – this was his first win as a professional boxer. He danced around the ring, stopped, then ran back and hugged Louie and Huey. "I did it! I did it!" he kept saying over and over again.

"We never doubted it for a second," said Huey as he slid off Mercy's gloves and cut the tape off his hands. Then Louie handed Mercy his red, white and blue sweatband and they all walked over to Albany's corner to see if he was all right.

"Congratulations," said McGill, shaking Mercy's hand. "You must have some Irish in your blood, because you hit like a mule. I didn't even see those punches coming."

Mercy beamed. Savoring the praise from his fellow fighter, he felt as if he had made it as a professional boxer. Mercy, Louie and Huey returned to their corner. Huey gathered their towels, water bottle and first aid kit, placing them in a cardboard box. Then they started to walk down the aisle, on their way back to the locker room.

Some people yelled, "Mercy! Mercy! Mercy! Mercy smiled and waved to the crowd.

On the drive back to New York, they discussed the fight, then the conversation turned to Mercy's dancing career.

"So, are you still set on being a Broadway dancer, champ?" asked Huey, patting Mercy's shoulder.

"Well, right now my dancing is on hold," replied Mercy. He felt a little disappointed about not pursuing his dream of becoming a dancer. But with his busy training schedule, he hadn't had much time to think about it lately. Mercy continued, "It is very expensive and I need more money if I want to continue. I've already used up the thousand dollars that I won from fighting Percy, on dancing lessons. I tried out for a Broadway show, but the producer didn't want me because I can't sing. He told me that my dancing was fantastic, but he also needed someone who could sing. But, I'll fight anytime, anywhere."

Louie reached over and grabbed Huey's hand and squeezed it hard. They were both ecstatic. Mercy had just agreed to fight for them *Anytime, Anywhere*.

Chapter 10

The phones were ringing off the hooks. Promoters had heard about Mercy's first professional knockout and were eager to arrange a fight with one of their own. Mercy's next fight would be held in New Jersey. His challenger, another hometown fighter by the name of Mike "Jersey" Mead, had a record of four wins, three by knockout. With only three weeks to train, Mercy didn't waste a second. He had had a taste of victory, and was eager to repeat the performance.

Huey was pleased with Mercy's jabs and combinations. His footwork was incredible; he could move to the right, left, forward and backward quickly and gracefully, like a cat. His dancing background was paying off in the ring. He seemed to get stronger every day. The muscles in his arms, legs and chest bulged.

The day of the fight arrived, and the three friends drove to Hoboken, New Jersey, in Mercy's car. Arriving at the Hoboken Arena, where the fight was scheduled to take place at 10 PM that evening, they stowed their boxing gear in the locker room, then headed to the weigh-in room where Mercy tipped the scales at 175 lbs.

"Okay, we got about 4 hours to kill," said Louie as they left the weigh-in room, "let's grab some dinner."

"Sounds good," said Huey. Mercy nodded, although he was feeling too nervous to eat.

They settled on a nearby diner and soon Louie and Huey were tucking in to a full meal, of soup, salad, steak, and dessert. Huey allowed Mercy to order a minute steak and a salad, but Mercy merely picked at his food, his thoughts on the upcoming fight. Mead was a formidable opponent – Mercy's strongest challenge yet.

After dinner, they drove back to the arena. Louie parked the car and the three of them sat back, listened to the radio and closed their eyes. Time passed slowly for Mercy. Too nervous to sleep, his thoughts wandered to his family back home in Michigan. He wished they were there to watch him fight. He hadn't told them yet that he was a boxer. He knew they would be shocked when they found out. Still disappointed that he hadn't made it as a dancer yet, Mercy's hopes were slowly fading as he became more involved in his boxing career.

Louie's booming voice interrupted his reverie. "It's eight thirty – time to head to the locker room to get ready for the fight. Let's hit it."

As they waited in the locker room, Mercy could hear the crowd yelling and booing at the other fighters who were in the ring. A security guard called time, and the three friends marched toward the ring, displaying their red, white and blue sweatbands.

Chants of "No Mercy," assailed their ears. Louie yelled back, "Mercy, Mercy, Mercy." He didn't like the crowd yelling at his fighter. But the crowd continued to boo. Mercy climbed into the ring and started to shadow box as he waited for his opponent.

"No Mercy," yelled the crowd.

"You'll be sorry," yelled back Louie.

Mike "Jersey" Mead strutted down the aisle toward the ring and the crowd's chants switched to "Jersey, Jersey, Jersey." As Mead climbed into the ring, Louie and Huey appraised his well-built physique. A few inches taller than Mercy, with a strong muscular chest and powerful looking arms, Mead exuded strength and power. Mercy had his work cut out for him.

"Go for his ribs and then start using your combination," Huey whispered to Mercy.

After the announcer had called for a moment of silence, and introduced the two fighters, the referee called them to the center of the ring and issued his instructions. Mercy returned to his corner.

"Feel out Jersey in the first round to see what he's got," said Huey. "Then in the second round we'll start putting the pressure on. Don't forget, he's in his home state."

Mercy remembered Huey's advice, but Jersey had other plans. He charged across the ring, reminding Mercy of his fight against Percy. Jersey wanted to brawl. Mercy was caught by surprise. He expected a boxing match, not a barroom brawl. Jersey landed some good clean shots to Mercy's body and head. Mercy covered up his head and backed away, throwing a few jabs at Jersey to keep him away. Jersey refused to let up. He attacked Mercy again, throwing different combinations of punches. But then he made a mistake. Jersey dropped his left guard and Mercy landed a powerful, crushing punch to his jaw. Mead went down for the count. Mercy had won his second professional boxing match by knockout.

Huey and Louie ran across the ring to congratulate him. Huey placed Mercy's sweatband around his head for him. Then, the three friends posed for photographs, Huey and Louie holding up Mercy's arms in victory. Six sports reporters clambered into the ring and rushed over to Mercy. "When's your next fight," they asked in unison. "Were your two wins by knockout due to plain luck?"

"You'll have to ask Louie and Huey," Mercy said. "They gave me the chance to fight."

Mead walked over to Mercy and they gave each other the fighter's hug. "Good luck with your boxing career," Jersey said as his trainer walked over and shook hands with Louie and Huey.

Louie and Huey were proud of their protégé. Mercy was like a son to them. "I am proud of the way you covered up when Jersey came after you," said Huey, "and for waiting for that opening so that you could give him a good punch."

"Way to go, kid," said Louie, patting Mercy on the back, "way to go."

Back at the locker room, four reporters were waiting by the door. Mercy and Huey slipped inside the room, while Louie stayed outside to talk to the reporters. The reporters fired questions at Louie in rapid succession. "Why do you wear red, white and blue sweatbands? How did you find him all the way from Michigan's, Upper Peninsula? How did he get the name, "Mercy"? Do you think he can become the light heavyweight champion of the world?"

Louie responded to the reporters' questions one at a time. "We wear the red, white and blue sweatbands because Mercy used to wear one when he was a lumberjack back in Michigan. We found him at a bar here in New York City. He got into a brawl with a couple of obnoxious patrons and we liked the way he moved and threw his punches. He came to New York hoping to become a Broadway dancer. We chose his name because of something that was said one day. And yes, if things go like they are now, then maybe Mercy can become the light heavyweight champion of the world," Louie finished as he turned and entered the locker room.

It was after midnight when Mercy, Louie and Huey drove back to New York, stopping at *Your Favorite Place* to celebrate Mercy's victory. Mike was tending bar, as usual, and after congratulating Mercy, he asked him, "Do you still work at the florist?"

"Yes," Mercy replied.

"I was wondering," Mike said, "because I haven't seen Corinne lately. Anyway, how's your dancing coming along?"

"Well, Corinne is going with somebody, and I'm doing most of my dancing in the ring." Mercy and Corinne were good friends and dancing partners, nothing more.

"I'll drink to that," said Louie, and they all raised their glasses to salute Mercy's victory.

Mike noticed Mercy's eye. "Boy, that's a nice black eye you have," he said. "The next drink is on me."

A few days later Louie told Mercy that his next fight would be against a black boxer from Brooklyn, who had a record of five wins; three by knockout. "He's an older fighter, about 35, who goes by the name of Harold "I'm Not Old" Brown," said Louie.

Over the next four weeks, Mercy trained rigorously for the fight, sparring with Garcia, hoping for his third win. Although still not enthusiastic about boxing, he needed the money for dancing lessons. Mercy liked Garcia. He was the best fighter in the gym, but not as fast with his hands as Mercy. Nor did he move as quickly.

As the two fighters sparred, Huey kept a close watch on Mercy, making sure that he didn't develop any bad habits, like dropping his hand and not protecting himself. Huey would shout, "Move, move, move. Combination, combination, combination. Step back, step back, step back." He was pleased with Mercy's jab; it was quick, and hard enough to knock someone out in the later rounds.

On a balmy Saturday night in summer, Mercy entered the ring in the Brooklyn arena as shouts of "No Mercy" echoed around the crowded stadium. In contrast, when Harold "I'm Not Old" Brown entered the arena, the crowd greeted him enthusiastically, clapping their hands and cheering, "He's not old, he's not old." Born and raised in Brooklyn, Brown was popular with the local fans. He looked much younger than his thirty-five years. Lean and muscular, with a solid physique, Harold proved to be a tough opponent. It took Mercy until the fourth and final round to knock him out.

After that fight Mercy went on to win twenty-one consecutive fights by knockout. He quit his job at the florist because he was so busy training, and would often be gone for days, depending on how far he had to travel, to fight in a match. However, he wasn't ready to sever all ties with the florist shop and occasionally helped out during their busy seasons. He was grateful to the owner for giving him a job when he first came to the city.

Mercy, Louie and Huey were all afraid to fly, so they drove to the boxing matches, staying overnight in local motels, if it was a long trip. Mercy's fear stemmed from all the stories he had heard about airplane crashes; Louie's and Huey's because a close friend had died in a small plane crash.

The three friends were growing rich off Mercy's earnings. Money was dropping in like falling leaves. Louie sold his beloved Cadillac, Betsey, and bought a new car. Huey moved into a bigger apartment, a block away from his old apartment. And Mercy bought a new convertible, a 2006 light blue Ford Mustang. He decided to stay at the rooming house, with Mr. and Mrs. Keely, because they treated him like a son and it felt like home. But he did deposit $50,000 in his savings account to perhaps buy a house someday.

Mercy continued working out at the gym, sparring with Garcia and practicing his jabs and combinations. His jabs were strong, but his combinations were still weak. He worked on strengthening his muscles: lifting weights, doing sit-ups and skipping rope. Huey was pleased with Mercy's quick footwork and the power he was generating from his punches. Each day, he was becoming stronger and stronger. Huey and Louie still had dreams of Mercy becoming the light heavyweight champion of the world.

After his workout session, Mercy would usually grab a seat and sit outside, enjoying the fresh air. Sometimes he would fall asleep, other times he would just daydream – Gil Aller, from Michigan, light heavyweight champion of the world. Huey and Louie weren't the only ones with dreams!

One day, while Mercy was sitting outside, taking a nap, three beautiful girls walked by. Victoria, who was Caucasian, had flowing, black hair, which fell below her shoulders. Tall and willowy like a model, she had striking hazel eyes and full rosebud lips. Sabrina, Hispanic, with short brown hair and dark brown eyes, was of medium height, and wafer thin. The third girl was black and her name was Carol. Her wiry black hair was woven in cornrows, interspersed with different colored beads. She had soft brown eyes and a radiant smile that lit up her whole face, revealing pearly white teeth. Unlike her two friends, Carol was short and stocky. All three girls were in their early twenties.

Mercy was not wearing a shirt. It was a hot day in July, with the temperature in the mid eighties. The girls stared at Mercy's strong, muscular body, the sweat glistening on his arms and shoulders, and the ripple-like muscles in his stomach.

They also stared at his black eye, courtesy of his last fight, and the red, white and blue sweatband adorning his head.

As the three girls ate lunch in the luncheonette, across the street from the gym, they talked about Mercy.

"What is that red, white and blue sweatband all about?" Carol said, in her street-smart voice.

"He must belong to some gang or something," Sabrina piped in. She was the sassy one of the group. Her brother had belonged to a gang, until he was shot and killed.

"I have a different impression of him," Victoria said. "I can't see him belonging to a gang. I can see him as being very patriotic, and maybe he got a black eye from trying to break up a fight."

Carol and Sabrina smirked. They didn't share Victoria's opinion of Mercy. They thought he was a roughneck, who got into lots of fights, and that he was sitting outside waiting for his next prey. Back at their office, they continued to talk about Mercy. All three were administrative assistants, who worked nearby for Parkington Inc., an insurance company.

Louie had watched the girls walk past the gym, and pointed them out to Huey. "I have plans for these girls," he whispered as he looked at his watch and scribbled something on a piece of paper.

"What's going on?" asked Huey.

"I just had a brainstorm," Louie answered.

Huey sighed. When Louie had a brainstorm, trouble lie ahead.

Mercy had finished his nap. Picking up the chair, he entered the gym and walked past Louie, who was sitting at his desk. "Hey, Mercy," called Louie, "I'd like to have a word with you."

"OK." Mercy wondered what Louie wanted.

"Someone phoned for you, but they didn't leave a message," Louie said. "I had no idea you were outside, so I couldn't find you to tell you. Anyway, to stop this from happening again, would you mind taking your break at noon? This way, I'll always know where you are. That could have been the president of the United States calling you."

"Yeah, right," Mercy chuckled, never believing that the president would call him. "All right, I'll take my break at noon," he said, turning away from Louie's desk and walking toward the men's room. Once inside, he closed the door behind him.

Huey looked at Louie. His face held that certain grin, the one that told Huey he was up to no good. Huey knew that there had been no phone call for Mercy - Louie had made it up. Now Louie was kissing his arms, up and down. "I love myself. I love myself," he said between kisses, followed by, "I'm brilliant. I'm brilliant. I'm brilliant."

"What in hell are you up to?" Huey asked.

"Don't worry about it, Huey," Louie said, "You'll find out tomorrow and I promise you're gonna love it."

The next morning, when Huey arrived at the gym, he noticed that Louie had the same shit-eating grin on his face. He kept looking at his watch and as noontime approached, his grin grew bigger. At noon exactly, Victoria, Sabrina and Carol walked past the gym, on their way to lunch. Louie, who was standing by the window, waved to Huey to come over and pointed to the three girls.

"So what?" Huey asked as he looked out the window and saw the girls.

"So what?" Louie said, practically shouting at his friend. "Wait and see what's going to happen."

Huey had no idea what Louie had planned, nor did he care.

Then Louie walked over to Mercy and told him, "It's time for your break."

Mercy didn't notice the grin on Louie's face, which started at his lips and seemed to travel up to his ears. "Thanks for letting me know," he said.

"Anytime," Louie replied.

Mercy picked up one of the chairs and walked outside. Placing the chair to the left of the front door, he sat down and took his break.

Louie was looking out the window as Victoria, Sabrina and Carol emerged from the luncheonette, munching on Macintosh apples. Louie called out to all the guys in the gym.

"Watch what is about to happen," he shouted.

As the three girls walked past Mercy, they glanced at him, but didn't stop or say anything. They realized that this was the same guy they had seen yesterday.

Suddenly, Louie yelled out, "Hey, you bunch of bitches."

Mercy heard Louie and practically shot up out of his chair like a rocket. He was shaking his head and saying, "No, no, no. It wasn't me."

"You have some nerve calling us a bunch of bitches," screamed Sabrina.

"And now you're lying to us," said Victoria.

The girls hurled their half-eaten apples at Mercy, hitting him in the chest and arms. "That's what you get for calling us bitches," yelled Carol.

Mercy shook his head in disbelief. Walking inside the gym, he found Louie lying on the floor, laughing. The other guys, including Huey, were wiping tears of laughter from their eyes. "Louie," Garcia asked, "where did you come up with that one?"

Louie tried to stand up, but when Mercy said to him, "I think those girls really hate me," he fell back down on the floor.

"I think I'm having a baby," said Louie, clutching his stomach. It was as if Louie's laughter were contagious because soon Mercy was laughing along with the rest of them.

"That was a good one, Louie. But those girls are pissed," Mercy said as he realized that he had been set up by Louie. Mercy wasn't angry - he knew that Louie liked to play practical jokes on his friends. But he was disturbed that the girls

thought he had called them bitches. He would never call a woman a bitch. Never!

Chapter 11

Mercy started training rigorously for some upcoming bouts. To build up his strength and endurance, Huey had him running laps at a neighborhood park. Mercy had been fighting four- and six-round fights, but the next two fights would be eight-round matches. And soon, Louie would be arranging a twelve-round fight.

After the incident with Victoria, Carol and Sabrina, Mercy didn't sit outside for about a week. Anytime he saw the girls, he tried to explain that it was Louie who had called them a bunch of bitches. But the girls told Mercy to can it. "That cute little Louie would never call us a bunch of bitches," they said, glaring at Mercy. They had known Louie for over a year now, since they first started working for the insurance company. Louie would chat with them, tell them funny jokes as they passed by the gym on their way to lunch. They thought he was funny and cute.

118

Mercy won his next two fights by knockout. His first opponent, Jack "Fast" Martin, definitely lived up to his name. Instead of fighting, Fast would run around the ring, throwing a few punches whenever he felt like it and then run around the ring again. Sometimes, Mercy was nowhere near him when Fast threw his punches. He could barely keep up with him. Finally, in the seventh round, Mercy pinned Fast against the ropes and delivered a couple of hard and fast punches to his head and rib cage. The spectators, along with Louie and Huey, didn't know if Fast went down because of Mercy's punches, or from fatigue.

After two eight-round fights, Mercy was a little fatigued himself. Noontime found him sitting outside in his chair, relaxing in the fresh air. Meanwhile, inside the gym, Huey noticed that Louie and Garcia were planning a prank involving Mercy and the three girls.

Huey saw Louie looking across the street, toward the luncheonette, as Victoria, Carol and Sabrina walked out, clad in high heels and short skirts. *It must be Carol's birthday*, thought Huey, noticing that she was carrying a silver balloon with the words *Happy Birthday* emblazoned in red letters.

Louie scurried around the gym, rounding up all the men. "Quick, go over the window and look outside," he urged as the three girls approached the gym. Then he walked over to the front door and stood next to Garcia. Still half asleep, Mercy didn't notice the three girls walking toward him. They glared at Mercy as they passed by, then continued on their way, laughing and joking. Suddenly

Louie opened the front door and yelled out, "Loose pit bull! Pit bull! Pit bull! Run for your lives!" as Garcia started barking and growling like a mad dog.

Carol screamed, "Pit bull! Loose pit bull! Run for your life!" and in her fright she let go of the balloon and it flew up into the sky. Then all three girls started running down the block in their high heels, almost tripping over their own feet.

Louie stared, his eyes wide with delight, as the girls clip-clopped down the street, breasts and bottoms bouncing up and down as they ran for their lives. Carol led the pack, with Victoria and Sabrina running close behind her. Upon reaching their office, they turned and looked around, realizing that no mad dog was chasing them. Hands on hips, they shook their heads, angry at having been duped, and stared down the block at Mercy.

Mercy woke with a start because he heard a dog barking and Louie yelling. Jumping to his feet, he looked down the block at the girls and shook his head. "No. No. No," he shouted as he pointed to his chest. " It wasn't me." But to no avail. The girls just stood there, glaring at him, not believing a word. *If looks could kill, I'd be a dead man now,* he thought.

Mercy picked up the chair and carried it inside the gym. Once again, he found Louie lying on the floor, laughing. "Well, you got me again, Louie," said Mercy. "Now they really hate me. I may be mistaken, but I think one of them gave me the finger." Mercy felt ashamed because he thought that the girls hated him for playing a joke on them. He also felt embarrassed because all the guys in the gym were laughing at him. Being young and naïve, Mercy was the perfect foil for Louie's practical jokes.

Louie laughed so hard that he said to Huey, "I think I'm having twins this time."

Huey was laughing too. "I have to hand it to you, Louie," he said. "That was one beautiful sight; seeing those three gorgeous girls clacking down the street in their high heels and tight skirts, with their little rear ends swaying and their breasts bouncing up and down. I'm sorry I didn't have a camera." By now, everyone was laughing, including Mercy.

The next day, Huey and Mercy were working on Mercy's upper cut. This was a good punch to use if the other fighter was covering up. Usually, the fighter covering up would leave an opening between his two elbows allowing his opponent to forcefully place his glove in between the fighter's elbows, and hit him on the jaw. Huey wanted Mercy to learn this punch because it could be used as a natural weapon.   Mercy repeated the following moves over and over again: 'Right, left, upper cut. Right, left, upper cut.' The quicker and more powerful his upper cut became, the easier it would be to knock out his opponent.

Mercy's first ten-round fight would be against John "The Biker" Mueller. It was scheduled in two weeks, in Dover, Delaware. A tough, scrappy fighter, Mueller had learned how to fight on the streets of Dover, by challenging others to fight him. He had a reputation as a bully, and at nineteen, decided to see how

well he could do in the ring. He was on Sparkey's list to fight Percy "Mean"

Williams for the light heavyweight championship. Politics play a big part in the

boxing world. Sparkey had a lot of influence with officials in the world boxing

commission. If he thought that a particular fighter had a chance of beating his

prize fighter, or if he didn't like someone - a fighter, a promoter, a manager or a

trainer - then that fighter might not get an opportunity to fight for the

championship. If Mueller won the upcoming fight against Mercy, Sparkey and

the world boxing commission might consider him to fight Williams for the

championship. So the fight against Mercy was an important fight for John "The

Biker" Mueller.

If Mercy won the fight, there would be no chance of his fighting Williams

for the championship. Although, smart and powerful, with quick hands and feet,

Mercy was still an unknown in the boxing world, still working his way up.

Besides, Sparkey hated Louie and Huey, and he had not forgiven Mercy for

calling him an asshole. Mercy's chances of fighting Percy were almost

nonexistent.

The night of the fight arrived. Mercy waited in the locker room, with

Louie and Huey, for the call to the ring. He had been warming up for the last 15

minutes, dancing and shadow boxing around the room, and now Louie was

delivering his usual pep talk to ease Mercy's nerves. "Now don't forget, he puts his pants on the same way you do," said Louie, referring to Mueller, "and he goes to sleep just like you do." Then Louie added, "Last night "The Biker" didn't get any sleep. And do you know why he didn't get any sleep?" Louie asked rhetorically. "Because he was thinking about you all night."

As Louie finished his pep talk, an official rapped on the door and called time. Donning their trademark sweatbands, the three men made their way to the ring.

The auditorium was filled to capacity with spectators, cheering and yelling, "No Mercy," followed by chants of "Biker." Mueller was the hometown favorite, and his fans were hoping that he might have a chance to fight against Williams for the light heavyweight championship.

A few minutes after Mercy had entered the ring, a big roar resounded throughout the auditorium and five Harley Davidson motorcycles rolled down the aisle toward the ring. Each bike had the logo, "The Biker," with two boxing gloves underneath it, painted on top of the gas tanks. Forty more bikers walked behind Mueller and his entourage, following him into the auditorium. The riders on the Harley Davidsons gunned the engines, causing the building to shake. The noise was deafening.

Mueller shadowboxed around the ring, then walked over to ropes and whispered to the bikers at ringside. "This is going to be an easy one," he said,

123

covering his mouth with his boxing glove. "This so-called "Mercy" looks like a
pussy to me."

The bikers responded by standing up and shouting, "John. John. John,"
followed by chants of "Go Biker, Go Biker," their arms raised to form the letter
V for victory.

The announcer, Bill White, with microphone in hand, walked to the center
of the ring to announce the beginning of the fight. In his early forties, Bill was tall
and thin, with light red hair, and a voice as smooth as velvet. "Ladies and
gentlemen," he began, "Green and Brown Inc." is proud to sponsor this ten-round
light heavyweight fight. In the blue corner, all the way from the Upper Peninsula
of Michigan, wearing the red, white and blue trunks, weighing in at one hundred
sixty eight pounds; with a record of twenty wins, by knockout; no defeats and no
draws, I give you, Gil "Mercy" Aller."

The people in the auditorium yelled and screamed and stamped their feet.

"In the red corner," Bill continued, "hailing from Dover, Delaware;
wearing the blue trunks, with white stripes; weighing in at one hundred seventy
pounds; with a record of twenty-three wins, eighteen by knockout, and two losses;
I give you, John "The Biker" Mueller." Once again, the crowd erupted, cheering
on their hometown boy.

The referee, Joe Cucci, stepped over and called the two fighters to the
center of the ring. "Follow my commands," he said, "and may the best man win."

The fighters returned to their respective corners, and the bell rang for the start of the fight. As they met in the middle of the ring., Mercy couldn't help but notice all the tattoos on Mueller's body – the snake on his right arm, a red heart with "Mother" on his left arm, and a large eagle tattooed on his chest.

The first three rounds passed with little action. Both men were feeling each other out, trying to gauge each other's strength and speed. Before the fourth round began, Huey said, "Mercy, let's get the ball rolling. I want you to put some pressure on Mueller. I want you to add more punches and start throwing more jabs." Mercy realized that he would have to speed things up to increase his chances of winning the fight.

The bell rang and Mueller pounced on Mercy like an attack dog, pinning him against the ropes. *His trainer must have told him to pick up the pace too,* Mercy thought to himself as he struggled to free himself from the ropes.

Now in the middle of the ring, the two boxers continued to slug it out, delivering quick jabs, right and left, as well as body punches. Mercy's right eye was swelling up after a right hand punch from Mueller. And Mueller's lip was bleeding thanks to a hard left jab from Mercy. The bell rang signaling the end of the round. When Mercy returned to his corner, Huey told him, "Keep the pressure on. Start using your left jab and throw some combinations."

The bell rang for the start of the fifth round. Mercy pinned Mueller against the ropes. Mueller covered up, so Mercy, recalling what Huey had told him to work on during practice, landed a right, left and an upper cut and punched his opponent in the jaw. Mueller fell backward against the ropes. *Bingo!* Mercy knew his opponent was in trouble. The bell rang to end the round.

The next two rounds, both boxers battled hard, throwing powerful body shots, and right and left combinations. Mercy's swollen eye throbbed painfully, and Mueller's eyes and nose were now bleeding profusely. Before the eighth round, Huey told Mercy, "I want you to go for Mueller's ribs and stomach and continue giving him upper cuts."

The bell rang for the start of the eighth round. Mercy danced across the ring and forced Mueller against the ropes, punching him sharply in the rib cage and stomach. Then Mercy delivered a swift upper cut, snapping his opponent's head back. "The Biker" was down.

"Go to the farthest neutral corner," Joe Cucci told Mercy.

Mercy didn't like hurting people, but when the bell rang he knew that it was either he or the other guy, and this was business. He had to do whatever it took to win.

Cucci counted, "One, two, three, four, five, six... Are you all right?" he asked Mueller.

"I'm fine," Mueller replied, staggering to his feet.

The bell rang signaling the end of the round.

"Keep up the good work," said Huey as Mercy returned to his corner. You got Mueller in trouble, so you should finish him off in the next round." Mercy nodded as Louie gave him a sip of water and wiped the sweat from his forehead.

At the bell, Mercy charged across the ring like a bull and pushed Mueller against the ropes. He hit his opponent high in the head and low in the rib cage and stomach. But Mueller refused to fall down. Pushing Mercy aside, he maneuvered his way off the ropes and the two fighters ended up in a clinch in the middle of the ring. The referee told them to separate. They moved around the ring, throwing punches at each other and shuffling backward and forward. Mercy sensed that Mueller was tiring; his punches were weak and he was moving sluggishly around the ring. "The Biker" was losing steam.

Back in his corner, Mercy listened attentively as Huey said, "Okay, it's time to go for the kill. Try to knock him out because you never know how the judges will see the fight; sometimes they favor the hometown fighter. So if the fight goes a whole ten rounds, you could lose on points."

"I'll try my best," said Mercy. He was ready to finish this off.

The tenth and final round would decide the victor. This time Mueller came charging across the ring, pinning Mercy against the ropes and throwing wild punches to Mercy's head and stomach. Mercy fought his way off the ropes by pushing Mueller aside and stepping sideways away from his opponent. Mueller covered up his face and head. So, Mercy delivered a right, left and an upper cut, which bounced off Mueller's right arm. However, on Mercy's second attempt, he struck Mueller on the jaw, causing him to fall down. This time, "The Biker" was out for the count. Gil "Mercy" Aller had won his first ten-round fight and his twenty-first win by knockout.

Silence reigned in the auditorium. The fans were in shock. Their hometown boy had been knocked out by an unknown fighter from Michigan. Their dream of a light heavyweight championship, now in tatters.

Huey and Louie were so excited, they literally fell into the ring. Scrambling to their feet, they ran to Mercy and lifted him up off the mat. "He did it! He did it! He did it!" they shouted in unison.

The crowd was still sitting in shocked disbelief. Then a few tentative voices shouted out, "Mercy, Mercy, Mercy."

Louie turned toward Huey and said, "They better remember the name, "Mercy."

Chapter 12

Mercy had taken quite a beating from the Biker. His right eye was swollen shut and a deep gash marred his left eyebrow. It would take about a month for the injuries to heal. Louie and Huey knew how hard Mercy had trained for the fight, so they decided to cut him some slack.

"Why don't you and Garcia hit the beach tomorrow," Louie said to Mercy. "Take a break from training."

"Yeah, good idea, Louie," agreed Huey, "the salt air will work wonders on those open wounds, speed up the healing process."

"Besides, it will give you guys a chance to relax and get to know each other," said Louie.

Mercy nodded. A day at the beach sounded like heaven to him.

Louie turned to Garcia. "Mercy's never been to Jones Beach, so take him there. Relax and get yourselves a suntan. But make sure that Mercy buys a bottle of sunblock, otherwise with his fair skin he'll burn to a crisp.

"Will do, mon," said Garcia, grinning, pleased to have a break from training.

Early the next morning, Garcia drove his 1993 Toyota Corolla to the gym and picked up Mercy about 7 a.m. "Jump in, mon," said Garcia, leaning over and opening the passenger side door for Mercy. "We're gonna have us a little sightseeing tour first, before we hit the beach."

"Sounds good to me," said Mercy as he tossed his bag in the backseat and hopped in beside Garcia.

Garcia took the Midtown Tunnel into Queens to the Long Island Expressway and then to the Meadowbrook Parkway, exiting onto the Southern State Parkway. "I'll take you to the Nautical Mile in Freeport, first, show you around a little," said Garcia.

Mercy looked around at all the shops and restaurants, and then stared in amazement at the number of boats in the bay. Fishing boats bobbed up and down, alongside sailboats, cigarette boats, gambling boats, and private yachts. Mercy turned to Garcia. "Gee "I've never seen such a wide variety of boats," he exclaimed. "Just look at those gambling boats, they sure are big."

"Yep, they sure are," agreed Garcia. "Gambling is legal out in the Atlantic Ocean, so they usually have a full load of people every day."

After touring the Nautical Mile, Garcia drove to Jones Beach, parking near the J.F.K. Memorial, where all the different sections of the beach converged. He chose Section 4, which was south of Bay Shore, in Suffolk County, one of his favorite parts of Jones Beach. It was now approaching ten o'clock.

Although still early, the temperature had already soared into the mid-seventies. Mercy squinted up at the sun, blazing down from a cloudless sky. "It's gonna be a scorcher," he said to Garcia. "Good thing I brought that sunblock."

"Yeah, mon, otherwise you'd be toast. Me, I don't have to worry, I already dark," he said. And the two men broke into laughter.

Mercy looked up and down the long, sandy beach, impressed by the white sand. Stepping around a couple of guys who were throwing a football back and forth, he squeezed the warm sand between his toes. It felt good. He looked around, surprised to see that the beach was already crowded. A group of boisterous teenagers were playing volleyball; children frolicked in the ocean, while others played in the sand, building sandcastles and kicking beach balls, as their parents looked on. A sea of brightly-colored umbrella, some striped, some solid, dotted the beach. It reminded Mercy of a garden in spring, with all the myriad of shades and colors.

131

And presiding over all, sat the lifeguards in their towering highchairs. Their muscular, sun-bronzed bodies glistened in the early morning sun, as their heads swiveled back and forth, scanning the beach for any sign of trouble. "I wouldn't mind a job like that," said Mercy, looking up at one of the young lifeguards. "Sitting in the sun all day, and getting to meet all the pretty girls." Mercy pointed to a group of tanned, bikini-clad girls lying spread-eagle in the sand, soaking up the sun.

Garcia nodded. "I hear ya, mon, I hear ya. Beats training in a sweaty gym all day long."

Mercy and Garcia spread their blanket on the warm sand and stripped down to their bathing trunks. For the next few hours, they relaxed in the sun, occasionally plunging into the ocean, to cool off. Both men were strong swimmers. Mercy had spent countless hours swimming in the pool and lakes, back home in Michigan, but this was his first time in the ocean. And he loved it! Especially the feel of the waves slapping against his body and the buoyancy of the salt water. "This is heaven," he yelled to Garcia as he floated on his back and gazed up at the sky. "I feel as light as a feather."

"Yep," agreed Garcia, floating alongside him. "Sure beats training in a sweaty gym."

Back on the blanket, the conversation turned to girls. "So, mon, have you found a girlfriend yet," Garcia asked Mercy.

"Nope," replied Mercy, "but I haven't been looking very hard." He paused. "Besides, my heavy training schedule doesn't leave much time for girls."

Garcia nodded. "I hear you, mon," he said. "Huey certainly puts us through our paces. He's tough but fair. And Louie is one helluva promoter."

Mercy agreed. "Yeah, and Louie is quite a comedian, too," said Mercy, recalling some of Louie's practical jokes. "I didn't know he could bark and growl like a real mad dog."

Garcia chuckled. "You should have seen the look on your face, when you were trying to explain to those three girls that it wasn't you barking."

"Well, at the time I was embarrassed," Mercy said. "But I can see that to those who were watching, it was funny."

Garcia had brought a cooler, packed with soda, ice, chips, fresh fruit and a couple of roast beef sandwiches on whole wheat bread. "Time for lunch," announced Garcia, and the two friends tucked into the food, still laughing about Louie and his practical jokes.

At 3.00 p.m., they decided to drive back to New York City, to avoid the rush hour traffic. "If we leave any later," said Garcia, "we'll be stuck in a traffic jam."

"Yeah, let's go," said Mercy, rolling up the blanket and placing it under his arm. "It's been a perfect day and I don't want anything to spoil it." Little did he know what lay ahead!

As they walked back to the parking lot, Mercy and Garcia noticed a young woman, about twenty-five, lying face down on a bright orange beach towel, her black bikini top unfastened. The two men couldn't take their eyes off her. She had long, shapely legs and her blonde hair, tied in a loose ponytail, cascaded down her bare back.

Garcia nudged Mercy. "She looks like a model," he said. "Just look at those long legs, they practically go up to her neck."

"She's gorgeous," said Mercy.

"Do you want to see her tits?" said Garcia.

"Oh sure," said Mercy, laughing. "Just walk over to her and ask her."

Garcia remained silent. "You're not serious," said Mercy, his face turning red. He was embarrassed. "No way, Garcia," he pleaded.

"Stand next to her towel and keep your eyes on her tits," Garcia told him.

Mercy complied, standing like a dummy, next to the girl's towel, while Garcia yelled at the top of his lungs, for the whole beach to hear, "Pit bull! Loose pit bull! Run for your life!" Then Garcia barked and howled like a mad dog.

Startled, the woman jumped up, leaving her bikini top on the towel.

Mercy stood there with his mouth open and his eyes wide with amazement as he watched the beautiful blonde woman jump up, her bare breasts bouncing up and down.

"Pit bull! Loose pit bull! Run for your life!" she screamed, kneeling down to retrieve her towel and her bikini top. Surprised to see Mercy standing there, staring at her, she tripped and fell over her tote bag, chipping her front tooth on the bag's steel clasp.

Garcia grabbed Mercy's arm. "Let's get the hell out of here," he said.

The two men raced toward the parking lot. A crowd of beach goers followed in ho pursuit. "Stop them! Stop them!" they yelled.

On reaching the car, Mercy and Garcia jumped in and slammed the doors shut. As Garcia revved the engine, a police car drove up behind, blocking them from leaving.

"I think we're in trouble, mon," said Garcia as he watched a police officer emerge from the car and walk toward them.

"Get in the back of the police car," said the officer. He pointed to the angry mob that had now gathered in the parking lot. "You'll be safe from the crowd in there."

About forty people, including the young bikini-clad woman, were screaming and yelling at Mercy and Garcia. Many of them were frightened of dogs, and had believed that a pit bull was running loose on the beach, especially when they heard the growls and Garcia's warning cries. Realizing that Garcia and

Mercy had played a practical joke on them, they were angry and wanted to voice their complaints to the police.

As Mercy was sitting in the backseat of the police car, he recognized the officer – it was Officer Wells, the same police officer, who had arrested Louie and Huey. After his divorce, Wells had left New York City and moved to Bay Shore to work for the Suffolk County police department. Wells still carried a chip on his shoulders. Despondent over his divorce, he rarely smiled, and lately a sad look seemed to be permanently etched on his face. But when he saw the beautiful, blonde woman, with the chipped tooth, standing outside the police car, his lips curled up into a smile. Turning to her, he asked, "Are those the men you saw?" and pointed at Mercy and Garcia.

"Yes," she said. " I chipped my tooth because of him," she continued, glaring at Garcia. "He was yelling, 'Pit bull! Pit bull! Loose pit bull!' And then he started barking like a mad dog."

"Would you like to press charges?" Wells asked.

"Yes, I would." The young woman was adamant. "Oh, and Officer…"

"Yes, ma'am?"

"I would like to have these two men spend the night in jail. Is that possible?"

Wells, clearly smitten with the beautiful blonde, was ready to oblige. "Oh, of course, they'll spend the night in jail. They had no right scaring you and causing you to chip your tooth. If you come to the jail tomorrow and ask for me, I'll make sure you get their addresses if you decide to pursue this case any further." Then Wells turned to Mercy and Garcia. "Okay, you two, step out of the car and hand me your driver's licenses."

Mercy and Garcia did as ordered. Wells wrote down their addresses on a piece of notepaper and handed it to the young woman. "Call me in the morning and I'll give you their telephone numbers," he whispered, handing her his business card.

By now, another police car had arrived. Wells walked over to the police car and told the officer, "Everything's under control. You can leave. There's no need to stick around."

He walked back to Mercy and Garcia and read them their rights. "I'm placing you under arrest for disturbing the peace and causing a riot." Then he handcuffed the two men, bundled them into the back of the police car and drove to the village jail in Bay Shore.

En route to the jail, Mercy asked Officer Wells, "Do you remember taking two men to jail, by the name of Louie and Huey, because they couldn't stop laughing?"

Wells turned around briefly and glanced at Mercy. He had a puzzled look on his face. After a few seconds, Wells realized who Mercy was talking about and said, "Oh, yeah. You're the guy who came with the bail money to get your buddies out of jail."

Mercy had never been arrested before, much less spent a night in jail. *Gee, I wonder if they'll only serve us bread and water.*

The next morning, the telephone rang at the gym and Louie answered. It was Garcia's wife, Maria. In broken English, she tried to describe what had happened to her husband and Mercy. "Artie no come home last night. He in jail in Bay Shore with Mercy. They say he need bail money."

Louie called the jail and spoke to the desk sergeant. "I hope you gave them more than bread and water," he screamed into the phone when he heard that it would cost $500 to post bail. "Make sure you feed them steak and lobster. Those are my two boys. So make sure you take good care of them." He scribbled down the address of the jail. "I'll be there as soon as I can."

As Louie was hanging up the receiver, Huey walked in the front door. "Get in the car," Louie told him. "We're going to Bay Shore." Louie threw the keys of the gym to one of the regular patrons. "Here's the keys. If we're not back by closing time, lock up."

"To Bay Shore?" Huey asked. "What for?"

"Yes, to Bay Shore," Louie answered. "I'll explain on the way there."
Once they were in the car, Louie told Huey what had happened, adding, "They had to spend the night in jail because of some blonde."

"I think it best, if from now on, we don't give them any days off," said Huey.

Louie nodded in agreement. "I hear ya, I hear ya."

When they arrived at the jail, Mercy and Garcia were still wearing their bathing suits. "They made you stay like that all night," Louie asked.

"No, they gave us blankets to cover ourselves," Garcia said, "but it got damn cold in there. There's some crazy person in there. Let's get the hell out of here."

Mercy had not enjoyed his night in jail. The cell had been cold and damp, and had smelled liked wet, sweaty tee shirts. "Yeah, let's get the hell out," he said, walking toward the exit. "One night was enough for me."

Louie drove Mercy and Garcia to Jones Beach so that Garcia could pick up his car. On the way there, Mercy asked Garcia, "Where did you learn to bark like a mad dog?"

"I used to make all kinds of sounds, when I was in high school, for all the school plays," Garcia said. "My specialty was barking and growling like a dog.

Huey, who was sitting in the front seat, turned around and said to Garcia, "You sure could scare the hell out of somebody in a dark alley."

"Yeah, mon," said Garcia. "And my turkey ain't half-bad, not to mention my rooster." And Garcia proceeded to gobble like a turkey and crow like a rooster for the rest of the journey.

Chapter 13

Mercy had one month to train before his next fight. Every fight was important because of the standings. If he were to lose a fight, he would go down in the standings and his chances of fighting Percy "Mean" Williams for the light heavyweight championship would diminish. He was now fighting boxers of a high caliber – the more fights he won, the tougher his opponents.

Louie had no problem lining up fights for Mercy, thanks to Sparkey. Or so Louie believed. He thought that Sparkey wanted someone to stop Mercy. This way Mercy would never get another shot at his best fighter.

Huey noticed that Louie was acting strangely. He had that grin, the one that started on his lips and extended up to his eyes; causing his lips to curl upward, his checks to puff out and his eyes to take on a devilish look. *What could Louie have on his mischievous mind?* Huey wondered.

One sunny afternoon, Mercy was sitting outside the gym, taking a well-earned break, when Victoria, Carol and Sabrina walked past and stuck their tongues out at him. Mercy tried to explain that he was innocent. But they wouldn't believe him. Mercy felt desolate – how could he convince them that Louie was the real culprit?

A couple of days later, Mercy was back outside, taking his break in the sun. He had just fallen asleep, when the three girls walked by. In the meantime, Louie had called all the male patrons over to the window. "Watch this," he said as he yelled out, "Hey, you bunch of lesbians."

Startled, Mercy quickly opened his eyes, and shrugging his shoulders, he said, "Goddamit, Louie got me again."

Victoria, Carol and Sabrina spun around. "That's it," they cried in unison.

"It wasn't me. It was Louie," Mercy tried to explain.

"Sure, try to blame it on poor, cute little Louie," Carol said. "Okay, girls, let's get him."

And with that, the three girls launched an attack. Sabrina kicked Mercy's right leg, while Carol punched him in the stomach, and Victoria smacked him in the face.

Mercy tried in vain to defend himself. "Ouch. That hurt. No! No! No! It wasn't me. It was Louie!" Mercy cried out. His pleas fell on deaf ears.

"That should teach you to stop blaming things on cute little Louie," said Sabrina.

"Maybe now you'll think twice before calling us names," shouted Victoria. And the girls stomped off in a huff, and headed back to their office.

Poor Mercy was devastated. Louie's "little joke" had gone too far. *Enough is enough*, he thought to himself. Snatching up the chair, he stormed into the gym to find everyone laughing at his expense. Louie lay on the floor, rolling around like a beach ball. "I think I'm having triplets this time," he said, clutching his stomach.

"Hey, Louie, you better cut that out," Huey said. "The next time they may have a gun or a knife." Huey's tone was serious. "You really got those women worked up."

"Gee, I'm having so much fun. But you're probably right. I'll lay off for a while," he said. Then, seeing the forlorn expression on Mercy's face, he quickly apologized. "I'm sorry, kid, I'll never do that again," he said sheepishly.

Mercy didn't trust Louie. "Apology accepted. But I sure hope you're telling me the truth."

Louie decided to play it safe. "Okay, everyone, listen up," he said, addressing all the patrons in the gym. I've been bad and I wanna make it up to Mercy. You're all invited to *Your Favorite Place* – the drinks are on me."

Mercy had arranged to meet Corinne at the club at nine o'clock. People started trickling in at this time, and by eleven, the place would be packed.

Corinne arrived early. She looked for Mercy at the bar, but didn't see him. Glancing around the crowded club, she spotted three girls she had known from high school, and decided to walk over to their table and say hello.

"Hi, Corinne, long time, no see. Sit down and join us for a drink," said Victoria, motioning for Corinne to sit down.

"Thanks," Corinne said, "but I'm waiting for someone."

"Oh, who are you meeting?" Sabrina asked.

"A friend, who used to work with me at the florist shop," Corinne explained to her friends. "He likes to dance, so we meet here on Friday nights to dance and have a few drinks."

Mercy arrived at the bar promptly at nine, and stood near the entrance waiting for Corinne to arrive. He glanced around the club and saw Corinne sitting at a table with three girls. All were deep in conversation.

Mercy walked over to the table and said, "Hi, Corinne. How are you tonight?"

"Oh, I'm fine," Corinne said. "Gil, I'd like you to meet some of my friends from high school."

Mercy blanched as he realized that these were the same three girls who had walked past him at the gym. Fortunately for Mercy, the girls didn't recognize him. Now dressed in a dark blue collared shirt, with black pants and black shoes, he bore no resemblance to the sweatsuit-attired boxer lounging in the chair outside the gym.

"Girls, this is the friend I was telling you about," Corinne said, turning toward Mercy. "Gil, I want you to meet Victoria, Sabrina and Carol," Corinne said, pointing to each girl in turn. "Gil wants to be a dancer in a Broadway show," Corinne continued. "But now he's a boxer, as you can see from his black eye." Garcia had accidentally given Mercy a black eye while they were sparring earlier. "Girls, I would like you to meet Gil."

"Hi," the girls said, not realizing who he was.

"He works out at L&H Gym," Corinne said. "Not far from where you work. I'm surprised that you don't know him."

A pause. Then Carol suddenly sprang out of her chair. "He's the guy who barks like a mad dog," she said, wagging her finger at Mercy. Victoria and Sabrina jumped up and joined in the chorus. "He called us a bunch of bitches, and told us we were a bunch of lesbians," they yelled.

Corinne stood there in shock, her mouth wide open and her cheeks bright red. She couldn't believe what she was hearing. Rallying to Mercy's defense, Corinne insisted, "You have the wrong person. Gil would never do anything like that. Besides, he seldom swears. The only time I hear him swear is when the Detroit Tigers lose a game, which is quite often."

"He tried to blame everything on cute little Louie," said Sabrina. Victoria and Carol nodded, anger suffusing their faces.

"Believe me, girls, you have the wrong the person," Corrine pleaded with her friends as she led them over to a far corner in the club, trying to calm their anger, and explain that Mercy was a nice guy.

Mercy remained standing next to the table. Although innocent, he was still worried that the girls wouldn't believe Corinne. He would rather be inside a boxing ring, instead of standing there by himself, having his fate decided by three women.

Five minutes later, Corinne and her friends returned to the table. Victoria, Carol and Sabrina seemed calmer. Victoria looked into Mercy's eyes and said, "We'll give you a chance to prove yourself."

Mercy felt a flood of relief. "Well, I can tell you one thing," he said. "Sabrina, you kick like a mule. Carol, you punch like a kangaroo. And, Victoria, you gave me this black eye," Mercy said, pointing to his left eye. Garcia had given him the black eye, but Mercy wanted to see Victoria's reaction.

"I gave you that black eye?" Victoria asked in disbelief.

"You hit me. Didn't you?" Mercy asked.

Victoria, Sabrina and Carol all had blank expressions on their faces. They thought that maybe Corinne was telling them the truth about this guy, Gil.

Corinne stood there in astonishment, listening to Mercy admonish her friends. She was surprised to hear that they would treat him that way. To break the tension, she grabbed Mercy's hand and said, "Let's dance."

"I thought you'd never ask," said Mercy, and the two of them walked over to the dance area, and were soon caught up in the music.

Victoria, Sabrina and Carol watched the couple gliding effortlessly across the floor. Perhaps Corinne was right about Gil, they asked each other – he seemed like a nice person. And what a dancer! They were amazed at how gracefully he moved around the dance floor.

After the music stopped Mercy walked over to the bar and ordered screwdrivers for all the girls. A waitress walked over the table. "The drinks are on Mercy," she told them, placing the glasses on the table.

Victoria, Carol and Sabrina looked at the waitress in puzzlement. "Who's Mercy?" asked Sabrina.

Corinne explained, "His real name is Gil Aller. But his professional boxing name is Mercy."

The girls held up their glasses to Mercy as a gesture of thanks. Mercy, who was still standing by the bar, raised his glass in salute. Then a tall girl, with short blonde hair, who was sitting at the bar, got up and grabbed Mercy by the arm. "I saw the way you danced just now," she said. "And I want to dance with you."

Mercy glanced over at Corinne, wondering if she would mind him dancing with another girl. But Corinne was busy chatting with her friends. *Why not?* he thought. Besides, the blonde girl wasn't about to take no for an answer – she was determined to take a turn around the dance floor with Mercy.

Corinne sat at the table, looking annoyed. When she and Mercy made plans to meet and go dancing, Mercy danced with her, and with her friends, if they present. But Corinne didn't know this woman, so she was a little miffed. After the dance was over, she waved for Mercy to come back to the table.

"Thank you," the blonde said to Mercy. "I really enjoyed that dance. If you want to dance again later, just ask." And winking flirtatiously, she returned to her stool at the bar.

When Mercy returned to the table, Corinne, who had calmed down, said to him, "The girls want to apologize to you."

Victoria, Sabrina and Carol immediately sprang to their feet and said in singsong voices, "We apologize, Mercy."

"I accept your apologies," Mercy said, but on one condition."

"What's that?" they asked.

"If I can have a dance with each one of you."

"That's a deal," said Sabrina, grabbing Mercy's hand and pulling him toward the dance floor. After dancing with Sabrina, he then danced a fast dance with Carol, and a slow number with Corinne. But Mercy saved the last dance for Victoria – he was smitten with her. They danced to *Pretty Woman*. "This is one of my favorite songs," Mercy whispered in Victoria's ear.

"What is it about the song that you like?" Victoria asked. "The lyrics? The beat? Or is it rhythm?"

"Well, it's a little bit of all three," Mercy said. "But the real reason I like this song is because it has my name, Mercy, in it."

"I've never met anybody with that name before," Victoria replied, thinking to herself, *Mercy's arms are so strong. I like the way he places one arm around my neck and the other around my waist. He's so light on his feet. I feel like I'm floating on air. It sends chills down my spine. Ooh, I like the way he smells. And the way he speaks to me. I think I could really get to like this guy.*

This Victoria can really dance, *Mercy thought to himself.* She feels so soft and she smells delicious; her tall, thin body seems to fit perfectly in my arms.

At the end of the evening, Mercy walked Corinne and her friends to Carol's car, to make sure they were safe. Then he walked back to the boarding house. He decided not to ask Victoria for her phone number because he was afraid that she might still believe that he had actually called her and her friends names. He wanted Victoria to have time to think about what happened outside the gym, before he made a move on her.

The next morning, after finishing his workout, Mercy called to Louie and Huey, "I'm going out for a while. I'll be back soon."

Louie was curious, but he shrugged his shoulders and said nothing. He didn't want to create more tension between himself and Mercy.

When Mercy returned, he was holding three long stemmed red roses, with baby's breath and leather leaf, each wrapped separately in cellophane, and tied with a red ribbon.

Louie and Huey exchanged glances. "Who are those roses for, Mercy?" asked Huey.

"You'll find out in a few minutes," Mercy said, grinning. Louie returned to his desk, and Huey went back to the exercise machines to monitor the patrons.

After about five minutes, Mercy, holding the three roses, walked outside and waited for Victoria, Sabrina and Carol to return from lunch. He had seen them pass by earlier on their way to the luncheonette.

Louie thought that Mercy was trying to make amends with the three girls. Glancing outside at Mercy, he thought to himself, *Does Mercy want another beating? Those girls are going to hit him on the head with the roses.* Then Louie called all the guys in the gym, over to the window. "Mercy is trying to make amends with the three roses. Did you ever see a fighter get banged over the head with a red rose?" he chuckled. Little did he know that the girls now knew the truth about his prank.

The guys all stood at the window and watched as the girls crossed the street. They approached the gym and Mercy stood up. "Here's a little something I bought for the three of you," he said as he handed each girl a rose.

Carol kissed Mercy on the cheek, as did Sabrina, and Victoria kissed him on the lips.

Louie was shocked. "What the hell's going on out there?" he said. "I can't believe what I'm seeing."

All the guys laughed, except for Louie. Louie opened the door a crack, trying to eavesdrop on Mercy's conversation with the girls. He heard the word, cute, and his name. Then he noticed that Carol and Sabrina had left, leaving Mercy talking to Victoria.

"Would it be all right if I took you out to dinner on Friday night? We could see a movie afterward?" Mercy asked Victoria, his voice quivering, the palms of his hands sweaty.

"Yes," Victoria said, smiling. "I'd like that." Her cheeks were flushed.

"You're sure?" Mercy said, wondering if she now believed he had nothing to do with the name-calling. "Would seven o'clock be all right?"

"Oh, seven o'clock would be fine," Victoria said sweetly.

"I'll pick you up at your place, but I don't know where you live."

151

Victoria wrote her address and telephone number on a piece of paper, and handed it to him. "I'll see you on Friday," she said, kissing him lightly on the cheek.

"Well, that's great," Mercy said, smiling. "See you on Friday." Then he turned, picked up the chair and carried it back inside the gym.

Louie was now sitting at his desk, pretending to work on some papers. He couldn't believe what he had just seen and heard.

"Hey, Louie, the girls want to talk to you about something, when you have time," Mercy said loudly so that all the guys in the gym could hear him.

Louie's face turned red and all the guys laughed. "What do they want with me?"

"I have no idea," said Mercy, winking at the others. "Perhaps they have a surprise for you."

Mercy took Victoria to an expensive restaurant, noted for its steak and seafood. He wanted to impress her, so money was no object. His uncles had taught him to respect women and to treat them well. Mercy ordered a T-bone steak and Victoria ordered lobster. The evening was going well. Victoria was impressed with the restaurant, and with Mercy's impeccable manners. He was the perfect gentleman. The more she got to know him, the more she liked him. And, she seemed genuinely interested in his boxing career. Over coffee and liqueurs, she asked him about his family and how he got started in boxing.

Mercy told her how he came to New York from Michigan to pursue his dream of becoming a dancer in a Broadway show. And how he had hooked up with Louie and Huey after they had seen him handle the two hecklers at the club.

"I have a fight coming up in Manhattan, in a month," he said. "If you're interested, I'll get tickets for you, Carol and Sabrina."

"I'd love to come and see you fight," Victoria said. "I'll have to check with Carol and Sabrina, first, to see if they can come. But you can count me in."

"There's a catch," Mercy said.

"What's that?" Victoria asked, her curiosity piqued.

"You have to cheer for me," Mercy said, with a grin on his face.

"That's no problem. Besides, Sabrina and Carol like you now. But, Mercy, I still have one question."

"Oh, what's that?" Mercy said.

"Are you sure you didn't call us a bunch of bitches?"

"Honest, Victoria, I would never do that," Mercy replied.

They both laughed. Victoria believed Mercy now and she wouldn't ask him about the incident again.

After that first date, Mercy and Victoria became inseparable. They ate lunch together in the park; walked on the beach, went to the movies, saw a couple of Broadway shows. They also dropped by *Your Favorite Place* and danced the night away. Victoria had natural rhythm. She kept in step with Mercy, and he loved how she felt in his arms, so soft and warm.

Victoria changed jobs and became a fashion designer, a career she had wanted to pursue since high school. She enrolled in night classes at the Fashion Institute of Technology and during the day she worked for a small, clothing design house. Now she would be working about two blocks from the gym.

One day, when they were eating lunch at the park, Victoria turned and saw Mercy grinning at her. They had just bought hot dogs, and Victoria was busy peeling the bun and throwing the crust to the birds.

"Mercy, I can see that you think I'm crazy, but I just don't like the crust," Victoria said, with a serious face.

Mercy laughed. "Do what you want," he said. "The birds love you and so do I."

Victoria turned to face Mercy and kissed him on the lips. "I love you even more," she said, adding, "Don't forget, tomorrow we're eating lunch with Carol and Sabrina."

The next day, when Mercy was working out at the gym, he found himself thinking about Victoria. He just couldn't imagine life without her now. They had

so much fun together and he counted the hours until he would see her again.
Victoria was equally enamored of Mercy. She felt as if she had known him
forever, not just a few weeks.

At lunchtime, Mercy and Victoria met Carol and Sabrina, in the park, as
arranged. They sat around a picnic table underneath two sturdy oak trees, eating
hot dogs. A soft breeze blew, cooling the hot summer air.

"I've got three tickets to my next fight," Mercy announced proudly.

Sabrina and Carol seemed excited, but Victoria looked worried.
Although she wanted to go to the fight to cheer on her man, she was worried that
he might get hurt.

Mercy read her thoughts. "Don't worry, I'll be fine," he said, "as long as
you are there to cheer me on."

Victoria forced a weak smile. And Carol and Sabrina chimed in, "You'll
have your very own cheerleading section – count on it!"

Mercy trained harder than ever for the upcoming fight. Victoria, Carol
and Sabrina would be there rooting for him and he was determined not to let them
down. His opponent would be Sam "The Man" Taylor," a tall, black man, with a
knockout punch. Taylor was in contention to fight Percy "Mean" Williams.

The night of the fight, Huey told Mercy, "Remember, stay away from
Taylor. He has a killer knockout punch. I think that your dancing skills will
come in handy because of your quick feet."

Mercy's bout with Taylor was scheduled for ten rounds. At fight time, Mercy headed toward the ring, flanked by Louie and Huey. Once in the ring, he scanned the crowd and spotted Victoria, Carol and Sabrina sitting in the fourth row. They were shouting, "Mercy, Mercy, Mercy," but the other spectators drowned out their voices by yelling, "Sam The Man, Sam The Man," as their hometown hero made his grand entrance.

Several days before the fight, Huey had explained to Mercy that if a fighter gets punched hard and he has long hair, his hair will shoot out from the back of his head from the force of the punch, making it look as if he has been hit hard, and he could lose points. Thus, a fighter with a shaved head will have an advantage. After hearing this, Mercy had shaved off his golden locks. The only thing on his head was his red, white and blue sweatband.

As the fight progressed, Victoria, Carol and Sabrina continued to scream out Mercy's name, only to be drowned out by the chanting of the crowd. But Mercy knew they were there, cheering him on, and that's all he needed.

Mercy knocked out Taylor in the fifth round, with a straight right punch to the jaw. This win put his record at twenty-two wins by knockout. Louie knew that Sparkey would be watching and he wouldn't like it. "No siree," murmured Louie to himself, "Sparkey won't like it at all!"

Chapter 14

It was a beautiful Sunday in August, a perfect day for the beach. After church services were over, Mercy and Victoria left St. Mary's Catholic Church, to pick up Carol and Sabrina and their dates. They were looking forward to spending a lazy afternoon in the sun with their friends.

Mercy drove his new Mustang convertible. With the top down, he and Victoria felt the warmth of the breeze as they drove to Carol's apartment on Eighty-sixth Street.

Carol and Sabrina were waiting outside Carol's apartment building, with their dates, Paul and Carlos, when Mercy pulled up.   After clambering inside the car, Paul and Carlos congratulated Mercy on winning his twenty-second fight. Since the backseat only held three people, the two girls had to sit on their dates' laps.

"Hey, man," Carlos commented to Mercy, "you know, you could get in trouble having four people in the backseat. And besides, two passengers are not wearing seatbelts."

Mercy didn't argue and decided to put the top up.

Arriving at Jones Beach, they all piled out of the car and headed for the ocean. A refreshing swim would cool them off before they had their picnic. After swimming, Mercy, Paul, and Carlos joined in a game of volleyball, while the three girls relaxed on their towels, soaking up the sun.

Later, Victoria, Carol and Sabrina spread out the picnic. They had brought two coolers: one filled with a selection of sandwiches: Liverwurst and American cheese, salami and Swiss cheese, turkey, along with potato salad and coleslaw. And the other packed with iced Coke, root beer and ginger ale.

As they tucked into their food, Victoria said, "Mercy, you know how you told me that Louie and Huey have been getting telephone calls and letters from fans, asking if you had a fan club? Well, while you guys were playing beach volleyball, Carol, Sabrina and I were talking and we have come up with a name for your fan club."

"Okay, what is it?" asked Mercy, grinning.

"Well, we decided to call your fan club, *The Bitches and Beasts*. What do you think?"

Mercy smiled. "That's a good name," he said. "*The Bitches and Beasts.* I like it. But first I'll have to talk it over with Louie and Huey. I have a feeling that Louie will love the name." Everyone in the group laughed.

The next day, at the gym, Mercy told Louie and Huey about the girls' name for the fan club. Louie liked the name so much that he started dancing around the gym, singing, "Bitches and Beasts. Bitches and Beasts. Oh, oh, oh, I love that name."

Huey said, "Well, it sounds like a great name. We should get a lot of fans."

And so was born the *Bitches and Beasts* fan club.

Mercy and Victoria had fallen deeply in love. At first, Louie and Huey were worried that Mercy's boxing career would suffer, that he would be distracted by his newfound love. But Mercy was training harder than ever, with Victoria's full support. They were the perfect couple, and Louie and Huey loved both of them.

Mercy won his next four fights by knockout. He was getting smarter and smarter with his punches, delivering them at lightning speed. And Victoria and the girls were there at every fight, cheering him on. He had his own personal cheerleading team, complete with the trademark red, white and blue sweatbands. In fact, as Mercy continued to win, Louie started calling Victoria, Victory. It was the perfect nickname, and it stuck.

The *Bitches and Beasts* fan club was growing like wildfire. It seemed that everywhere Mercy looked, people were wearing red, white and blue sweatbands: at the gym, at the club, on the street, at the park. The fans loved Mercy. He was a clean fighter - no big show or entourage, no bullshit. Before each, fight, it would be just Mercy, Louie and Huey walking up to the ring.

Some television and newspaper reporters were saying that Mercy could become the next light heavyweight champion of the world. Others thought that Percy "Mean" Williams was too strong to lose his title. All were anxiously awaiting a rematch of Mean vs Mercy.

Chapter 15

Mercy walked into the gym one morning and asked Louie and Huey to look at a summons he had received to appear in small claims court. "Does this mean I have to appear in court?" Mercy asked, handing the summons to Louie.

Louie perused the document then handed it to Huey. "Yeah, kid, it sure looks like it," said Louie. "What do you think, Huey?"

Huey nodded. "This woman, Belle Anderson, wants you to pay her one thousand dollars to fix a chipped tooth," he said.

"I don't know anybody by the name of Belle Anderson," said Mercy.

Garcia, who was standing nearby, had overheard their conversation. She's probably the blonde woman who was Jones Beach, the day we got arrested. You know, the one with the nice boobs, he said, smiling.

"Oh no, not her," Mercy said with a panicked look on his face.

"This is wonderful. This is great. This is one beautiful day," Louie said.

"How can this be a beautiful day?" Huey asked Louie. "It's going to cost Mercy one thousand big ones?"

"Well," Louie said, this Belle with the big boobs sounds like a real "beach bitch," so we're all gonna back Mercy up."

Garcia walked over to Mercy and patted him on the shoulder. "Hey, Mercy, it was all my fault. But I don't have a thousand dollars, with Maria being sick and all, and the two kids." His wife Maria was recovering from a nasty bout of pneumonia.

"Don't worry about it," said Mercy. "I want you to be there with us."

"That's a deal," Garcia said, flashing a smile of relief. "I'll be there with Louie and Huey."

Three days before Mercy's court date, Louie was kissing himself and telling everyone at the gym how much he loved himself and what a wonderful world it was. Mercy and Huey just looked at him and shook their heads.

On the day of the trial, Mercy, Louie, Huey and Garcia met at the gym bright and early. They all wore dark blue suits and matching ties. And the red, white and blue sweatbands around their heads.

On reaching the courthouse, they walked inside and passed through a metal detector. One of the guards looked closely at Louie. "Hey, didn't I see you on the Friday night fights?" he asked. "I remember seeing those sweatbands." He turned to Mercy. "And your name must be Mercy." Mercy nodded.

"That's right," Louie said. "Keep watching the Friday night fights and you'll see us again."

"Well, you'll have to take off your sweatbands before you go into court," the guard told them. "Just put them in your pockets."

Louie, Huey and Garcia walked inside the courtroom and sat down at the front. Mercy sat outside in the hallway, waiting to be called by the judge. The courtroom was beginning to fill up with people. The bailiff walked in and said, "Would you all please rise, the Honorable Reginald White, presiding."

Judge White walked in from behind a door at the front of the courtroom and sat down in the judge's seat. Tall and stately looking with a shock of thick, white hair, the judge was considered to be a fair and just man.

Once the judge was seated, the bailiff told everyone, "You may now be seated." Then he walked up to the judge's desk and handed him a stack of papers. "The case number is two hundred and eleven, Anderson vs. Aller."

The doors to the courtroom swung open and in walked Belle Anderson, her big breasts bouncing up and down in unison with her long blonde hair. She wore a tight black miniskirt and a low cut pink blouse, which showed off her ample cleavage. Mercy followed meekly behind.

Louie nudged Huey and Garcia and uttered, "Meow. Meow," as if he were a cat.

Judge White picked up his gavel and banged it on the desk. "Quiet, please," he ordered. "Quiet in court." He turned to Belle Anderson, who was now sitting on the witness stand. "Ms. Anderson, you have been sworn in, could you please tell the court what happened the day you chipped your tooth?"

"Yes, your honor," Belle said, in a soft, breathy voice. "I arrived at the beach at around eleven o'clock. I put my blanket down on the sand, as well as a small tote case, where I keep my sunblock and other items. Then I put sunblock all over my body because I burn easily, your honor."

"This is a real *beach bitch*," Louie whispered to Huey and Garcia.

Judge White hit the gavel again. "Quiet, please." He paused and looked around the courtroom. "Please continue, Ms. Anderson. What happened next?"

"Well, your honor," Belle said, giggling, "I was lying on my back and I decided to turn over and lay on my stomach. So I took off my bikini top, so I could get tanned all over. That way I would not have a bikini bra line."

"Ms. Anderson, was this a topless beach?" the judge asked.

"Well, no, your honor. But the law allows you to take your bikini top off if you're lying on your stomach."

The judge turned to a female court bailiff. "Is that true?" he asked her.

"Yes, it's true, your honor," replied the bailiff.

"Very interesting. I never knew that. But, of course, I never go to the beach," Judge White said, smiling.

"Please continue Ms. Anderson. What happened next?"

"Well, your honor, I spent most of the day putting my bikini top on, and taking it off, putting it on, taking it off, putting…"

"All right, all right, that's enough," the judge cut in. "Please continue."

"Well, it was afternoon and I had my bikini top off. I was asleep, when all of a sudden…," Belle turned her head and pointed at Mercy who was sitting at the front of the courtroom. She shook her finger at him and said, "You're bad. You're bad. You're bad."

The judge banged his gavel and told Belle, "Don't be giving the defendant the finger. I mean, don't shake your finger at the defendant. This is a court room."

"I'm sorry, your honor. It won't happen again," Belle said, smiling.

"Please continue, Ms. Anderson," said the judge.

"Well, all of a sudden, I heard somebody yelling, 'Loose pit bull! Loose pit bull! Run for your life!' I was scared, your honor," Belle said, starting to cry. "Can I have a tissue?"

"Give her a tissue," the judge told the female bailiff. The bailiff handed Belle a tissue, and she dabbed at eyes.   The tissue fell to the floor. "Oops," sniffed Belle, bending over to pick it up and revealing her cleavage. "I've lost the tissue."

"Are you all right, Ms. Anderson?" the judge asked, his eyes fixed on her ample bosom.

"Yes, I'm fine, your honor. Sorry..."

"What happened next?"

"Then he starts barking like a mad dog."

'Who starts barking like a mad dog?"

"Him. Whatever his name is?" she said, pointing at Mercy. "They called him Mercy, but the report said his name was Gil...Gil Aller."

"Go on, Ms. Anderson."

"I jumped up, off my towel, with no bikini top on and I'm looking straight into "Mad Dog's" eyes."

Laughter erupted in the courtroom. Even the bailiffs and court officials were sniggering. Of course, Louie was laughing the hardest. "My sides are aching," he said to Huey and Garcia. "That Belle's a riot."

The judge banged the gavel again. "Order in the courtroom," he shouted. "Please be quiet, otherwise I'll have the courtroom cleared." He turned to Belle. "Ms. Anderson, please refrain from referring to the defendant as "Mad Dog." I won't warn you again," he admonished.

"Sorry, your honor, it just slipped out," said Belle meekly, batting her eyes at the judge.

"Proceed, Ms. Anderson, and remember, you have been warned."

"Well, I stood there for a few seconds, before I realized that "Mad...,

oops, I mean the defendant, wasn't looking at my eyes, your honor. So I reached

down to pick up my blanket," Belle bent over as if to pick up something from the

floor and exposed her cleavage once again, "and I tripped on my blanket and fell

on my case. That's how I chipped my tooth. And it's all "Mad Dog's" fault."

Once again, everyone in the courtroom started laughing. "Order, order,"

shouted the judge, banging his gavel on the table.

"Ms. Anderson, I won't tell you again," said the judge angrily. "Refrain

from using that epithet when referring to the defendant?"

"What's an epithet, your honor?" asked Belle innocently.

"Never mind," said the judge. "You will refer to the defendant by his

proper name."

"Sorry, your honor, it won't happen again. But he does sound like a mad

dog," said Belle.

"That's enough." The judge turned to Mercy. "Mr. Aller please step

forward." Mercy rose to his feet and stood in front of the judge.

Now, Mr. Aller, you have been sworn in, what can you say in your

defense?" the judge asked. "Ms. Anderson has told the court that you can bark

like a mad dog. Is that true, Mr. Aller?"

"Yes, he can," shouted Belle. "He sounds just like a mad dog and he's good at it."

Once again, the judge banged his gavel hard against the wood. His face was like thunder. "Ms. Anderson, this is your last warning," he said loudly. "Any more outbursts and I will order you to leave the courtroom. Do you understand?"

Belle bowed her head meekly. "Yes, your honor," she said softly. "Sorry, your honor."

The judge turned back to Mercy. "Now, Mr. Aller, let's try again. Will you please bark like a mad dog," the judge asked.

"Pardon me, your honor?" said Mercy. He couldn't believe what the judge was asking him to do.

"I said, please bark like a mad dog. The plaintiff has accused you of barking like a mad dog, so the court wants to hear you barking," said the judge.

"But, your honor, I can't bark like a mad dog," said Mercy.

Belle jumped to her feet and was about to yell out, but one look from the judge, and she sat back down.

"I insist, Mr. Aller. Bark like a mad dog," the judge said.

Louie started barking, howling and panting like a dog.

Judge White banged his gavel. "Order! Order!" he shouted. "Bailiffs, remove that man from my courtroom," he said, pointing at Louie, who was still barking.

Two bailiffs grabbed Louie by his arms and dragged him toward the exit. Louie struggled and kicked, trying to break free of the bailiffs' grasp. "Please, your honor, I don't want to leave. I don't want to leave," he panted.

After the bailiffs had dragged Louie from the courtroom, Huey stood up and addressed the judge. "Your honor, it wasn't right throwing Louie out of the court room," he said.

Judge White was rapidly losing his patience. "Sir, you are out of order," he bellowed at Huey. "I will not tolerate interruptions in my courtroom. Bailiffs, escort this gentleman from the courtroom."

Then Garcia stood up and said, "It was my…,"

Before Garcia could finish his sentence, the judge cut him off. "Silence!" he shouted. "Any more interruptions and this court will be adjourned." He pointed at Garcia. "Bailiffs, escort that gentleman from the courtroom, too."

The bailiffs strode over to Huey and Garcia and led them from the courtroom. Unlike Louie, they didn't put up a struggle. At the door, Huey turned and gave Mercy the thumbs up, as if to say, 'It's gonna be okay, kid.'

Judge White banged his gavel and addressed the courtroom. "Settle down. Maybe we can get something done here today." He paused, then turned to Mercy. "Well, Mr. Aller, maybe now you can bark like a mad dog."

"Arf, arf, arf," Mercy said in a weak voice.

"Well, that doesn't sound much like a mad dog," the judge said. "But you did spend the night in jail for disturbing the peace, and causing a riot. So I'm awarding Ms. Anderson five hundred dollars for each br... Excuse me, I mean one thousand dollars for her chipped tooth. That's my judgement." He banged the gavel. "Next case!"

Mercy sat there in shock. He opened his mouth to speak; after all, he was innocent. But one glare from the judge and he thought better of it. He walked out of the courtroom, $1,000 lighter, but relieved that the trial was over.

He found Louie, Huey and Garcia waiting for him outside. "I lost," he said. "I had to pay a thousand dollars."

Huey patted his shoulder. "Oh well, it's over now, let's go get a drink."

"I just have one question, Mercy," said Louie

"Yeah, what's that?" asked Mercy.

"Just how big were Belle's tits?"

Chapter 16

After winning twenty-six fights by knockout, Mercy was receiving

coverage in the sports section of all the major newspapers. His next fight would

be against Billy "The Goat" Nelson. Nelson was a dirty fighter who threw hard

punches, many of them below the belt. He would do anything to win because he

was looking for a shot at Percy.

At Mercy's fights, Louie and Huey noticed that Victoria and her

girlfriends always sat in the third row, wearing their red, white and blue

sweatbands. Mercy would look over at Victoria just before the fight started and

they would exchange a knowing glance. It was as if they had their own secret

language.

Once the fight began, however, Mercy became focused and determined,

his eagle eyes fixed firmly on his opponent. He was in great shape; his jabs were becoming hard and quick, giving him an opportunity to use his combination punch.

A few days before Mercy's fight with Nelson, Louie walked over to the ring, where Huey and Mercy were practicing. "Billy "The Goat" Nelson got into a car accident. So you'll be going to Philadelphia to fight against Buck Curtis.

Mercy had an easy fight in Philadelphia, mainly because his opponent had little experience in the ring. Mercy knocked him out in the fourth round, winning his twenty-seventh fight by knockout.

Unfortunately, Victoria and her friends had decided not to attend the Philadelphia fight, so it was just Louie, Huey and Mercy driving back to New York that night. Louie felt good as he drove down the road – his protégé was getting closer and closer to the light heavyweight championship. *It's just a matter of time*, he thought to himself, *so look out Sparkey, look out Percy Mean Williams! Our boy is on his way.*

They were driving down a dirt road, following a crow. As Louie always said, "I drive the way the crow flies. They will always lead you home." As Louie made the turn, a sign appeared, which read, "Homemade Cherry Pie, Made Fresh Everyday."

"Let's stop," said Mercy, spotting the sign. "I have to find out if the pie is as good as my grandmother's cherry pie." They were all hungry, so it wasn't hard for Mercy to talk Louie into stopping.

The café was small but clean, with red and white checkered tablecloths on all the tables. The three friends sat down at a table near the window and Mercy ordered two pieces of cherry pie.

"Well, if he's having two pieces of cherry pie, then I'll have two pieces myself," Louie told the waitress, a kindly looking lady with twinkling blue eyes. She reminded Mercy of his grandmother.

"I'll have two also," Huey said.

The waitress scurried back carrying three plates and six pieces of cherry pie, covered with a white glaze.

"Be careful of the pits," she said as she placed the pie in front of them.

"What does she mean, be careful of the pits?" asked Louie.

"Well, sometimes they don't get all the pits out and you could chip a tooth," Mercy explained. "So be careful."

Louie took his first bite and said, "My first bite and I got a pit." But instead of taking the pit out of his mouth, Louie blew it across the table at Mercy, hitting him in the chest.

"I've got one, too," said Huey, blowing the pit at Louie and hitting him in the arm. Then Mercy blew a pit at Huey, hitting him in the neck. Now all three of them were trying to find more pits. They were laughing so hard that Louie got a pit stuck in his throat and started choking. One good hit on the back by Huey took care of that. He slapped Louie on the back and the pit flew out of Louie's mouth. Louie took a glass of water and the pit blowing started again. They were running out of cherries; Louie had the last pit.

Louie's cheeks looked like a bullfrog's. He was going to blast this one right at Mercy. Building the air pressure in his cheeks, he let it fly. The pit was headed to strike right between Mercy's eyes, but at the last second, Mercy moved his head slightly to the right and the pit missed him by a hair.

Seated at the next table, just behind Mercy, were Sonny McGill and his friend, Willie Washington, both ex-cons. They had been released from jail three days ago and were in no mood for horseplay. Anger and resentment had built up during their time in prison – it was always the other person's fault, not theirs - and they were looking for trouble.

The pit hit Sonny in the back of the neck. Grabbing the pit, he spun around in his chair and stared menacingly at Louie, Huey and Mercy. "What the hell?" he said. "That hurt," and he clutched at his neck. Louie, Huey and Mercy just sat there, frozen.

McGill and Washington sprang to their feet. They were both tall and burly-looking, the muscles rippling in their tattoo-covered arms. They'd had plenty of time to hone their bodies in the prison gym. They walked over to the table, where the three friends were sitting

"Hi there," said Huey as he slowly stood up. "We're sorry. We were just having some fun." Then he added, "Do you know who we are?"

"Yes, we know who you are," said Willie. "They call you the "Pit Boys" and your cousins are the "Pep Boys." And he and Sonny laughed and gave each other high-fives.

"Look, I'm sorry, but do you really know who we are?" Louie said, now standing.

"Yes, we know who you are," said Sonny, pointing toward Louie. "Don't they call you "the Midget"?" Again the two ex-cons laughed and gave each other high-fives.

Then Sonny turned and looked at Mercy and said, "Don't they call you "the Faggot"?"

"And you," said Willie, looking at Huey, "don't they call you "the Nigger"?"

Huey stared in astonishment at the ex-con – Willie was black himself! Angry, he stepped toward Washington.

Willie took a swing at Huey causing him to crash into the next table. Sonny grabbed Louie by his shirt, and Mercy hit Sonny with a left hook to his head, followed by another to his chest. Sonny fell to the floor. Then Huey hit Willie with a straight right hand, knocking him to his knees. But Willie picked himself up and came charging back toward Huey. Mercy intervened, hitting Willie with a powerful right hook. Willie went down.

Meanwhile, Sonny had recovered from Mercy's punch, and now had Louie on the floor. Huey ran to Louie's aid, pulling Sonny off him and hitting the ex-con with a powerful right hand. McGill crumbled to the floor. Huey then turned to see Willie rising to his feet. Fueled by anger at Willie's earlier comment, Huey hit him with a right hook, sending Willie flying across the room. Both ex-cons were now lying on the floor, out for the count.

The three friends dusted themselves down and walked over to the waitress. Louie handed her a hundred-dollar bill. "Thanks for the cherry pie," he said, "it was delicious. And sorry about the fight. Hope this will help to pay for the mess."

The waitress smiled. "Thanks."

"Let's get out of here," said Huey.

As they headed to the car, Huey walked over to the two lone motorbikes in the parking lot and pulled loose a few wires. "They won't get far now," he said, referring to Sonny and Willie. "The walk will do them good." And the three men burst into laughter.

Chapter 17

Mercy's next fight was in Rhode Island. Garcia was also fighting the same night, in the same arena. So he, Mercy, Louie and Huey would drive there together, in Louie's car.

Victoria told Louie, "No stopping for cherry pie." Mercy had told her all about their last little adventure.

"No way," Louie laughed.

The four men left early on Saturday morning to miss some of the traffic. The night before Mercy had taken Victoria for dinner at her favorite restaurant. And as they dined by candlelight, the music playing softly in the background, Mercy had proposed.

"Victoria," he said, gently slipping the engagement ring on her finger. "I want to spend the rest of my life with you. Will you marry me?"

For a while, Victoria was speechless as she stared at the glittering diamond on her finger. She couldn't believe this was happening – it was just as she had imagined.

"Oh, Mercy, of course I'll marry you. Yes, yes, yes," she cried as she reached over and kissed him tenderly on the lips. "I can't wait to be your wife."

Mercy beamed. He felt as if he were the luckiest guy in the world.

\-

That night Victoria couldn't sleep. She was excited about the engagement, but she was also worried about Mercy. She had read about boxers getting killed in the ring, or ending up with brain damage. So after tossing and turning all night, she decided to drop by the gym, to see Mercy before he left for the fight in Rhode Island.

"Be careful," she told him, as she planted a wet kiss on his lips. "I want you to come home in one piece. After all, we have a wedding to plan."

"Don't worry, I'll be fine," replied Mercy, gathering her in his arms and returning the kiss.

"What's this about a wedding?" asked Louie, Huey and Garcia, who were standing nearby and had overheard their conversation.

178

Mercy and Victoria gave them the good news. And soon it was bear hugs and congratulations all round for the happy couple.

"We'll be your best men," said Louie and Huey in unison.

As the four friends prepared to leave, Victoria asked, "Why don't you ever take a plane? It would be faster." Learning of their fear of flying, she wondered to herself, Where *will Mercy and I end up on our honeymoon?*

Louie stepped on the gas pedal and a few hours later they were in Rhode Island. Once again, Mercy was victorious, winning his twenty-seventh bout by knockout. Garcia also won by knockout, so Louie and Huey were doubly proud of their two boxers.

Mercy's fan club was continuing to grow at an alarming pace. They now had over 5,000 members and counting. There was so much fan mail that Louie hired Victoria, Carol and Sabrina to work on Saturdays to answer all the letters, and include a red, white and blue sweatband with the reply. In addition, a block of seats was always reserved at every fight, for the *Bitches and Beasts* fans. No matter where Mercy fought, he would always see his fans, wearing the trademark sweatbands, and waving the American flag.

Mercy went on to win his next three fights by knockout. Thirty wins. He was inching closer and closer to the light heavyweight championship. But the fights had not been easy. He had taken quite a beating in the last bout, and Victoria had been distressed beyond belief. She fussed and fretted over him, not letting up until all his cuts and bruises had healed.

After Mercy's thirtieth win by knockout, the sports reporters were asking, "Why can't Mercy get a shot at the light heavyweight title, against Percy "Mean" Williams?"

Louie had called Sparkey dozens of times, asking him to give Mercy a shot at the title. But Sparkey would have none of it, so Louie stopped calling. He became tired of hearing Sparkey call him an asshole, and he couldn't stand it when Sparkey told him that Mercy had never fought any big-name fighters. Louie decided to leave it to the press. If they kicked up a big fuss, Sparkey would have no choice but to agree to a match with Williams.

Jatun Wanbe, an unknown fighter from Africa, would be Mercy's next opponent. Huey learned that he had an awkward, ungainly style of fighting, but he was strong, and could take a punch.

On the night of the fight, Louie, Huey and Mercy sat in the locker room, waiting to be called to the ring. Finally the call came, and they walked into the arena, surprised at the huge number of *Bitches and Beasts* fans sitting in the stands. "Mercy! Mercy! Mercy!" they yelled as they waved their American flags.

Louie, Huey and Mercy swelled with pride. Shivers ran up and down Mercy's spine – he was proud to have the fan club there cheering him on.

The yelling continued until Mercy climbed into the ring. Jatun was already dancing around the ring. His fans were also cheering for him. Mercy could hear the shouts of, "No Mercy! No Mercy!" but the cries were being drowned out by shouts of "Mercy! Mercy! Mercy!" Mercy stood there, feeling the fans' adulation – he would not let them down. Everything hinged on this fight. Mercy knew it, Louie and Huey knew it, and the fans knew it. If Mercy won this fight, he would have a credible shot at the light heavyweight title.

Jatun was tall, with a lean, muscular body. He looked calm and relaxed, while Mercy was feeling the pressure.

"Go for the body first to slow him down," Huey advised. "Then get on the inside and lean on him." Mercy nodded as he took a couple of deep breaths to calm himself.

As soon as the bell rang, Mercy and Jatun met in the middle of the ring. Mercy tried to follow Huey's advice, but he was having a difficult time with Jatun's awkward style of fighting.

By the end of the eighth round both fighters were cut and bleeding heavily. Blood was streaming from a cut above Mercy's right eye, and pouring from Jatun's nose. As Mercy sat in his corner, waiting for the start of the next round, Huey told him, "Jatun is getting tired and you only have two more rounds to go. Try to finish him off in the next round."

At the bell, Mercy came out swinging and knocked Jatun to his knees. But, on the count of eight Jatun was back on his feet. The two fighters continued to slug it out until the bell rang to signal the end of the ninth round.

When Mercy returned to his corner, Huey said, "You have one more round. Jatun is still reeling from that last knockout – I can tell by the glazed look in his eyes. Go for the knockout."

The bell rang for the final round. The two fighters circled each other in the middle of the ring. *Huey was right*, Mercy thought to himself, *Jatun is definitely feeling that last knockout. I've got to finish it off now.* Mercy worked his way in, but Jatun covered up, trying to get his legs back after Mercy's last knockout punch. Mercy caught him with a combination punch. Still the African fighter stayed on his feet. *He's tough*, thought Mercy as he pinned Jatun against the ropes. Exhausted and dazed, Jatun didn't throw any punches back at Mercy. He sagged against the ropes, barely able to stand, his nose bleeding profusely. The referee stepped in and promptly stopped the fight. Mercy had won his thirty-first fight.

The *Bitches and Beasts* fan club went wild, stomping their feet and yelling out Mercy's name. The stadium was raining red, white and blue sweatbands as the fans waved the bands above their heads, then threw them up in the air. Mercy had not let his fans down – this victory was for them.

Louie and Huey walked over to Jatun's corner to find out if he was all right. "I'm fine," said Jatun, in a precise British accent. He obviously hailed from one of the former British colonies. "I'm just dazed – Mercy packs quite a punch," he said wryly. Then he walked over to Mercy and congratulated him on his victory by giving him a sportsman's hug.

"That was one hell of a fight," Louie and Huey told Mercy in unison.

"You earned that one," said Huey, slapping Mercy on the back.

"Do you think you have a shot at the title?" asked a reporter from The Daily News, directing his question at Mercy.

Before Mercy could answer, Louie walked up behind the reporter and said, "That's up to Sparkey Morrison. Why don't you go and ask him?" Louie smiled to himself, thinking, *Get out of that one, Sparkey.*

Sparkey had watched the fight from his apartment in Manhattan, with a few close friends. Turning to one of his friends, he said, "What a bunch of assholes. Percy could kick that lumberjack's ass and send him back to Michigan in a wooden box."

Chapter 18

Mercy's next fight was against Billy "The Goat" Nelson. Billy had

recovered from his car accident and was spreading vicious rumors about Mercy.

"He's a has-been. If it wasn't for my car accident," said Nelson, "Mercy's

record would have at least one loss recorded on it." Then he added, "I'm gonna

knock the living daylights outta him, when we meet in the ring." He thumped his

chest proudly. "Then I'm gonna take on Percy."

Nelson was next in line to fight Williams for the light heavyweight title.

Louie thought that Sparkey was probably behind this, hoping that Nelson would

beat Mercy, or better yet, knock him out. Whoever won would be considered for

the title.

For the next two months, Mercy pursued a grueling training schedule:

Sparring with Garcia and other fighters, running 10 miles every day, and working

out practically to the point of exhaustion, until his body was a fine-honed fighting

machine. Nelson was considered to be one of the best fighters around, so Mercy had to be in tip-top shape. He was determined to beat "The Goat," especially after all the nasty comments Nelson had made.

The time flew by and before Mercy knew it, he was walking out to the ring, flanked by Huey and Louie. *Am I ready to take on The Goat?* he thought to himself. *Yes, you're ready,* replied his inner voice.

As they walked into the arena, the *Bitches and Beasts* fan club cheered wildly, yelling out Mercy's name, while Nelson's fans tried to drown them out by yelling, "Goat! Goat! Goat!" It was pandemonium. The fans of both fighters were working themselves into a frenzy. Louie and Huey were relieved to see a large number of policemen and security guards patroling the stadium.

Mercy climbed into the ring as the crowd continued to yell. Seconds later, Nelson and his entourage entered the arena, followed by two goats bleating, "Baa, Baa." The crowd erupted; the noise was deafening. *What a circus!* Mercy thought to himself as he shadowboxed around the ring.

Nelson clambered into the ring and glared at Mercy. "Maa. Maa," he bleated like a goat. Mercy ignored him and continued dancing around the ring. He was determined to stay focused and not be distracted by all the theatrics. Nelson shrugged and ambled over to his corner. He was short, about 5'5", but extremely powerful. And if things didn't go his way, he would fight dirty – hitting below the belt, using his elbows, and stepping on his opponent's toes.

The crowd continued yelling, "Mercy! Mercy!" followed by chants of "Goat! Goat!" Mercy looked over at the stands where Victoria, Carol and Sabrina were sitting. They were wearing their red, white and blue sweatbands. Victoria looked nervous. She was chewing on her nails, and flicking her hair back and forth. But when she caught Mercy's eye, she smiled brightly and waved her hand. Mercy returned the wave. He knew she was putting on brave face, and it made him all the more determined to win.

Victoria wasn't the only nervous one. Louie and Huey were practically trembling but trying hard to hide their jitters from Mercy. This was a crucial fight – Mercy had to win.

Louie walked up to Mercy and said, "Sparkey and Percy are seated near Victoria. Over to the left, about 3 rows behind her." Mercy scanned the stands and sure enough, there was Sparkey. He appeared to be staring directly at Mercy and Louie.

"What's he doing here?" asked Mercy.

"We have him running scared," replied Louie. "He's obviously here to check out the competition. If you can beat Nelson tonight, he has no choice but to give you a shot at Williams for the title." And Louie raised his hand and waved at Sparkey. Sparkey scowled.

"Yep," said Louie, "he's definitely running scared. Show him what you got, kid." Mercy exhaled slowly and looked over at Nelson. Showtime!

186

Nelson was shadowboxing around the ring, still uttering, "Maa! Maa! Maa!" The crowd loved it. Usually, Mercy, Louie and Huey got a kick out of the other boxer making a fool of himself, but this crowd had them worried. They had been drinking heavily, and most of them were rooting for "The Goat." Things could get out of hand, especially with Sparkey in crowd, to stir up trouble.

Joe Cucci, the referee, called the boxers to center of the ring and said, "Follow my instructions, and protect yourselves at all times. Touch gloves and let's get it on."

As Mercy and Nelson touched gloves, Nelson bleated like a goat again, "Maa, Maa," then turned and pretended to head butt the crowd. His fans leapt to their feet. "Maa, Maa," they screamed in response. Mercy just shook his head. *What a stupid goat*, he thought to himself.

Back in the corner, Huey had some words of advice for Mercy. "Stay away from him, use your jab and watch the head butts. As you just saw, he thinks he's a goat!"

The bell rang and Nelson charged toward Mercy, backing him into a corner. Mercy pushed his way out and the two fighters circled each other. This was a ten-round fight, so they had plenty of time to feel each other out.

After four rounds, Nelson was ahead on points. Mercy was still worrying about a head butt. If he sustained a serious injury from a head butt, the fight would be stopped and he would lose on points.

"Use your jabs and watch the head butts," Huey reminded Mercy when he returned to his corner. As if Mercy needed reminding – he couldn't think of anything else.

In the fifth round Nelson backed Mercy against the ropes and tried to give him a head butt. The referee cautioned Nelson. "Watch your head."

Louie was watching the fight at ringside, when suddenly, a man with a black sweatband grabbed him from behind. Louie cried out, and for a split second, Mercy took his eyes off Nelson. Nelson seized his chance. He delivered a swift right hook to Mercy's chin, and Mercy was down for the first time in his career.

Meanwhile, Louie was wrestling on the floor with this crazy man who kept yelling "Goat! Goat!" Security rushed over and hustled the man out of the arena. Louie staggered to his feet and looked over at Sparkey and Percy. They were both laughing. *I should have known that no-good Sparkey would pull a stunt like that,* thought Louie to himself.

Mercy was up at the count of eight and Nelson came after him again. Although still dazed, Mercy made it through the fifth round, thanks to his dancing skills and powerful jab.

After the sixth round, Huey told him, "Pick up the pace. We're behind on the scorecards. Stay on the outside and circle away from his power. Use your jab and work your way in."

Time was running out for Mercy. He was bruised and battered, and behind on points. It was time to take charge. Now on the offensive, Mercy started taking the fight to Nelson, instead of waiting for Nelson to make the first move. And it was working – "The Goat" was starting to feel Mercy's power.

By the end of the seventh round, Mercy was catching up on points. Then during the eighth round, Nelson headbutted Mercy and opened up a big cut under Mercy's left eye. "Nelson, one point deduction," shouted the referee. "This is your last warning."

The bell rang to signal the end of the round. *Thank God,* thought Mercy as the blood flowed down his cheek. *I literally was saved by the bell!*

Seated in his corner, Mercy took a sip of water, while Huey tended to his eye. "This should hold it," said Huey as he smeared ointment on the cut. "Now listen, I want you to back away. Step in quickly. Throw your combination. Then step back fast so he doesn't open up that cut."

Mercy nodded. He knew that if Nelson opened up the cut, the referee might stop the fight. He looked over at Victoria and they locked eyes. And in that moment, he knew he could win.

At the bell, Mercy stepped in quickly, threw a five-punch combination, backed out fast and then stepped right back in, throwing a three-punch combination. It worked. Billy "The Goat" Nelson went down.

Nelson got up at the count of eight. He pushed Mercy against the ropes and kicked him hard on the left leg. Taken by surprise, Mercy stumbled and almost went down. Unfortunately, the referee's view was blocked and he didn't see the kick. Mercy was limping. Nelson tried to take advantage by pushing Mercy against the ropes, but Mercy took two quick side steps and now had Nelson against the ropes. Mercy threw a three-shot combination and "The Goat" was down for the second time. He too was saved by the bell.

The bell rang for the start of the tenth and final round. The noise in the stadium was deafening, with both sets of fans screaming out their champion's name. Nelson came charging across the ring and pinned Mercy against the ropes. And with a sharp right hook, he opened up the cut below Mercy's left eye. Once again the blood flowed down Mercy's cheek. He could hear the crowd yelling, "No Mercy! No Mercy! No Mercy!" And in the distance, he heard Victoria and her friends yelling, "Mercy! Mercy! Mercy!" He had to finish this off now, before the referee stopped the fight.

Now running on pure adrenaline, Mercy pushed himself off the ropes. Nelson tried kicking Mercy again but this time he missed. The blood continued to pour from Mercy's eye – he knew it was now or never. Both fighters were now in the middle of the ring. *This is it*, thought Mercy as he started throwing punches with everything he had. Mercy's punches came so fast and so hard that Nelson went down for the count for a third time. And this time, he didn't get up. Gil "Mercy" Aller had won his thirty-second fight by knockout.

The stadium erupted. All Mercy could hear was "Mercy! Mercy! Mercy!" Even some of Nelson's fans were cheering for him. Fights broke out among the rival factions, but security and the police soon had things under control.

Mercy stood in a daze as Huey walked over to him and placed a red, white and blue sweatband around his head. Victoria, Carol and Sabrina raced down from the stands and literally tumbled into the ring. Victoria threw her arms around Mercy and kissed him squarely on the lips. Carol and Sabrina hugged him. Reporters and sportscasters crowded into the ring, along with boxing officials, security and fans, all trying to get close to the champion.

Suddenly a piercing scream rang out. The crowd turned to see Percy "Mean" Williams charging toward the ring. "I'm going to kick your ass, Gil "Mercy" Aller, or whatever it is you call yourself," he yelled.   "I'm going to kick your lumberjack ass all the way back to Michigan." And he waved his arms wildly above his head.

A reporter yelled back, "You're going to kick Mercy's ass. When?"

"When? When? When?" Williams yelled, shaking his fist at the reporter. "I'll tell you when," said Williams. "Right here, right now!"

Victoria grabbed Mercy's arm and held on tight, while Carol and Sabrina held on to her.

191

"I'm scared," said Victoria, "and so are Carol and Sabrina."

"Don't worry," said Mercy, squeezing her hand, "I'll take care of Williams."

Then Louie yelled to Percy, "Get your ass up here. Get your ass up here."

Huey joined in. "That's right, Percy, get your ass up here. And bring Sparkey with you."

Mercy paled. *What are Louie and Huey doing?* he thought. *I couldn't possibly fight Williams right here and now.*

Sparkey rushed down from the stands and stood by Percy's side. "We're going to kick all your asses," he shouted. "We're going to kick all your asses." The police and security guards raced over and tried to lead them away.

"Take your hands off of me," yelled Sparkey. "Don't you know who I am?"

"Don't know and don't care," replied one of the cops. "I just know you're creating a disturbance. Now let's go."

Huey, Louie and Mercy looked on as Percy and Sparkey were escorted from the arena, kicking and screaming all the way. The ring was still crowded with reporters and officials.

"When are you going to fight Williams for the title?" a reporter asked Mercy.

192

"Any time, any place," replied Mercy, "but it's going to be in a ring, not in the streets. And now if you'll excuse us, we have some celebrating to do."

Chapter 19

Several days after the fight, Louie was sitting at his desk when the phone

rang. He picked up the receiver and said, "L & H Gym. Can I help you?"

"Yeah, you might be able to help me, asshole." It was Sparkey.

Louie knew why Sparkey was calling – he wanted a championship fight

between Percy and Mercy. The press was putting a lot of pressure on him after

Mercy's last fight. Mercy's record spoke for itself. Thirty-two wins by knockout

– Sparkey had to give him a chance at the title.

"Yeah, whaddya want?" drawled Louie, as if he didn't know.

"I'm meeting with the boxing commission and I want you come, alone.

Don't bring Huey or Mercy with you," said Sparkey.

Louie was silent. *What's Sparkey up to?* he thought to himself.

" Did you hear me, asshole?" shouted Sparkey. "Don't bring Huey or Mercy with you, otherwise Percy's going to tear Huey and that asshole from Michigan, two new assholes."

"All right," Louie said, "I hear you, keep your hair on."

"Meet us at the Hilton on 54th, Suite 16 – one o'clock sharp. Don't be late," snapped Sparkey. "I'll see you then, asshole," and he slammed down the receiver.

Louie hung up the phone, then danced around his desk, kissing his arms and yelling, "I'm a genius! I'm a genius! I'm a genius!"

Hearing all the commotion, Huey walked over from training ring and asked, "What's going on, Louie?"

"We may have the title fight," Louie said excitedly. "Sparkey just called." And he told Huey about the phone conversation, and how Sparkey had insisted on his coming alone.

Huey couldn't believe his ears. "We may have the title fight! We may have the title fight!" he shouted, grabbing Louie's arm and dancing around the table with him. Then he suddenly stopped and said, "I don't like the idea of you going alone, Louie. Sounds fishy to me."

"Yeah, but what can we do?" said Louie. "You know Sparkey, he calls the shots."

195

Just then Mercy walked into the gym and Louie and Huey gave him the good news. Mercy was speechless. "Are you serious?" he said finally. "I don't believe it – me, Gil Aller from Michigan, fighting for the light heavyweight title?" Mercy shook his head in disbelief.

"You better believe it, kid," said Louie, patting Mercy on the back. "And believe this, you're gonna win!" Mercy continued to shake his head back and forth – it would take a while for this to sink in.

"Call Victory and her two friends and have them meet us at *Your Favorite Place*," Louie told Mercy. "We're gonna celebrate."

....

The day of the meeting arrived. Louie was excited and a little nervous. They had been waiting for a chance at this fight for a long time and Louie didn't want to screw it up.

"I'm nervous," he told Huey and Mercy. "The press and TV will be there. And the mayor and the boxing commission."

"My father used to go to lots of meetings," said Mercy. "And he always said that the best way to ease the tension was to tell a joke."

"You do know a few jokes, don't you, Louie?" asked Huey facetiously.

"Yeah, I'll think of something," Louie said, a note of trepidation evident in his voice.

Louie arrived at the hotel early and headed straight to the bar. *A drink will settle my nerves,* he thought to himself as he ordered a Scotch on the rocks. Twenty minutes later, Louie had finished his drink and was now standing outside suite sixteen. He knocked on the door.

A tall, swarthy-looking man, gold earring hanging from his left ear, opened the door. Come in, Louie," he beckoned, opening the door wider.

As Louie entered the lavishly decorated suite, Sparkey grabbed his arm and walked him into a private room. "Look, asshole," Sparkey said, "To get this fight you have to give up something."

"Like what?" Louie asked nervously. He didn't trust Sparkey.

"Your fighter," Sparkey said, "Mercy, or whatever the hell you call him, goes down in the tenth round and Percy wins. Then we have a rematch and Percy goes down in the fifth. The third fight is the real match, and we all make a bundle." Sparkey smirked triumphantly.

Louie didn't utter a word. He just stood there and glared at Sparkey. Then he turned on his heel and stomped toward the door. Sparkey grabbed him from behind.

"Get your hands off of me," Louie said, breaking Sparkey's grip. "You know damn well that Huey and Mercy won't go for that."

"All right. All right, asshole, have it your way. But Percy will win this fight. So don't be looking for no rematch," Sparkey said, raising his voice.

"Go to hell," Louie shouted, and walked back into the main suite.

The suite was now filled with people: the mayor and his entourage, the boxing commissioner, reporters and commentators from TV and radio, and various other hangers-on in the boxing world. A makeshift podium had been set up by the far wall of the suite.

"Okay," said the boxing commissioner, "let's get this press conference started. Louie, you have the floor."

Louie walked toward the podium and stood behind the head table. Nervously rubbing his hands together, he scanned the room. Sparkey was standing by the window, puffing on a cheap cigar, some of the reporters were drinking beers, others mixed drinks, the mayor nursed a coffee. All were waiting for him to begin.

"I'd like to tell a joke before we get started," Louie said. "Johnny walks up to his father and says, 'Dad, what's this thing they call love?' Johnny's dad scratches his head and says, 'Love? That's a pretty hard thing to explain, son. But, I can tell you this, son, tonight your sister Nellie has a date with Billy. So this is what I want you to do. Get down here before Nellie does and hide behind the couch. I'm pretty sure you will find out what love is.' The next morning, Johnny's father asks, 'Well, did you find out what love is, son?' 'Yes, I did and if that's love, then I want no part of it.' 'What happened, son? You get there too late?' 'No, I did what you told me. I got behind the couch before Nellie came downstairs. She had on that perfume that disgusts me and then she turned on the television. You know how Nellie likes to blast the television and it was right in my ear. When Billy came, Nellie invited him in and told him to have a seat on the couch. Then she asked him if he'd like to have beer. Well, Billy had a beer and then another and another. Then he reached over and held Nellie's hand and they start hugging and kissing. That's when I got this horrible cramp in my leg and I wanted to scream, but I kept quiet. The next thing I know, Billy pulled out this big cigar and started puffing away.'"

Louie stopped talking for a second, to see how his joke was coming across. They all seemed to be enthralled, waiting expectantly for the punchline.

Louie continued, "So Johnny said to himself, 'I don't care if I suffocate from all that cigar smoke, I'm going to find out what love is.' Then Billy reached over and whispered something in Nellie's ear. So Nellie gets up and goes upstairs to her room and closes the door. No sooner did she close the door, than Billy started letting them go. He started with three atomic bomb blasts, *Boom, boom, boom*, and finished with machine gun fire that went, *Taa, ta, ta. Taa, ta, ta.* Then Nellie opened her door and asked what the noise was. 'Did you hear that? It sounded like the Vietnam War broke out again.' 'Oh, that noise?' Billy said, 'That was just the TV.' Nellie walked down two steps, stopped and said, 'I could swear I smell gun smoke.'"

Louie paused and looked around the room; they were still hanging on to his every word. He continued. "Johnny told his father, 'That's when I passed out. The next thing I remember was Nellie sitting back down on the couch, whispering something in Billy's ear. Nellie got up off the couch and turned the TV off. Then she and Billy headed outside to the garden. Gasping for air, I crawled out from behind the couch and limped out behind them. I watched them from the bushes. Nellie pulled down her slacks and Billy pulled down his pants. Well, I didn't have to take a dump, so I went to bed.'"

The room erupted in laughter. Louie no longer felt nervous – he was ready to begin the press conference. "First, I would like to thank the mayor, the boxing commission and everyone assembled here today." Louie paused and looked over at Sparkey. "And now I'd like to know why my fighter can't seem to get a shot at the title championship?"

The boxing commissioner stood, and turned to Sparkey. "Sparkey, I believe this is your question. Over to you…"

Sparkey cleared his throat. "Well, I guess Louie's fighter has proved himself. So, let's set up a date."

The press and TV reporters surged toward the podium, bombarding Sparkey and Louie with questions. This was the fight they had been waiting for: Percy vs. Mercy.

Louie was ecstatic. Mercy would be fighting Percy "Mean" Williams for the title. It was a dream come true. He couldn't wait to tell Huey and Mercy. The fight would be held in four months, in Percy's hometown of Philadelphia.

Back at the gym, everyone cheered when Louie gave them the good news. Mercy and Huey hugged each other, then threw their arms around Louie.

"I must call my family back in Michigan," said Mercy, heading toward the phone. "They are not gonna believe this in a million years."

"He's got that right," Louie said to Huey. Our young lumberjack has come a long way!"

After the TV and press broke the news about the upcoming fight, membership in the *Bitches and Beasts* fan club doubled. Victoria, Carol and Sabrina could hardly keep up with the fan mail. The press was hailing the fight as the fight of the century.

Mercy's entire camp bustled with activity. Huey worked with Mercy day and night, preparing him for the fight. With Sparkey's connections and influence in the boxing world, Huey knew it would be difficult for Mercy to win a decision on points, in Percy's' hometown. Mercy had to knock out Percy – it was the only way.

The next four months flew by and before they knew it, Mercy, Louie and Huey found themselves sitting in the dressing room, waiting to be called to the ring. Mercy was thinking about his family, back home in Michigan, and wishing they could be there to support him.

A knock at the door interrupted Mercy's reverie. Showtime! There was no going back now. He stood and smiled at his two friends. He owed it all to them, and he wouldn't let them down.

As the three friends exited the dressing room, they were surprised to see so many fans waiting by the door. All of them were wearing their red, white and blue sweatbands, and waving American flags.

"Mercy, Mercy, Mercy," they yelled, some trying to touch Mercy as he passed by.

Louie led the way into the arena followed by Mercy and Huey and the huge entourage of fans. It was a sight to behold - a sea of red, white and blue.

Mercy jumped into the ring. Dancing lightly on his toes, he shadowboxed around the ring as he waited for Percy to make his grand entrance. Cries of "Mercy, Mercy," echoed around the stadium followed by shouts of "Percy, Percy, Percy." The noise was deafening. Mercy blocked it out – he had to stay focused.

Every seat was taken. The crowd had waited a long time to see this fight. And now they were growing restless. Where was Percy? Mercy had already been dancing around the ring for about five minutes. Now seated in his corner, he took a sip of water as he scanned the crowd.

In one section of the stadium, Mercy noticed a group of people wearing black sweatbands. *Percy's fan club*, thought Mercy as he heard them yelling Percy's name followed by cries of "No Mercy." *Come on, Percy, where are you? Let's get this show on the road.*

As if on cue, the lights suddenly dimmed and about one hundred people marched into the stadium holding lit candles. In the center of this large group, walked Percy and Sparkey. Percy's fans jumped to their feet and started yelling out his name. Percy soaked up the adulation -- this was his hometown. As he clambered into the ring, the lights came back on and his fans sat down.

Dozens of sports reporters and television announcers were in attendance, as well as a smattering of movie stars and celebrities. One commentator addressed his TV audience, watching at home. "Notice Percy's black sweatband. Could this be a send-up of Mercy's red, white and blue sweatband? I'll let you viewers decide."

Mercy looked on as Percy strutted around the ring and raised his arms in victory. The crowd was working itself into a frenzy. Fighting broke out between the rival fans. And the security guards and police had to surround the ring when one of Percy's fans grabbed Louie's pant leg. Several minutes passed before they had the situation under control.

Huey reminded Mercy about the last time he fought Percy in the exhibition fight. "Remember, Percy will charge across the ring and try to knock you out in the first round," said Huey as he rubbed Mercy down with a towel.

The announcer, a tall, rugged man, with a velvety voice, walked up to the microphone. "Ladies and gentlemen," he began, "P&H Associates is proud to announce a twelve-round, light heavyweight championship fight. In the blue corner, wearing the red, white and blue trunks, hailing all the way from Michigan, weighing in at 168 pounds, with a record of thirty-two wins by knockout, no draws, no losses, I give you the challenger, Gil "Mercy" Aller."

Mercy's fans cheered, yelling out his name and drowning out the boos from the Williams' camp. The announcer paused, waiting for the cries to die down. "Ladies and gentlemen," he continued, "in the red corner, wearing the black and gold trunks, straight from Philadelphia—" The hometown fans roared, cutting off the announcer in mid-sentence. He signaled for quiet then began again. "Weighing in at 171 pounds, with a record of thirty-six wins – thirty-one by knockout - two draws and one defeat, and thirty-one wins by knockout, I give you the light heavyweight champion of the world, Percy "Mean" Williams."

The noise from the crowd was thunderous – both sets of fans trying to outdo the other. More fights broke out, but once again the police and security were quick to act, soon bringing the troublemakers under control.

The crowd finally settled down. This was the fight they had been waiting for: the light heavyweight championship of the world. And each and every fan had to come to see their champion win the title. Would it be Percy, or would it be Mercy?

With a flourish, Percy suddenly ripped off the black sweatband around his head. His fans cheered wildly because painted in the middle of Percy's forehead was a red circle with a crossed black M. This meant that Williams was going to knock out Mercy.

Mercy, Louie and Huey looked on in amazement as Percy strutted around the ring like a peacock, inciting his fans and pointing to the red circle on his forehead.

Mercy turned to Huey and Louie. "What is he doing?" he asked. "What does that red circle mean?"

"Don't worry about it, kid," said Louie. "He's just trying to freak you out. Make you nervous before the fight."

"Yeah, it's all a big show," said Huey, exchanging glances with Louie. They didn't want Mercy to know what the red circle and black cross signified.

The referee called Mercy and Percy to the center of the ring. "Follow my commands," he said, "and protect yourselves at all times. Now touch gloves."

Instead of touching Mercy's gloves, Percy turned and walked away. His snub did not go unnoticed. The referee walked over to the red corner and whispered something in Sparkey's ear, after which a reluctant Percy walked back to the center of the ring and touched gloves with Mercy.

The bell rang for the first round. True to form, Percy came charging across the ring, but this time Mercy was ready for him. Sidestepping to the left, Mercy threw a couple of punches to Percy's body. Caught offguard, Percy ended up pinned against the ropes in Mercy's corner. Mercy let him turn around - he would never hit an opponent in the back - then delivered two more punches to Percy's body. The two fighters slowly worked their way to the middle of the ring.

In the first seven rounds both fighters scored points, with some hard punches. Just before the eighth round, Huey told Mercy, "I want you to concentrate on the red circle on Percy's forehead. It looks like a big, red bull's-eye. Makes a perfect target."

Mercy had been hitting Percy on his body, hoping that Percy would bring his hands down to protect himself, thus leaving his head exposed. But Percy was a tough, hard fighter and he held his hands high.

Both fighters had sustained injuries: Blood flowed down Mercy chin from a busted lip; Percy's left eye was swollen shut, and the body shots were starting to show. His arms were now dropping to protect his lower body, chest and ribs.

By the end of the eighth round, word had reached Percy's corner about the red bull's eye and now his trainers were trying to rub it off with water. But to no avail – the circle would not come off.

The bell rang for the start of the ninth round. Mercy was now starting to pound the bull's eye on Percy's forehead. One, two, three, four hits right on the red circle. Stunned and dazed, Percy staggered to his corner at the end of the round.

"Get it off! Get it off!" yelled Sparkey, pointing to the circle on Percy's forehead. The trainers frantically rubbed and scrubbed the mark with soap and water, but it was hopeless. The red circle would not come off.

During the tenth round, the two boxers danced around the ring, trading punches and trying to go for the knockout. By the start of the eleventh round, they were both feeling the punches. The blood was now gushing from Mercy's lip and he had a cut over his left eye. Percy had a cut on his right cheek and his left eye was had now swollen to the size of a golf ball.

Mercy continued to pummel the red circle on Percy's forehead. Then, with a quick left body shot and another blow to Percy's forehead, Mercy staggered Percy, causing him to stumble and lose his footing. But Percy was hanging on – he refused to give up. The bell rang for the end of the eleventh round.

When Mercy returned to his corner, Huey said, "This is a close fight. It could go either way. Remember, we're in Percy's hometown and the decision could go in his favor."

Mercy glanced over at Victoria who was sitting in the front bleachers. He could tell by the look on her face that she was worried about his injuries. He wiped the blood from his chin and gave her the thumbs up. She smiled weakly and blew him a kiss. Beside her, Carol and Sabrina were yelling, "Mercy, Mercy, Mercy."

The bell rang for the start of the twelfth and final round. *This is it*, Mercy thought to himself as he jumped to his feet. *Would Sparkey get his wish, or would Louie and Huey get their wish?* Percy charged across the ring, hoping to surprise Mercy. But Mercy was ready for him, his eyes fixed on the red bull's-eye in the center of Percy's forehead. As Percy approached, Mercy landed a powerful right hand, right on the red circle. Percy went down.

A deathly hush descended over the stadium. The referee turned to Mercy. "Go to the farthest neutral corner," he ordered as he started to count, "One, two, three, four, five, six, seven..." Percy tried to stand up, but fell back down. The referee continued to count. "Eight, nine, ten. The fight was over. Mercy had won.

Louie and Huey rushed to Mercy's side and placed his red, white and blue sweatband around his forehead. The *Bitches and Beasts* fans were jumping up and down and screaming Mercy's name. Percy's fans sat in shocked silence – they couldn't believe that their champion had been beaten.

Mercy was overjoyed. *Am I dreaming?* he thought to himself. *Am I really the light heavyweight champion of the world? What will the folks back home think?*

Louie and Huey wrapped their arms around him. "We did it, kiddo," said Louie, beaming from ear to ear. "It's a dream come true."

"Yeah, a dream come true," repeated Huey, hugging Mercy even tighter.

Victoria and her two friends practically fell into the ring in their rush to reach Mercy. Victoria threw her arms around him and kissed him full on the lips. Carol and Sabrina hugged Louie and Huey, and then embraced Mercy and Victoria. They were all drunk on excitement.

By this time, the ring was crowded with people, all trying to get to the champion. Reporters shouted out questions and photographers clicked cameras, their flashbulbs lighting up the arena. Mercy's victory would be headline news tomorrow.

The announcer took the microphone and called for quiet. "The time of the knockout was in the final second of the final round. Then the referee placed the light heavyweight championship belt around Mercy's waist and raised Mercy's arm in victory.

"Ladies and gentlemen," continued the announcer, "I give you the light heavyweight champion of the world, Gil "Mercy" Aller."

The crowd erupted. Cries of "Mercy, Mercy, Mercy," echoed around the stadium. Mercy could hardly hear himself think as he soaked in this moment of victory. Swelling with pride, he turned to Victoria and lifted her off her feet and swung her around the ring. He was so happy, he wanted this moment to last forever, and he wanted to share it with the woman he loved.

Meanwhile, in the red corner a bruised and battered Percy was bemoaning his loss. "The referee hurried the count," he said. "I was about to get up."

"Yeah, Percy, I hear ya," said Sparkey. "We'll get Mercy in the rematch."

Mercy and Louie walked over to Percy's corner, and Mercy extended his hand. But Percy refused to take it. "You got lucky," he said.

"Yeah," sneered Sparkey, "one lucky punch, that's all." He turned to Louie and brought his face up close so that their noses were almost touching. "One lucky punch, asshole."

"Yeah, but we got the title belt," said Louie, grinning. He grabbed Mercy's arm. "Come on, champ, let's go celebrate."

After about fifteen minutes the fans finally settled down. Mercy and his entourage slowly made their way back to the dressing room, stopping briefly while Mercy signed a few autographs for his fans. Too tired to drive back to New

York, they decided to spend the night at a local hotel. They would have a full-blown celebration when they returned to the city.

That night, Mercy and Victoria shared a quiet dinner together, while Louie and Huey escorted Carol and Sabrina to one of the nearby bars. They hadn't had a chance to be alone together for weeks. As they held hands across the table, they talked about their upcoming wedding and their future plans.

"What about your dream to become a Broadway dancer, Mercy?" Victoria asked him. "Have you forgotten all about that?"

"No, I haven't forgotten. It's still my dream, but tonight I feel as if I'm living the American dream." He looked deep into her eyes and smiled. "Here I am, Gil Aller, a small-town boy from Michigan, light heavyweight champion of the world, sitting across the table from the most beautiful woman in the world. Who would have thought it? Let me hold on to this dream for a little while longer."

Victoria clasped his hand tighter. "I fell in love with that small-town boy from Michigan." She paused, her eyes filling with tears. "And no matter what, he will always be my champion."

Chapter 20

When Mercy arrived back at the gym, with Louie and Huey, the building was surrounded by the media: reporters, TV camera crews and photographers were everywhere. They wanted to hear from the champion. *Could they hold a press conference? Would Mercy grant them an interview?*

Louie stepped in. "Okay, fellas, you got five minutes. Fire away."

Mercy handled the press conference like a pro, answering all their questions and posing for photographs. Finally, Louie called a halt to the proceedings. "That's it, guys, time's up. Our champ is tired – he needs some time to himself."

Mercy took a week off – his first break in months. He would meet Victoria for lunch every day – some times at the park, other times at a nearby restaurant. In the evening they would catch a movie or eat dinner at one of their favorite restaurants. One night they went to Radio City Music Hall, to see the Rockettes.

Mercy's cuts and bruises were healing quickly, thanks to Victoria and Huey, who took it in turns to dress the wounds. "You'll soon be as good as new," remarked Huey one day as he tended to the cut above Mercy's eye. "Sparkey will be thrilled – he can't wait to get you back in the ring."

Sparkey had called Louie many times since the fight, demanding a rematch.

"The only reason that asshole won was because of the red circle on Percy's forehead," he insisted.

After many arguments and phone calls, Louie finally agreed. "Anything to get you off my back," said Louie. He was too tired to argue any more.

"Okay, asshole, lets make it six months from now, in New York," said Sparkey. "Don't forget, you got lucky last time. Now it's our turn. See you at ringside, asshole."

Louie remained silent. *I'll let Mercy's fists do the talking for me,* he mused.

Mercy was looking forward to the rematch. He wanted to prove to himself, and to the world, that he could beat Percy, without the red circle as a target.

Six months later. on a cold November night, Mercy once again found himself in a packed stadium, facing Percy "Mean" Williams. Only this time, he was the defending champion.

Before the fight began, Percy strutted around the ring, hanging his head over the ropes so that everyone could see that he had no red circle on his forehead. "I'm getting my belt back," he bragged. His fans roared their approval.

Percy was out of shape. Although he had trained hard over the last six months, his body had never fully recovered from the last fight. The referee stopped the fight in the tenth round.

Although Mercy was the victor, he had taken a devastating beating from Williams. Percy did not accept defeat easily, or gracefully, and he put up one hell of a fight.

Huey treated Mercy's injuries as best he could. "You got a few bad cuts, kid," said Huey, surveying Mercy's battered face and body. "But I don't think you need stitches." He patted Mercy on the back. "You'll be sore for days, but you're young. Nothing a bit of lovin' care won't fix," he said, winking at Victoria who was standing nearby.

Victoria took one look at Mercy's bruised and battered body, and refused to let him go back to the rooming house.

You're staying at my apartment tonight," she said, tears welling up in her eyes. "And I won't take no for an answer."

Mercy shrugged. "Yes, ma'am," he replied meekly.

When they arrived at Victoria's apartment, she handed him a robe and directed him to the bathroom. "Why don't you take a shower," she said. "The hot water will help to soothe the cuts and bruises."

Mercy nodded. "Good idea. What would I do without you?" *How little did he know he would soon be put to the test?*

Victoria grinned. "Oh, you'd manage somehow."

After his shower, Mercy walked into the kitchen and found Victoria sitting at the table.

"Come, sit down," she said, pointing to a chair.

"Yes, ma'am, whatever you say. You're the boss."

Victoria punched him playfully on the shoulder. "Ouch! that hurt," he cried.

"Oops, sorry, I forgot about your bruises. Here--- "

She placed his feet in a pail of warm water and started to gently bathe his legs.

"How did you get that?" she asked, pointing to a big, black-and-blue mark on Mercy's leg.

"Well, that's what you call a real low blow," Mercy replied.

"Percy kicked you?"

"That's right," said Mercy. "Percy will do anything to win."

"Let me get some ice for that," said Victoria as she retreated to the freezer and took out an ice pack. "Here, hold this over the bruise, it will help to reduce the swelling. She placed the ice pack on his leg. "I'll be right back."

When Victoria returned she was wearing a white satin robe. "How are you feeling?" she asked.

"Much better," said Mercy, taking his feet out of the pail of water. "The swelling has definitely gone down."

As Victoria bent down to remove the pail, her robe fell open, exposing her beautiful breasts. "Oops," she said, pulling the robe closed.

Mercy didn't speak. Instead he reached down and kissed Victoria gently on the lips. Then, he stood up and slowly opened Victoria's robe. Slipping his hand inside, he placed his hand on Victoria's left breast and gently massaged the nipple. A small sigh escaped Victoria's lips as she welcomed his touch. Then Mercy leaned down and kissed Victoria's right breast, teasing the nipple with his lips.

Victoria let out another sigh, and pressed Mercy's head closer to her breasts, running her fingers through his soft blond hair. "I love you, Mercy," she whispered.

Mercy raised his head and looked into Victoria's emerald green eyes. "And I love you, Victoria," he said, holding her gaze. "More than you will ever

216

know." And taking Victoria in his arms, Mercy picked her up and carried her into the bedroom.

As he lay Victoria down on the bed, her robe fell open, exposing her supple, silky body.

Mercy sighed. "You are so beautiful, you take my breath away."

Standing in front of the bed, Mercy sucked on Victoria's toes, then slowly kissed his way up her long, shapely legs. She quivered beneath his touch, her breath coming in quick short pants. "I love you, Mercy, please don't stop."

"Are you sure you want to do this?" he asked, holding her gaze.

"Oh yes, my love, I've never been surer of anything in my life." And she reached up and slowly slid the robe from his shoulders. Her eyes explored his muscled torso, finally coming to rest on his throbbing member. Victoria gasped. Although she had indulged in heavy petting before, she was still a virgin. This would be her first time.

He's so big, she thought to herself. *He'll rip me apart.* But she loved this man, and was ready to give herself to him, heart, body and soul. Her whole body ached for him. She drew him closer. "Now, Mercy, now," she whispered. "I'm ready."

Mercy placed himself between her legs and gently pushed himself inside her. "I don't want to hurt you," he said as he penetrated deeper, slowly moving his cock up and down.

Victoria sighed. Although she felt the pain, she held him tighter, spreading her legs wider and pushing herself against him. "I love you, Mercy. You can never hurt me. Don't stop – I want to feel every inch of you."

Mercy continued to thrust, slowly at first, then faster and harder. He was close to the edge, ready to explode, but he held back, waiting for Victoria to catch up with him.

Victoria was now panting breathlessly. The pain had now given way to an exquisite pleasure. She felt like a fluorescent light, flicking on and off. Suddenly the light seemed to gain in intensity and time seemed to stand still.

"Oh, Mercy, I want this moment to last forever," she cried. "Take me, take me now!"

Mercy groaned. He could not hold back any longer. Thrusting harder and harder, his lips brushed her cheek. "Come with me, my love, come with me now."

And together, the lovers fell over the edge, into the arms of ecstasy. They were one.

Chapter 21

The next few months passed quickly for Mercy. Since becoming the light

heavyweight champion of the world, he had defended his title twice, winning both

fights by knockout. And, along with Louie, Huey and Victoria, he had also

attended several other fights.

One night the four friends decided to watch the fight between Percy

"Mean" Williams and Billy "The Goat" Nelson. Percy was on a comeback trail,

hoping to have another shot at Mercy. Since his loss against Mercy, he had won

his last three fights by knockout.

Once the fight started, Mercy could tell that Percy was intent on regaining

his title. So far he had won every round. His punches were solid, his footwork

impeccable. He danced around the ring, dodging blows, and looked to be in the

best shape ever. The only way that Nelson could win was by knockout.

Don't tell me I'll have to fight Percy again? Mercy thought to himself.

It was the seventh round and Percy continued to pummel Nelson, well on his way to victory. The Goat was looking for an opportunity to land one big punch to knock out Williams. Suddenly, in the closing seconds of the round, one of the spectators lit a firecracker, setting off a loud boom that echoed around the stadium. Startled, Percy dropped his guard and turned to see what had caused the explosion. Nelson seized his opportunity. Stepping forward, he delivered a crushing blow to Percy's head. The punch was so powerful that it knocked Percy off his feet. He went down, hitting his head hard on the canvas, and lay motionless.

The referee knelt down by Percy's still body. Sparkey, and Percy's trainer also rushed over, followed by the in-house doctor. Percy lay motionless as the doctor felt for a pulse, then placed some smelling salts underneath Percy's nose. No reaction – Percy was still out cold.

A second doctor clambered into the ring. Holding a small flashlight, he lifted Percy's eyelids looking for signs of concussion.

"Bring a stretcher," yelled the second doctor.

At ringside, Percy's wife and mother were sobbing as two men rushed into the ring carrying a stretcher. They placed Percy on the stretcher and carried him off to the emergency room.

Victoria squeezed Mercy's hand so hard that his fingers became numb.

"If you continue to fight, I'm going to break off the engagement," she said as she watched the medics rush Percy out of the stadium.

"I'm a good fighter and I don't take chances," replied Mercy, trying to reassure her. "If somebody hadn't been playing around with firecrackers, then nothing would have happened. I like to fight and I like the excitement. What else can I possibly do, this is my life?" Mercy's voice wavered. "I will never make it to Broadway." Mercy's dream of becoming a dancer had faded over the last few months, until it was just that – a dream.

"That could be you, lying there in a coma," cried Victoria. And you either die or you're never the same."

That night Victoria broke off the engagement.

"I'm calling off the wedding," she said, her eyes filled with tears. "I never want to see you again," and she handed Mercy her engagement ring and walked away.

Mercy stood in stunned disbelief. He felt as if he'd been punched in stomach, the blow much harder than any he'd received in the boxing ring. Crushed and upset, he decided to drown his sorrows at *Your Favorite Place*.

When he walked in the door, Mike took one look at his face and knew something was wrong. "What's up, buddy, wrong time of the month?" said Mike. Mercy stared at him, puzzled.

"Sorry, bad joke. What's up, Mercy? You look as if you've lost your last penny?" He pushed a beer over the counter. "Here, the drink's on me."

"Not my last penny," replied Mercy, "my girl." And he proceeded to tell Mike all about the broken engagement.

"If she really loves you, she'll change her mind," said Mike. "If not, you are probably better off without her."

Mercy shook his head sadly. "I love her, Mike. I don't want to be without her."

Victoria couldn't sleep at all that night. Tossing and turning, she spent most of the night crying. The next morning she decided to call Mercy at the gym. Louie answered the phone. Mercy had told him about the break-up.

"Hey, Mercy," he shouted. "Some broad is on the phone and she wants to talk to you."

Mercy grabbed the phone, surprised to hear Victoria's voice. Louie overheard him tell Victoria, "I'm sorry, but I will not give up boxing. What else can I say?" Mercy was close to tears. "You know I love you."

"Don't you know that I love you too?" said Victoria. "I love you so much that I didn't sleep all night." She was crying into the receiver. "Do your fighting! Do your boxing! But, I'm coming to every fight. And I don't care if it is in a foreign country. If something happens to you, I want to be close by you," Victoria told him.

"I love you so much," Mercy said. You've made me the happiest man in the world. Does this mean that the wedding is back on?" he asked

"Yes, you foolish man," Victoria chuckled. "I love you," and she hung up the receiver.

"What was that all about?" Louie asked Mercy. "I couldn't help overhearing."

"Oh, it's a long story," said Mercy. "Listen, I have to go to the hospital and see Percy. Would you and Huey like to come with me?"

"I've spoken to Sparkey," said Louie, "and the doctors say there's no hope for Percy. He's brain dead. But, yes, kid, we'll go with you to the hospital."

An hour later, Louie, Huey and Mercy were walking down the hospital corridor when Billy "The Goat" Nelson stepped out of Percy's room.

"How's Percy doing?" asked Louie.

"The doctor says there's no hope. Nothing more can be done for Percy." Billy shook his head sadly and walked away.

The three friends entered Percy's room. Family and friends were gathered around Percy's bed, their faces solemn. Mercy walked over to Percy's wife, who was sobbing silently in the corner. Louie and Huey joined the others around the bed. Percy looked like a waxwork dummy – pale and lifeless – a shadow of his former self.

"I'm so sorry," Mercy said, placing his hand on Percy's wife's shoulder.

"Thank you," she mumbled, struggling to hold back the tears. "There is always the possibility of something like this happening, but you never think it will happen to you."

"I was at the fight with my fiancée," said Mercy, " and she told me that she never wanted to see me again, if I refused to give up boxing. But boxing is the only thing I know."

Percy's wife smiled sadly. Mercy's words seemed to lift her spirits. "Yes, I know what you mean. Boxing is the only thing that Percy knows; boxing is his life."

"My thoughts and prayers are with you," said Mercy. Then he walked over to the bed and placed his hand on Percy's forehead. Bending down, he whispered softly in Percy's ear. "You have to get better, Percy "Not So Mean" Williams." Brushing away the tears, Mercy headed to the door, followed closely by Louie and Huey. They had taken about four steps when they heard Percy's wife scream.

"Hurry! Get the doctor! Get the doctor!"

"Percy must have taken a turn for the worse," Huey said. "We should hurry up and leave. Let the doctors do their job." Mercy and Louie nodded, hoping for the best.

The next morning Mercy arrived early at the gym to work out. His next fight was against a tough Mexican called Chico Perez and he wanted to be in tiptop shape. He had just started his workout when Louie and Huey rushed into the gym, brandishing the local newspaper.

"Mercy, did you see today's paper?" Louie asked him.

"No, I usually look at the paper during my break," Mercy replied. "Why, what's up?"

"Well, let me read this to you," Louie said. "It's the headline, here on the sports page. It says, 'Mercy Saves Percy With Miracle.'"

"What? Let me see that," Mercy said, grabbing the newspaper. " "I didn't do anything."

"Well, that's what the doctors and Percy's family and friends are calling it," said Louie. "So, Mercy, what did you whisper in Percy's ear?"

"I just told him, 'You have to get better, Percy "Not So Mean" Williams,'" Mercy said defensively, feeling as if Louie had put him on the spot.

Good, because that's just the way Percy told the story," Louie said. "He remembered somebody calling him, Percy "Not So Mean" Williams. He opened his eyes, looked around and asked his wife who the hell had called him that name."

"Well, I'll be damned," said Mercy, grinning. "Percy must want a rematch real bad." And the three friends burst out laughing.

Later that day, Mercy met Victoria for lunch at the park. As they sat on a park bench, soaking up the sun and eating their usual hot dogs, an old woman approached them.

"Excuse me, but is your name Mercy?" she asked Mercy. "Aren't you the fighter who saved that other fighter, by performing a miracle?"

"Yes, my name is Mercy, but I don't think I performed a miracle," Mercy replied, embarrassed by his sudden fame.

"Yes, you did," Victoria chimed in, "even the doctors and the nurses said you did."

"God bless you," the woman said, and she walked away.

Chapter 22

It was the night of the fight. Chico Perez was already in the ring, when Mercy entered the arena, flanked by Louie and Huey. Thunderous applause and cries of 'Mercy, Mercy,' greeted his arrival. Looking around at the sea of red, white and blue sweatbands, Mercy felt emotionally overwhelmed. *All these fans are here to support me*, he thought to himself. *I still can't believe that I'm the light heavyweight champion of the world.*

Jumping into the ring, Mercy looked out into the crowd to see if Victoria was sitting in her seat. As he caught her eye, she smiled and threw him a kiss. *I'm the luckiest guy in the world*, he thought to himself. *That beautiful woman will soon be my wife.*

The bell rang for the start of the first round and Perez came charging across the ring. Mercy had no idea that his opponent was a southpaw, or a head butter. Perez pushed Mercy against the ropes and they butted heads.

"Watch your head," cautioned the referee as the bell rang for the end of the first round.

When Mercy returned to his corner, Huey said, "My contacts never told me that Perez was a southpaw." He shook his head. "And watch out for his head butts. Sorry, kid, I had no idea."

"Don't worry about it, Huey. How were you to know?"

"It's my job to know. I should know everything there is to know about your opponents. I let you down this time, Mercy."

"I can handle him," replied Mercy.

"They can stop the fight if a head butt is serious enough. If it happens after the fourth round, the three judges can go to the scorecards."

The bell rang for the start of the second round. Once again, Perez charged across the ring. He headbutted Mercy, opening up a gash above his right eye. Mercy backed away. Blood was running down his cheek onto his chest. His face throbbed

The referee walked over to Perez. "Watch your head," he cautioned. "I've already given you a warning. Do you understand English?" Perez nodded. But he did not understand a word the referee had said.

Mercy got through the second round, with the blood still streaming down his face. Huey and Louie were ready for him when he returned to his corner.

Huey worked on the cut, while Louie washed off the blood and cleaned up Mercy's face.

"Let's make sure we get all the blood off," said Louie. "It's bad for television and it's bad for the fans."

The doctor walked over to Mercy's corner and examined the cut. Huey had stopped the bleeding. "He's all right," said the doctor.

The bell rang for the start of the third round. Mercy and Perez met in the middle of the ring. Mercy knew that the cut above his eye would be like the red circle on Percy's forehead, providing a perfect target for his opponent.

As expected, Perez went for the cut and Mercy returned to his corner covered with blood. Once again, Huey was able to stop the bleeding, and Louie cleaned up all the blood. This time the doctor took longer to examine the cut, and whispered something in the referee's ear, before giving Mercy the go-ahead to continue fighting.

Mercy sensed that the doctor was concerned about the cut, hence his whispered conversation with the referee. He knew he had to do something, and quick, otherwise the referee could stop the fight. When the bell rang for the start of the fourth round, Mercy shot across the ring before Perez knew what was happening. Summoning every ounce of strength, Mercy hit Perez with a right and a left punch to his body, then a right and a left to the head. He followed this up with a right and a left to the jaw, and another right and a left to the head. Perez went down, hitting the canvas with a thud. The fight was over.

Cries of 'Mercy, Mercy, Mercy,' echoed around the stadium. The *Bitches and Beasts* were on their feet, waving their American flags and yelling out Mercy's name. "We love you, Mercy," they cried.

When Mercy, Louie and Huey returned to the dressing room, four people were waiting for them, two in wheelchairs and two on crutches, along with their aides. One of the aides stopped Louie outside the room, and said, "Can our loved ones have Mercy's blessing? We heard about the miracle he performed and we were hoping that he could cure our loved ones too."

Before Louie could respond, Victoria walked over. "What's going on?" she whispered to him.

"These people have read about Mercy's *miracle* and they're wondering if he'll be able to help them," said Louie.

"Well, let's see what he says," said Victoria, marching into the dressing room. Mercy was seated on the bench while Huey tended to the cut above his eye.

"I can't heal anybody," he said after Victoria told him about the people's request. "That was just a fluke."

"But they believe in you, Mercy. You have to do this," she pleaded.

All right. All right. I'll do it," said Mercy, "but I have to tell you, this is crazy! I'm no miracle worker."

Mercy walked over to the group of people and introduced himself. Then he turned to the woman in the first wheelchair and asked, "What is your name?"

"I'm Mary, and this is my husband, Tom," she said, pointing to the dark-haired man standing by her side.

Mercy put his right hand on Mary's forehead and whispered in her ear, "Mary, you have to get better." *This is what I said to Percy*, he thought to himself. *Maybe it will work for Mary too.*

Tom and Mary didn't know if Mercy had just happened to stumble over Mary's leg, or if he was weak from losing so much blood. Whatever the reason, he fell against her. "Sorry," he said, regaining his balance. "I must have tripped."

Mary sat in her wheelchair, watching Mercy bless the others, before he walked back into the dressing room. Then she looked up at her husband and said, "Honey, I just realized something."

"What's that, sweetheart," Tom asked.

"When Mercy tripped over my legs, I felt something," she said, her face flushed with excitement.

"That's impossible, sweetheart. You haven't been able to feel anything from the waist down, since before the accident," Tom said. "You're probably just excited."

"I felt something," Mary insisted as her husband wheeled her toward the exit. "I definitely felt something."

The next day Mary got out of bed and walked to the bathroom. *Was it possible that Mercy could perform miracles?*

. . . .

The cut above Mercy's eye needed twelve stitches, and it would take about a month to heal completely. Since Mercy was weak from losing so much blood, Victoria decided to take two weeks off from work so that she could be with him. And Mercy decided that it was time for Victoria, and Louie and Huey to meet his family. As the three men were afraid to fly, they opted to drive to Michigan in Huey's SUV, and take turns driving.

After a leisurely two-day drive, the four friends arrived at Mercy's home. Mercy had returned to a hero's welcome – the whole town had turned out to greet them. He was staggered to see so many people. Family, friends and townspeople were all waiting to greet the light heavyweight champion of the world, and to meet his friends.

Victoria nudged him. "Look, they're all wearing red, white and blue sweatbands."

"So they are," he said, his eyes brimming with tears. He felt like a returning hero. Never in a million years had he expected such a reception.

His mother flung her arms around and hugged him close. "Oh, Gil, I've missed you so much," she sobbed. To most people, he was Mercy, light heavyweight champion, of the world, but to his mother and the rest of his family, he would always be Gil – their Gil.

Mercy hugged her tighter. "I've missed you too, Mother. But not a day has passed that I haven't thought of you and all the family." He wiped away her tears. "Now, did I hear someone mention a pig roast?"

Louie and Huey were a big hit with the family, and everyone loved Victoria. Mercy's mother had been worried about meeting her beloved son's future wife. She had envisioned a spoilt, sophisticated city girl, who would probably look down on their simple country ways. Instead, she had found a warm, caring, down-to-earth young lady who was a perfect fit for *her Gil*.

Mercy's uncles told him that they had hired two buses to take them to New York City because so many people wanted to come to the wedding.

"The more the merrier," said Victoria, winking at Mercy. They had made her feel so welcome that she already felt as if she were a part of the family.

When the four friends returned to New York, it was back to work for all of them. Mercy's cut had healed and he started training for his next two fights, winning them both by knockout. Mercy now had thirty-eight fights under his belt.

Louie and Huey told all the trainers and promoters that Mercy would fight anyone, anytime, anyplace. So he was now fighting every six months. The sports writers and reporters were asking, "Is there anyone who can take the title away from Mercy?"

One day Sparkey phoned Louie. "Listen, asshole," he said gruffly, "I'm going to get that title belt back." Louie and Huey knew that Sparkey would do whatever it took to get the title belt back. Percy's fighting days were over, so Sparkey was travelling all over the world, looking for another fighter to take his place. Finally, after an exhaustive search, Sparkey found a local fighter in a small town in the Australian outback.

Bret Johnson was not well known. Sparkey had heard about him through his many contacts. For a training bag, Johnson used a steel drum filled with cement and covered with rubberized foam. He ran for miles in the hot sun, and trained for hours without tiring. He was fast, strong and extremely powerful. *But could he take the title away from Mercy?*

Chapter 23

One morning when Mercy was working out at the gym, Victoria called to say that she was going to be late for lunch.

"I have something important to tell you," she added. "Have the hot dogs ready so we'll have time to go to the park."

A couple of hours later, Mercy was talking with Danny, the hot dog vendor.

"I heard about Percy," said Danny. "That was some miracle you performed."

Mercy laughed. "Nothing to do with me, Danny boy, it was just a coincidence. I can't believe that people actually think I'm some kinda miracle-worker."

As the two men continued their conversation, Mercy glanced across the street and saw Victoria coming around the corner.

"You can start the hot dogs now, Danny," said Mercy as he watched Victoria waiting for the light to turn red.

"I'm one step ahead of you, kid," Danny said, "the dogs are almost ready."

"That's great," replied Mercy. He watched Danny put mustard and onions on the hot dogs, his back turned to the opposite side of the street where Victoria was standing.

The light changed, and Victoria and two men started to cross the street. Suddenly, a yellow cab came barreling down the street and shot through the red light, hitting all three pedestrians. One of the men died instantly, the other was seriously injured. Victoria was hit by the front of the taxicab. Her body flew up and over the hood, breaking the windshield. She was then catapulted twenty feet into the air, landing about forty feet down the street.

Mercy heard the squeal of tires, and people yelling, but that was common in New York City. He spun around expecting to see Victoria standing before him. But there was no Victoria. He could see people gathering on the street. Traffic was halted. Someone was yelling, "Call an ambulance. Call the police."

Victoria must be somewhere in that crowd, Mercy thought to himself as he started to walk across the street, hot dogs in hand.

The police had blocked off the area to traffic. Sirens could be heard in the distance. Mercy continued down the street, pushing his way through the large crowd and scanning the faces for Victoria. A sea of dark-haired women met his gaze, but there was no sign of Victoria. As he continued to scan the crowd, a fireman rushed by, knocking Mercy's hot dogs to ground.

"Damn," said Mercy out loud, "there goes our lunch. Now, where the heck is Victoria?"

Mercy broke through the crowd and saw Victoria's crumpled body lying on the street, in a pool of blood. He shook his head. "No, no, it's not possible. That's not Victoria. I just saw her standing on the corner."

A police officer was standing near Victoria. "Stand back!" he ordered as Mercy rushed forward.

"She's my fiancée," cried Mercy, choking back the tears. He was in total shock.

"Okay, son, come on through," said the officer, taking Mercy's arm and leading him toward Victoria.

This can't be happening, thought Mercy as he knelt down beside Victoria's still body. *It's all a bad dream and in a moment I'll wake up.* Tears were now streaming down his face.

"No, Victoria, no, this isn't you lying there. It's all a bad dream. No, no, no," he cried as he stroked Victoria's ashen face.

Victoria raised her hand and touched Mercy's face, brushing away his tears. "Come closer," she whispered.

Mercy leaned in close, his face touching hers. "Don't try to talk, honey. Save your strength. Everything's going to be fine – the ambulance will be here soon."

"I love you, Mercy," she said weakly, her hand still stroking Mercy's face.

"I love you, too, Victoria," he said, choking back his sobs. "Forever and always.

Victoria smiled. "I want you to kiss me," she said. "I want you to kiss me goodbye."

Mercy could barely speak. "Don't be silly," he croaked, struggling to gain control. "You're not going anywhere, you're gonna be fine. The ambulance will be here soon and they'll take good care of you. You'll be up and about in no time."

"Kiss me, Mercy," she said softly. "I want to feel your lips on mine one last time."

"My Victoria, my precious Victoria," he sobbed, "don't leave me." Then, cradling her gently in his arms, Mercy kissed her on the lips, one last time.

An ambulance screeched to a halt by the couple. Two paramedics dashed forward, carrying a stretcher. After quickly examining Victoria, they placed her on top of the stretcher and carried her to the waiting ambulance. Mercy followed behind. And with sirens blaring, the ambulance took off to the nearest emergency room. Twenty minutes later, Victoria lay in the operating theater undergoing

emergency surgery.

Mercy staggered around the hospital waiting room, in a daze, the tears still

streaming down his face.

"Don't leave me, Victoria," he muttered to himself. "You've got to fight,

fight, fight," he repeated. "Don't give up! Fight!"

Meanwhile, back at the gym, Louie had just received a phone call from

Danny, telling him about the accident.

"Victoria was hit by taxi," Danny said. "She's been rushed to hospital –

New Brunswick, the cop told me. Mercy's with her."

"Oh my God!" exclaimed Louie, shaking his head in disbelief. "I can't

believe what I'm hearing. Thanks, Danny, me and Huey'll head over there right

now."

"You got it. Tell Mercy that I'm thinking of them."

Louie and Huey wasted no time and within half an hour they were at the

hospital.

"What happened?" they asked Mercy as they burst into the waiting room.

Mercy was slumped in the corner, head in hands.

Looking up at his two friends, all Mercy could say was, "Victoria,

Victoria, Victoria." His eyes were glazed. Shock gripped his body.

"Don't worry, kid, she's gonna be okay. She's a tough cookie," said Louie, struggling to hold back the tears.

Huey walked over and embraced Mercy. "Louie's right, Victoria's a fighter – she'll come through this, just you wait and see," he said, wiping away the tears.

Silence. Then Mercy said, "She looked like a broken doll lying there in the street. And there was nothing I could do to help her. Nothing."

Now all three men were crying openly. They all loved Victoria.

"Okay, let's pull ourselves together," said Louie. "Crying isn't going to help Victoria. Has anyone called her parents?"

"Yes," said Mercy, "I gave the nurse their number and she called them. They should be here any time."

Victoria was the only child of Bill and Barbara Grant. Mercy had met them just after he and Victoria became engaged. The happy couple had spent a weekend at the Grants' family home, in Flushing. Bill and Barbara had been thrilled to hear of the engagement, and had welcomed their future son-in-law with open arms.

About an hour later, Victoria's parents entered the waiting room. They rushed over to Mercy and embraced him.

Mercy placed his head on Barbara's shoulder and asked, "Is she going to be all right?"

"We're waiting for the surgeon to come out," said Barbara, between sobs. "We just talked to one of the doctors – Victoria is still in surgery."

All they could do now was wait.

The hours passed slowly, and still no word. Finally, the surgeon entered the room and walked over to Bill and Barbara. He shook his head sadly. "Mr. and Mrs. Grant, I'm Dr. Roberts. We did everything possible to save your daughter, but her injuries were too severe. I'm deeply sorry," he said, placing his hand on Barbara's shoulder. Then, turning on his heel, he left the room.

Everyone was devastated by the news. Barbara collapsed in her husband's arms; Louie and Huey gasped; and all the strength seemed to drain out of Mercy's body. Stunned and shocked, he barely had the strength to walk over to Victoria's parents. Putting his arms around them both, he said, "I loved your daughter very much." Tears streamed down his face.

"She loved you very much too," said Barbara. Sobs wracked her body. "She was looking forward to her wedding day. It would have been a marriage made in heaven."

Louie and Huey had tears in their eyes as they expressed their condolences to Victoria's parents. Then they both grabbed hold of Mercy and helped him to walk out of the hospital.

They drove back to the gym in silence. Knowing that Mercy was in a state of deep shock, they stayed with him until late, then took him back to his apartment.

"We'll come up with you," said Louie. "Stay all night, if you want."

Mercy shook his head. "Thanks, guys, but I think I'd like to be alone for a while."

Unable to sleep, Mercy walked the streets, wandering aimlessly from block to block, until the sun came up. *Why, God? Why Victoria? Why didn't you take me instead?* he muttered.

Meanwhile, Louie called Mercy's family and told them about the accident.

"Tell Gil that we'll all be there for the funeral," said Mercy's mother. And, Louie, please take of Gil. He will need all his friends around him now. Give him our love and tell him to call us when he's ready."

As he hung up the phone, Louie thought to himself, *Instead of a busload of people for a wedding, it will be a busload of people for a funeral. How sad is that?*

Mercy ordered a big broken heart for Victoria's funeral. He had no idea how he got through the service. He remembered all the flowers, all the family and friends, and all the tears that were shed. But it was as if he were on autopilot. As if he were not really there – instead, just a spectator looking on from afar.

After the service, Louie and Huey took one look at Mercy and decided that he needed a few stiff drinks to loosen him up. He was still walking around in a daze, barely aware of what was going on around him. So after tearful goodbyes with Victoria's parents and the Aller family, the three friends headed to *Your Favorite Place*.

Mike was tending bar, as usual. He knew what Mercy, Louie and Huey were going through. He missed Victoria too.

"Okay, guys, what are you having? The drinks are on me," he said. "Looks as if you could use more than one!"

"Thanks, Mike, screwdrivers all round, please," said Louie. "And a stiff Scotch for Mercy."

Several rounds later, Mike looked down at the other end of the bar and saw the three friends slumped over the counter, passed out. It was now two a.m. *I'll let them sleep it off for a while*, he thought to himself.

Just then three young men walked into the club. "What are the three bums doing at the end of the bar?" one of them asked Mike.

"They're not bums," Mike retorted, "they just came from a funeral. Leave them alone."

As Mike turned to wait on a customer, Matt, the ringleader of the trio, walked over to Louie and poked him in the back. "Get up, you bum," he said.

Louie woke up and took a swing at the young man but missed and fell off the barstool, onto the floor. He was still half-asleep.

Mercy and Huey slept on, oblivious to the fracas going on around them.

"Get out, or I'm calling the police," said Mike.

"Okay, keep your hair on," said Matt. "We're leaving anyway, this place is a dive." He pointed at the sleeping men. "Full of bums. Come on, guys, we're outta here."

Mike went over to Louie and helped him get back on bar stool.

"Thanks, Mike," said Louie as he struggled to his feet. "Who the hell were those guys?"

"Never seen them before," said Mike.

"Good thing they didn't poke Mercy. He would have knocked them to kingdom come," said Louie, grinning.

At 4 a.m., Mike closed the bar and looked over at his sleeping friends. Louie had passed out again and was now slumped against Huey. "I'll let them sleep it off," he said to himself as he locked the door behind him. "Louie knows where the extra key is."

The next day, Louie and Huey arrived at the gym looking tired and haggard. They were both hung over after their drinking session the night before.

Chapter 24

Mercy was drinking heavily. Out of shape and overweight, he hardly stopped by the gym anymore. Instead, he spent most of his days sleeping and his nights drinking and walking the streets.

The fight against Johnson was drawing closer. Mercy had two months to pull himself together. Louie and Huey tried everything they could to shake him out of his depression. But it was hopeless – Mercy continued to wander around like a lost soul. Each day, he sank lower and lower.

One morning Garcia opened up the gym to find Mercy passed out in the ring, an empty bottle of whiskey lying next to him. He immediately phoned Louie and Huey, who rushed right over. When they saw Mercy, they told everyone to leave him alone.

"Let him sleep it off," said Louie, covering Mercy with a blanket. "Garcia, keep an eye on him. Make sure he's okay." Garcia nodded.

When Mercy woke up several hours later, Louie and Huey took him into the office and read him the riot act.

"Get your act together," said Huey. "Your fight against Johnson is in three weeks."

Mercy just stood there, shamefaced. "I'm sorry, guys, but when I'm sober, the pain is just too much to bear." He hung his head. "I miss her so much."

Louie placed his arm around Mercy's shoulder. "I know, kid, we all miss her. But you have to pull yourself together. Victory wouldn't want to see you this way. Do it for her."

Mercy nodded. "I promise to try to stop drinking and start working out," he told them, rubbing his sore head.

Apart from his emotional state, Mercy was in such bad physical shape that Louie and Huey didn't know if they had enough time to get him back into top form.

"It's gonna take a miracle," said Huey, shaking his head.

Mercy kept his promise. Although there were days when he yearned to lose himself in the oblivion of a drunken stupor, he did not touch a single drop. Louie and Huey were his best friends and he was determined not to let them down. He trained rigorously, pushing himself to the extreme. And by the time the night of the fight arrived he was in top shape.

The stadium was packed. As Mercy climbed into the ring, he looked out into the crowd, expecting to see Victoria's smiling face. Fans waved and yelled out his name. But there was no Victoria, no wave, no windblown kiss. He had lost the love of his life, his best friend, his soulmate, and life would never, ever be the same.

The announcer walked to the center of the ring and spoke into the microphone. "Ladies and Gentlemen, H&G Associates is proud to announce a twelve-round light heavyweight championship fight. In the red corner, wearing the gold trunks with the brown stripes, all the way from Sydney, Australia, weighing in at 170 pounds, with a record of eighteen wins by knockout, I give you the challenger, Bret "The Kangaroo" Johnson."

The crowd started yelling, "Mercy, Mercy, Mercy."

"In the blue corner," the announcer continued, "wearing the red, white and blue trunks, and now fighting out of New York City, weighing in at 174 pounds, with a record of thirty-six wins by knockouts; I give you the light heavyweight champion of the world, Gil "Mercy" Aller." Mercy's fans jumped to their feet, cheering and waving their red, white and blue sweatbands.

The bell rang for the start of the first round. Mercy and Bret met in the middle of the ring. During the first four rounds, Mercy's jabs were sharp and powerful, but in the fifth he started showing signs of fatigue. He had abused his body over the last few months, and now he was paying the price. Known for his speed and nimbleness, he now moved sluggishly around the ring.

In the sixth round, Mercy's breathing became ragged and labored. He was taking a beating from "The Kangaroo." His eyes were swollen and his nose was bleeding profusely. Mercy tried to stay away from "The Kangaroo," but his opponent was always in his face.

In the seventh round Johnson pinned Mercy against the ropes and overpowered him with punches. Mercy went down for the second time in his fighting career. On the count of eight, he struggled to his feet only to be knocked down again.

As Mercy staggered to his feet a second time, he muttered to Johnson, "Hit me harder, hit me harder." Before Johnson could react, the bell rang for the end of the round.

"What was that all about?" Huey asked Mercy as he returned to his corner.

"The harder I get hit, the closer I see Victoria's face," Mercy replied, looking over to the seat where Victoria once sat.

The bell rang for the beginning of the eighth round. Once again "The Kangaroo" pinned Mercy against the ropes and pounded him mercilessly. Mercy's left eye was now swollen shut, blood streamed down his face. Somehow he managed to hang on until the bell. Huey cleaned up his face, and the doctor examined the cut over his left eye. "He's all right," he said.

In the ninth round, it was all over in seconds. One powerful punch from "The Kangaroo" knocked Mercy to the floor once more. This time he didn't get up. Mercy had lost his light heavyweight title.

The Bitches and Beasts couldn't believe their eyes. Their hero had lost. "Rematch, rematch, " they yelled. "We love you, Mercy! Next time! Next time!"

Sparkey and his trainers climbed into the ring and lifted Johnson in the air, carrying him around the ring in triumph. When Sparkey passed Louie and Huey, he said, "I told you assholes that I would get my belt back."

"Yeah, yeah," Louie retorted, "we'll see you in the rematch."

Mercy was badly beaten. Not wanting the fans to see the injuries, Huey placed a towel over Mercy's head and he and Louie helped him back to the dressing room. "Next time, next time," Mercy's fans chanted as the trio passed through the stadium.

Outside the dressing room ten people were waiting for Mercy to bless them.

"No, not tonight," Louie told them.

"It's all right," Mercy said. "I'm okay."

Although weak and still bleeding profusely, he proceeded to bless all ten people. One man, Tony, had been in a terrible car accident, leaving him paralyzed from the neck down. Mercy placed his hand on Tony's head and whispered in his ear, "You have to get better, Tony." A drop of Mercy's blood fell on Tony's arm. Two weeks later, Tony regained feeling in his arms and legs, and after months of therapy, he finally walked again. *Had Mercy performed another miracle, or was it just another coincidence?*

Mercy was so badly beaten that it took a month for his cuts and bruises to heal. He could deal with the injuries, but his heart would never heal. Louie and Huey continued to let him fight, hoping that it would help to snap him out of his depression. But his condition only worsened. He lost his next two fights, making it three in a row. He was also losing his battle with the bottle. Once a social drinker, he was now a fully-fledged drunk. Sparkey was constantly badgering Louie for a rematch. But Louie refused, telling Sparkey that Mercy had to get back into shape.

The night after Mercy lost his third straight fight, he stopped by *Your Favorite Place*. Mike was tending bar, as usual. Several drinks later, Mercy passed out on his stool. Mike watched over him. He thought of Mercy as a son.

Two men walked into the club. Lenny and Carlos, the same two men whom Mercy had knocked out when he was protecting Corinne. Their last words to Mercy had been, "We'll get you, faggot."

"Who's that bum sleeping at the other end of the bar?" Lenny asked Mike.

"Some people call him Mercy, and others call him Gil," Mike said, not recognizing them. "And he's not a bum, he's a friend of mine, so watch your mouth."

When Lenny heard the name, Gil, he knew this was the guy who had kicked their asses several years ago.

"Do you remember when I tried to dance with that girl?" Lenny asked Carlos, not pausing to let him answer. "And we both got beat up?"

"Yeah, I remember," Carlos said. "And we told him that we would get him someday."

"Well, who do you think is sleeping down at the other end of the bar, stupid," Lenny scolded.

"That's him!" exclaimed Carlos, realization dawning. "Let's get him," and he pulled a knife out of his pocket and stepped toward Mercy, who was slumped over the top of the bar counter.

Lenny grabbed Carlos Jose by his shirt. "Wait a minute. We have to get this set up just right," he said, pulling out a sharp ice pick from his jacket. "I'll let you know when it's time for a little payback. First, we'll have a few drinks, then we'll make sure that the bartender's busy."

Carlos nodded, and the two friends slugged down two shots of tequila.

"I'll pull his head up," Lenny continued, "and you cut his throat. "Then I'll stick him in the back with this ice pick. And then we'll run like hell."

They downed two more shots of tequila, then Lenny stood and said,

"Okay, let's go."

Mike was busy at the other end of the bar as Lenny and Carlos started to

walk toward a sleeping Mercy, knife and ice pick at the ready. They had almost

reached their target when the door to the club opened and in walked Percy

"Mean" Williams and a big heavyweight boxer named Henry. Percy had fully

recovered from his near fatal injuries, but his boxing days were over.

Lenny and Carlos returned to their seats. "We gotta wait 'til those big

guys leave," whispered Lenny. "Don't want no witnesses. Carlos nodded.

As Lenny and Carlos brushed past him, Percy glimpsed the knife clutched

in Carlos's hand. *I wonder what these clowns are up to?* he thought to himself,

taking a seat in the middle of the bar and ordering a couple of drinks. Henry sat

down beside him.

"Who is that slumped over the end of the bar?" Percy asked Mike as he

brought the drinks.

"That's Mercy, the former light heavyweight champion of the world,"

Mike said.

Percy couldn't believe his ears. "What happened to him?" he asked.

Mike told him about Victoria's accidental death. "He's been drinking

heavily since her death," Mike explained. "He comes in here most nights to

drown his sorrows, to forget." Mike stared hard at Percy, a puzzled look on his face. "Hey, haven't I seen you someplace before?" Mike had watched the televised fight between Mercy and Percy.

"Well, I used to be the light heavyweight champion," said Percy. "That is until Mercy took the title away from me." He grinned. "Now I'm just happy to be alive."

Percy glanced over at Lenny and Carlos, who were still sitting at the bar. "I think those two guys want to harm Mercy," he said. "When we walked into the club, they were headed over to him and one of em' had a knife." Mike frowned. "I can't let that happen," Percy continued, "Mercy saved my life by performing a miracle. My wife and my mama would never forgive me if something happened to him."

"Yes, I heard about your miraculous recovery, but Mercy insists that it wasn't down to him," Mike replied. "Says it was just a coincidence."

"No coincidence, he's definitely a miracle-worker. Did he tell you about the other miracles he performed?" Percy asked.

Mike looked puzzled. "Nope, never said a word," he said.

"He blessed a woman, by the name of Mary. She'd been confined to a wheelchair for fifteen years. Now she can walk. Also a young man suffered from leukemia and now the doctors say that he's as healthy as a horse. They can't explain it."

"Well, I'll be damned," Mike said, "he never said a word about it."

"That's because he just laughs and tells everyone that their recoveries were flukes, not miracles," Percy replied, looking down the bar at Mercy. "We can't leave him here in this condition," he continued. Then he turned and glared at Lenny and Carlos. "Stay in your seats," he warned them, "otherwise there's going to be a big problem."

Lenny and Carlos jumped in surprise. "We're cool, man," said Lenny. "Don't want no trouble."

After finishing their drinks, Percy and Henry said goodbye to Mike, then walked down to the end of the bar and picked up Mercy, who was still passed out. Between them, they carried him out to Percy's car and plunked him in the backseat.

"Looks as if he got beat up pretty good," said Henry, eyeing the cuts and bruises on Mercy's face. Percy nodded.

When they arrived at Percy's house, the two men carried Mercy in the back way so as not to wake up Percy's two children. Percy's wife Rachel was sitting at the table drinking a cup of coffee.

"Who the heck is that bum?" she asked Percy, looking closely at the bruised and battered Mercy.

"You remember Mercy, the boxer who you claimed saved my life by performing a miracle?"

"That's Mercy!" exclaimed Rachel in disbelief. "He sure looks terrible. How did he get all those cuts and bruises?"

"From a fight he lost last night," replied Percy, who had watched the fight on television.

"You and Henry can put him in the spare room so he can sleep it off," said Rachel. The two men carried Mercy into the bedroom and lay him on the bed.

Percy then told Rachel about Victoria, and how she was pregnant at the time of her death. "Now all he does is drink," finished Percy.

"Poor Mercy," said Rachel, shaking her head sadly. "I'm calling your mother, she'll be delighted to see him again."

The next morning, Percy's two children awoke early. "You have to be very quiet," Rachel told them. "We have a guest in the spare bedroom. His name is Mercy."

"Mommy," asked Rachel's daughter, is he the man who saved Daddy's life with a miracle?"

"Yes, honey," replied Rachel, "he's the one."

The two children smiled, then crept silently into the guest room and sat on the bed, quietly watching Mercy as he slept.

A few minutes later, Mercy woke up to find the two children staring at him. He sat bolt upright and said, "Where am I?" Touching his head, he added, "Oh, my head."

The two children ran to their parents, who were having breakfast in the kitchen. "Mommy, Daddy," they cried in unison. "Mercy's awake and his head hurts."

Percy grabbed a couple of aspirins from the kitchen cabinet and filled a glass with water. Striding into the guestroom, he handed the aspirin and water to Mercy. "Here, take these, they'll help your head," he said.

Mercy took the aspirin and water from Percy's outstretched hands and gulped down the aspirin. "How the heck did I get here?" he asked, feeling dazed and confused.

"A couple of your old enemies were gonna do you in," said Percy. "And I'd have been in trouble with my wife if I hadn't helped you."

Percy's children ran back into the room, and Mercy gave them both a hug.

"What are your names?" he asked.

"I'm Bridgette," piped up the little girl.

"I'm Harold," said the little boy shyly. "You look just like my daddy after a fight."

Mercy and Percy laughed. Then Percy said, "Come on, I'll show you the bathroom – I expect you want to get cleaned up." Mercy nodded and followed Percy out of the room. "Oh, and if you need more aspirin," continued Percy, "just let me know. We'll have breakfast set for you in fifteen minutes."

"Thanks, Percy," said Mercy as he stepped into the bathroom and closed the door.

Fifteen minutes later, fortified by the hot shower, Mercy walked into the kitchen and took a seat at the table, across from Percy and Rachel. He was ravenous. As Louie always said, one thing Mercy never lost was his appetite.

Rachel stared at Mercy - she couldn't take her eyes off him. Finally, she said, "I'm so glad to have you here. I never had a chance to thank you for saving my husband's life by performing a miracle." Tears filled her eyes.

"I didn't perform a miracle," Mercy said, amazed that people still thought that he had a special power. "It was just something that happened. I had nothing to do with it. It was God's will," he insisted.

"I'm sorry, Mercy, but you're wrong," said Rachel. "Even the doctors and nurses said that they had never seen anything like it. Look at my husband," and she pointed at Percy, "he's healthy and strong, just like you. He just can't fight anymore."

Mercy shook his head – he realized it would be futile to argue with Percy's wife, her mind was made up. Mercy had performed a miracle and that was that.

"And now," she continued, "I'm going to cleans those cuts and bruises on your face." Before Mercy could respond, Percy stopped him and said, "Forget about it. Nobody can say "No" to Rachel."

"That's right," said Rachel, smiling. "And someday, somehow, I pray that we can make you a miracle."

After Rachel had tended to his wounds, Mercy thanked her and Percy for their kindness and hospitality. He hugged Rachel, then shook hands with Percy. "Thanks for everything," he said. "I owe you big-time. You saved my life and I'll never forget it."

"Well, now we're even," said Percy, grinning.

Finally Mercy bent down on one knee and said goodbye to Harold and Bridgette. He shook Harold's hand, surprised at how small it was. Bridgette threw her arms around Mercy and planted a sloppy kiss on his cheek. "Thanks for saving my da da," she said. "I love you, Mercy."

"Mercy, you're welcome here anytime," said Rachel, pecking him on the cheek.

"Thank you again," said Mercy as he hurriedly took his leave. He didn't want them to see the tears in his eyes. Their kindness had touched him to the core.

Chapter 25

Jane Shaw was standing on the subway platform, taking photos of her two best friends. A sportswriter from Cleveland, Ohio, she had just been hired to write for *Sports & More Sports*, a popular New York newspaper. And her friends, Doreen and Gloria, had accompanied her to the Big Apple to help her find an apartment.

The two girls were standing inside the subway car, giggling and making faces as Jane snapped one photo after another. "Okay, that's good," said Jane, continuing to click the camera. "Now, put your arms around each other." Her friends complied.

Jane had just taken her last shot, when the subway doors closed. Doreen and Gloria tried to pry open the heavy steel subway doors, but they were not strong enough. "Let us out," they screamed. But to no avail. The train pulled out of the station and disappeared into the darkness of the tunnel, leaving Jane standing alone on the station platform. She stood there in shock for a few moments, then suddenly realized how quiet it had become. Turning her head, she glanced up and down the platform. No one. She was all alone.

Myriad thoughts raced through Jane's mind. *This is supposed to be city that never sleeps. If so, why is it so quiet?* She shuddered. *Should I get on the next train? Or should I just stay where I am?* She decided to stay put and wait for her friends to come back to her.

Jane could feel her hands shaking, and she felt faint. But she had to keep her wits about her. This was New York City and she had heard all the stories about crime in the city. Clutching her purse and camera close to her body, she scanned the platform once again. No one.

A beer can rolling down the steps leading to the subway platform broke the silence. Jane heard voices. Someone was cursing. Three swarthy men came into view, striding along the platform toward her. Jane held her breath. *Stay calm,* she urged herself. *Stay calm.*

As the men approached, Jane could see that one of them was Latino. Short and heavyset, with dark beady eyes, he led the way, followed by a lanky black man, with swinging dreadlocks. Bringing up the rear was a stocky white man; tattoos emblazoned on his shaved head and muscular arms. They whistled at Jane and threw kisses at her.

"Hello there, baby," sang the Latino. "Watcha doin' here all alone? You want Miguel to take care of you?"

Jane trembled. "Hey, sugar, you're shaking. Forget Miguel, ole Leroy here will soon warm you up," laughed the black man.

Jane shivered again. She knew she was in trouble. "Keep your distance," she warned, using her camera and handbag as a shield.

"Aw, sweetheart, don't be like that," crooned the white man, whose name was Vince. "Me and my pals here are just trying to be friendly. We just wanna get to know you better, that's all." He winked at his two friends, then smacked his lips. "We could show you a good time, little lady," he leered. "Bet you've never had three at a time."

Terrified, Jane swung her bag forward. "Stay back," she gasped, "my friends will be here any second."

The three men laughed and continued to circle her, licking their lips and telling Jane what they'd like to do to her.

Jane was just about to scream, when she saw another man walk onto the subway platform. It was Mercy. After leaving Percy's house, he had wandered the street for hours, lost in thought, and was now making his way home. He continued down the platform, walking very slowly toward Jane and the three men.

What do we have here? he said to himself, shaking off his reverie and sizing up the scene before him: the pretty auburn-haired girl, brown eyes blazing, fending off the three thugs who were continuing to taunt her. *Not a good situation*, he mused. *Not good at all!*

As Mercy moved closer, Jane noticed his bruised and battered face, and the red, white and blue sweatband wrapped around his forehead. *Boy, he looks like shit*, she thought, *but at least he's not whistling at me or mouthing obscenities.*

Ignoring the three men, Mercy looked straight into Jane's eyes and said, "Sorry, I'm late, honey. But I got tied up with one of my buddies."

At first Jane was puzzled, then she realized what Mercy was trying to do. She went along with the charade. "I was getting worried about you, sweetheart," she said. "I thought maybe you forgot about me."

"Baby, how could I possibly forget about you," Mercy replied, taking her hand. "Now, how about introducing me to your three friends."

Miguel stared intently at Mercy. "Hey, you're that boxer, Mercy. You got the shit kicked out of you the other night. That's three fights in a row you lost," he sneered. "You can't fight worth shit lately. They knocked you out in all three fights."

"If we kick his ass right now, that will be the fourth fight he lost," said Vince. The three men burst into laughter.

Mercy knew he had to do something, and quick, otherwise there'd be trouble. He walked over to Miguel and extended his hand. "You know my name. But I don't know yours."

"I'm Miguel," he said, ignoring Mercy's outstretched hand.

"What are your friends' names?" Mercy asked.

Miguel called his friends over, but they hesitated. "Hey, get your asses over here and meet Mercy," he ordered.

The two men walked over and shook hands with Mercy. Miguel made the introductions. "This is Vince," said Miguel, rubbing Vince's shaved head, "and the black dude here is Leroy."

"Good to meet you," said Mercy.

"Good luck in your next fight, man," Miguel said. "Sorry about hassling your honey. We was just having a little fun." He turned to Jane. "No hard feelings, sweetheart," he said. "We was only kidding."

Jane grimaced. She wanted to lash out at him, but she held her tongue and gave slight nod.

Miguel turned to his friends and said, "Okay, guys, we're outta here, let's go." And with that, the three men set off down the platform, Vince kicking the beer can, and disappeared into the night.

Mercy and Jane stood alone on the subway platform. Jane was the first to speak. "Thank you. I was absolutely terrified of those thugs. God knows what they would have done to me if you hadn't come along. I'm still in shock." She shivered. "It was really clever of you to pretend that you knew me."

Mercy shrugged. "Well, it wasn't the greatest plan, but it was all I could come up with on the spur of the moment."

"It worked and that's the main thing," she replied, then went on to explain what had happened to separate her from her two friends. "I hope they'll come back for me soon." She extended her hand. "By the way, my name is Jane Shaw."

Mercy took her hand. But before he could respond, a train thundered into the station, and Jane's friends spilled out onto the platform. They ran to Jane and hugged her close.

"Thank God, you're safe," they both cried, still hugging her.

"Yes, I'm fine, thanks to…" Jane turned to Mercy. "Sorry, I didn't get your name."

Mercy grinned. "Well, my real name is Gil, Gil Aller, but most people know me as Mercy."

"Pleased to meet you, Mercy." She turned to her friends. "Gloria, Doreen, meet Mercy. If he hadn't come along, God knows what would have happened." And Jane proceeded to tell her friends about her encounter with the three thugs. "Mercy came to my rescue," she said. "My knight in shining armor."

Mercy blushed. "Any time," he said shyly.

When the next train roared into the station, Mercy boarded the train with the three girls and sat down. Doreen surveyed his battered face. "I hope you don't think I'm being rude, Mercy, but how did you get those cuts and bruises?" she asked.

"I was wondering the same thing," said Jane, "but didn't like to ask."

"Me, too," piped in Gloria.

Well, I'm a boxer," said Mercy, "and I got beaten pretty badly in my last fight."

"Ouch," said Jane. "I've never been a big fan of boxing, it's too brutal for me, and someone always gets hurt."

Mercy shrugged and said nothing. Finally, the train came to his stop. "Okay, this is where I get off," said Mercy, rising to his feet. "Goodnight, it's been nice meeting all of you."

"How can I ever thank you for saving me," Jane said, her eyes brimming with tears.

Mercy just smiled and waved his hand as if to say 'forget about it,' and disappeared into the darkness of the subway station.

"I wonder if I'll ever see him again," said Jane. "He truly was my knight in shining armor."

Chapter 26

It was Monday, Jane's first day at *Sports & More Sports*. As she settled

into her office, she could not stop thinking about Mercy. *If not for him, I shudder*

to think what would have happened, she thought to herself. *I don't suppose I will*

ever see him again.

Later that day, Jane was leafing through some old sports papers when she

came across an article that said, *Mercy loses three fights in a row*. Jane screamed.

"That's him," she cried, 'that's the guy who saved me on the subway."

One of the senior editors walked over to Jane's desk to see what all the

fuss was about. "What's going on?" he asked her.

Jane pointed to the article and told him about the incident in the subway,

and how Mercy had come to her rescue.

"Are you sure that's him?" he asked.

"Yes, I'm sure," said Jane excitedly. "He's the one."

The editor nodded, then turned on his heel and walked into the managing editor's office. A few minutes later he poked his head out of the office and beckoned for Jane to come over. "Freddy wants to see you," he said.

Jane felt her stomach tighten. Freddy Martini was the big boss. *Was she in trouble on her first day?* Rising slowly to her feet, she trudged over to his office and timidly knocked on the door.

"Come in," Freddy thundered. Jane took a deep breath and walked in.

"Grab a seat," he told Jane as he shuffled papers on his desk.

Jane lowered herself into the nearest seat, and clenched her fists tightly.

"I've been looking through your file," he began, "I see you have a nickname, *Jane, Jane, A Sportswriter's Dream*." Jane nodded, wondering where this was leading.

"What's with the nickname?" he asked.

"Well, you see, I have what they call a photographic memory. I can remember names and dates and statistics in practically in any sport: baseball, basketball, car racing, football, hockey, soccer, tennis – you name it," replied Jane.

"Yes, that's very good, but what about boxing, you didn't mention that?"

"Well, I don't like boxing," Jane said, "it's too violent."

"Wouldn't you consider boxing to be the ultimate challenge?" said Freddy, looking directly into Jane's eyes. "If you make a mistake, there's nobody to blame it on, but yourself." He paused. "I was told that Mercy may have saved your life in the subway station. Is that true, Jane?"

"Yes. I'm pretty sure he saved my life," Jane said. "If he hadn't come along, I don't know what would have happened." Jane shuddered, thinking back to that dreadful night in the subway station.

"Mercy used to be the light heavyweight champion of the world. And he also performed miracles. What do you think about that?" he asked, raising his eyebrows.

Jane was taken aback. "That's amazing. Is it true?" she asked.

"Well, that's what they say," replied Freddy. "Apparently, his first miracle saved the life of his bitter enemy – Percy "Mean" Williams - a former light heavyweight champion of the world, until Mercy took the title away from him. Percy sustained a head injury during a fight, and the doctors said there was no hope. Somehow, Mercy performed this miracle, and now Percy is walking around, as healthy as a horse."

"But how on earth did he do it?" asked Jane, her eyes as wide as saucers.

"Well, no one knows for sure," said Freddy, "but the word is, he just touched Percy and whispered that he would get better." Freddy waved his hands. "Lo and behold, he did!"

Jane shook her head. "Wow, that's incredible."

"Certainly is," said Freddy, nodding. "Percy will never fight again, but at least he's alive, thanks to Mercy. So, *Jane, Jane, A Sportswriter's Dream*, that's your first assignment. I want you to interview both of these fighters. Mercy doesn't like to talk to reporters, but I think he'll talk to you." He smiled knowingly. "After all, he did save you from those thugs."

Jane gulped. "Well...," she began nervously, "I'll give it a try, but I can't guarantee that he'll talk to me."

Freddy grinned. "Oh, I think he will. Now, see my secretary and she'll give you all the information you need." He waved his hand dismissively, signaling that the meeting was over.

Oh, my God, thought Jane as she left Freddy's office, *my first assignment. Hope I don't screw it up!*

In the reports provided by the secretary, Jane learned that Mercy had lost his fiancée, who was one-month pregnant, in a tragic accident. After reading this, Jane's stomach churned and she felt an emptiness in her heart. *Poor guy, he must be in his own private hell.*

The next day, Jane drove to the L&H Gym, hoping to set up an interview with Mercy, but he wasn't there. She introduced herself to Louie and Huey, and told them all about her experience in the subway, and how Mercy had come to her rescue.

"Well, I'll be damned!" exclaimed Louie, "he never said a word to us, did he, Huey?"

"Nope, but that's Mercy," replied Huey with a grin, "modest to a fault. Probably thought it was no big deal."

"Do you think he'll grant me an interview?" asked Jane.

Louie looked at the pretty, auburn-haired girl standing before him, her brown eyes sparkling. "Oh, I think he just might," said Louie, winking at Huey. "What do you think, Huey?"

Huey nodded. "But just remember that Mercy is still in mourning. He was a great fighter, but since Victoria died, he doesn't care about anything anymore, especially not boxing."

"I understand," said Jane.

"If you want to speak to Mercy," said Louie, "you'll have to go to *Your Favorite Place*. That's where you'll find him, propping up the bar."

"It's just around the corner," added Huey.

Jane didn't like the idea of going into a strange bar by herself. But she realized that this was a job and if she wanted to interview Mercy, she would have to do it.

"The bartender's name is Mike," Louie continued, "he'll help you. Just tell him that you've spoken to us, and he'll introduce you to Mercy."

"Thanks, guys. I'll go there right now," Jane said, walking towards the exit. She waved. "Thanks again for all your help."

Five minutes later, Jane walked into *Your Favorite Place* and approached the bar. Mike was busy washing glasses. "Excuse me," Jane asked him, "but is your name Mike? Louie and Huey told me that you could help me."

"Yes, I'm Mike. How can I help you?" said Mike, smiling.

"Well," began Jane, "I work for *Sports & More Sports*, and I've been assigned to interview the fighter, Mercy. Louie and Huey told me that I might find him here."

Mike pointed toward the end of the bar. "That's Mercy," he said.

Jane turned and saw a man wearing a red, white and blue sweatband, slumped over the bar. She recognized him immediately.

Jane walked over to Mercy. "Hi," she said, smiling, "do you remember me?"

Mercy looked up from his drink. "No, I don't remember you," he said curtly. "Leave me alone." And he fell back to staring at his glass.

Jane was taken aback by his rudeness. *Could this be the same man who had come to her rescue in the subway station?* "Well, my name is Jane, but some people call me honey." She paused. "But only in the subway…" She paused again, hoping that her words would jog Mercy's memory. No response. Mercy continued to stare at his glass, ignoring her.

Jane tried again. "And no, I'm not going to leave you alone," she persisted.

Still ignoring her, Mercy looked up from his drink and beckoned Mike. "Hey, Mike, give me a drink, and make it a double."

Jane refused to be deterred by Mercy's rudeness. "Honey, the subway. Honey, the subway," she repeated, determined to jog his memory.

Mercy turned and looked at Jane again. "Now I remember you," he said. "You're the lady from the subway."

Jane nodded. "That's me."

Mercy sat up straight. "Excuse me, where are my manners? Would you like a drink?" he asked.

"No, thanks," Jane said, relieved that he had finally recognized her. "I'm working."

"Working on what?" asked Mercy.

"They don't call me *Jane, Jane, A Sportswriter's Dream* for nothing," Jane told him.

"Oh, you're a dream, all right," replied Mercy. "What are you working on?"

Jane hesitated, unsure of Mercy's reaction. "I work for *Sports & More Sports*, and I'd like to interview you for an article I'm writing about you and

Percy "Mean" Williams," she said quickly. "We could talk at the gym, if you like." She could tell that he was in no shape to give an interview today.

Mercy shrugged and said nothing.

Jane handed him her business card. "I'll take that as a 'yes.' See you at the gym tomorrow," she said. "We'll talk then…" and before Mercy could respond, she waved goodbye and walked out of the club.

Mike grinned. "I think you've got your hands full with that one," he said to Mercy. "Don't think she'll take no for an answer."

"You got that right," said Mercy, nodding his head in agreement. "You'd better give me another drink, Mike. I think I'm gonna need it." And the two men laughed.

Mercy arrived at the gym around noon the next day, haggard and hung over. He had drunk heavily last night and was now paying the price.

Louie greeted him at the door. "That sportswriter, Jane something, has called about three times. Something about interviewing you today. That right?"

Mercy nodded. "My head hurts. If she calls again, tell her I'll be at *Your Favorite Place*. I need some hair of the dog."

"What about training?" asked Louie.

"I'll catch you later," replied Mercy, staggering out of the gym.

A couple of hours later, Jane phoned the gym again. Louie answered. "If you want to speak to him, he's at *Your Favorite Place*."

Jane stopped by the club again hoping that Mercy would be sober enough to give an interview. But she was too late – Mercy was bombed. Upset and disappointed, she turned on her heel and walked out of the club.

The next day, Jane stopped by the gym again, only to be told by Louie that Mercy was at the club. Once again, she found him propping up the bar, dead drunk. *There's no point talking to him in this state,* Jane thought to herself as she gazed at Mercy's hunched figure, the glazed eyes and vacant expression masking his face. *He doesn't even know I'm here.*

Jane sighed. She was beginning to hate Mercy for drinking so much. She felt a sense of desperation. Her job was on the line. Every time Jane wanted to interview Mercy, he was drunk out of his mind. *But I'm not giving up,* she mused, *come hell or high water, I'm going to interview Mercy Gil Aller!*

The following day Jane marched into *Your Favorite Place*, a look of determination etched on her face. Walking directly over to Mercy, she stared into his eyes and said, "Are you too drunk for an interview today? Or, are you too drunk, drunk, drunk?"

"Maybe I am. Or maybe I'm not," replied Mercy, taken aback by Jane's direct manner.

"You smell like cheap whiskey, whiskey, whiskey," she said, averting her face to avoid the smell of Mercy's breath.

Mercy did not miss a beat. "Well, you smell like cheap perfume," he replied. "Cheap, cheap, cheap."

Jane wasn't certain what came over her. Maybe it was the smell of the whiskey or Mercy's sarcastic comment about her perfume (she always wore expensive perfume), insinuating that she was cheap. Whatever it was, Jane raised her arm and slapped Mercy hard across the face with her open palm. Then, throwing her business cards on the floor, she turned and stormed out of the club.

Mercy rubbed his sore cheek. "Ouch, that hurt," he whined, stunned at being slapped by a woman he hardly knew.

Mike had watched the whole episode from behind the bar. He walked over to Mercy and handed him some ice for his face. "You sure have a way with women," he said, grinning.

Mercy nodded as he rubbed the ice on his throbbing cheek. "Yeah, I guess I do," he said wryly. "You know, Mike, for a little woman, she sure packs a wallop. She's a regular little firecracker."

Jane had dashed back to her office after leaving *Your Favorite Place*. She was now sitting at her desk, gathering up courage to tell her boss that she could not complete the assignment. *It's hopeless*, she thought to herself. *He's just a drunk – I'll never get through to him. And now I've ruined everything by slapping him across the face. He'll never grant me an interview now.* Suddenly the phone rang, jolting her from her reverie. Jane picked up the receiver. "Hello," she said wearily.

It was Mercy. "I apologize for acting like an ass," he said. "Can I make it up to you by granting you an interview over dinner tonight?"

Jane could hardly believe her ears. Instead of being angry with her, Mercy was inviting her to dinner. She would get her interview after all! "Call me back in ten minutes," Jane replied.

Jane was in shock. She needed time to gather her thoughts. Her body was trembling, and she felt dizzy. Walking over to the coffee machine, she poured herself a strong coffee. *Pull yourself together, girl,* she told herself as she sipped the bitter coffee. *He's calling back in ten minutes and you'd better be ready.*

Mercy called back exactly ten minutes later. "Hi, this is Mercy, do we have a date?"

"Yes, we have a date?" Jane said, still unable to believe her luck. *That slap to the face must have brought him to his senses,* she thought.

"We do? That's great!" exclaimed Mercy. "But, Jane, there's one condition, could you wear some of that cheap perfume? It really smells great."

Jane laughed. "Only if I can buy you a drink of that cheap whiskey," she replied.

"It's a deal," he said, laughing. "I'll meet you at the Steak House Inn around seven."

"See you then," said Jane, hanging up the phone.

That evening Mercy gave Jane an in-depth interview, answering all her questions without reservation. At the mention of Victoria, his eyes filled with such sadness that Jane quickly changed the subject. *How could I have been so insensitive?* she thought. *I could kick myself for being so stupid.*

After Jane turned in the article, Freddy called her into his office. "This is fantastic," he said, waving the article. "You've done an excellent job." Jane beamed.

After the interview, Mercy and Jane started seeing each other regularly. It was as if the slap to the face had shaken Mercy out of his depression. He started working out at the gym again. And he seemed to be sober. Louie and Huey were both surprised and encouraged by this sudden transformation. *Could Mercy possibly be over his devastating tragedy?* they wondered. *Would he start fighting again with the same aggressive style that he once had?*

Mercy's next fight was crucial. Losing four fights in a row would put him at the bottom of the standings, reducing his chances of getting a shot at the title. So far the Australian boxer, Bret Johnson, had defended his title three times, winning all three bouts by knockout. He was formidable opponent. But Louie and Huey knew that if they could get Mercy back into shape, Mercy could show Johnson a thing or two.

Sparkey continued to disparage Mercy at every opportunity. "That has-been Mercy is all washed up," Sparkey would tell the press. "He couldn't fight his way out of a paper bag. The only reason he won the championship belt was through the devil, and his so-called miracles."

Louie and Huey were itching to respond, but after Mercy lost three straight fights, the press didn't come around anymore. Mercy would have to prove his worth in the boxing ring. "We'll show'em," said Louie one day, after listening to yet another of Sparkey's tirades. "Then that asshole Sparkey will have to eat his words."

Christmas was fast approaching. Mercy had always loved the holiday season, but without Victoria to share in the festivities, Louie and Huey feared that he might start drinking heavily again. So far, he was training hard, and quickly regaining his regular shape and weight. They couldn't afford for him to relapse.

The two partners wondered about Jane. She had started coming to the gym regularly, to meet Mercy for lunch. At first, it had been once a week, then three times a week, and now, they were seeing each other every day. Jane liked pizza, so they would usually pick up a pizza and head for the park.

One day as they were sitting in the park, eating their pizza, Jane brought up the subject of miracles. "So, tell me about these miracles you performed," she asked him.

Mercy laughed and said, "I never performed any miracles."

"Don't say that, Mercy," Jane said, "I've spoken to some of the people whom you've cured. And I've seen some of the letters."

Jane convinced Mercy to speak to his priest, Father White, about the miracles. "Just see what he says. You have nothing to lose," she said.

"Okay," replied Mercy resignedly, "I promise to see him after my next fight." Mercy realized that he had found a beautiful, caring woman in *Jane, Jane, A Sportswriter's Dream*.

Jane learned all she could about boxing. She was a part of Mercy's life now, and she wanted to impress him with her newfound knowledge. She read books and articles about old boxing legends and up and coming fighters; watched footage of boxing matches, and old movies like "Ali" and "Rocky." She now realized what Freddy had meant when he asked her if fighting wasn't the ultimate challenge. *Fighting was the ultimate challenge,* she thought to herself. *Two fighters, alone in the ring. One the ultimate winner and one the ultimate loser.*

Chapter 27

Mercy's next fight was one month away. He continued to workout everyday, arriving at the gym early in the morning and leaving late at night. To Louie and Huey, he looked stronger and faster than before. His jabs were quick and powerful, and Huey could feel their power against the punching bag as he held it during Mercy's training sessions. Now 26 years old, Mercy was in his prime.

Mercy's opponent was Dale "Alligator" Jones. A cold, hard fighter from Florida, Jones was hoping for a title shot against Johnson. A win against Mercy, the former light heavyweight champion, might give Jones this opportunity. And he was ready.

Meanwhile, Johnson was bragging that nobody in the world could beat him. Sparkey was always by his side. Be it TV, radio, press conference or sporting event, Sparkey was there, making sure his fighter said all the right things. And Sparkey himself continued his verbal assault against Mercy, telling the media that Mercy was a washed up has-been. "He don't stand a chance against my boy," he bragged on one of the late night talk shows. "Chopping down trees is the only thing that hillbilly lumberjack is good for."

Sparkey's remarks angered the three friends, especially Louie. "We'll show that asshole," he said, shaking his fist. "We'll show him…"

The night of the fight arrived. Mercy, Louie and Huey strode toward the ring, heads held high. Over three hundred members of the *Bitches and Beasts* fan club were sitting in the arena, wearing their red, white and blue sweatbands. "Mercy, Mercy, Mercy," they yelled. "You can do it. You can do it."

Mercy glanced over to Victoria's seat, half-expecting to see her sitting there. Not a day passed that he didn't think of her. But he knew now that she wanted to set him free. He had to start fighting again. He would always love Victoria, but he had to go on with life. It was at this moment, as he scanned the crowd and saw all the people in the stands waving and cheering, that it dawned on Mercy: he had the will to box again, the will to go on living his life.

Mercy jumped into the ring and glanced over at Alligator Jones. He was a powerful looking man – tall and muscular with a finely-honed body. *I have my work cut out for me*, he thought to himself. *He's looks as if he's as strong as an ox.*

"Fire his jab," Huey told Mercy. "Feel the Alligator out."

Mercy nodded as he listened to his fans yelling, "Mercy, Mercy, you can do it! You can do it!" The old embers of fire and passion ignited within him. *He could win this fight.* Tears threatened his eyes. The outpouring of support was overwhelming. *Yes, he would win this fight.*

He turned to Louie and Huey, his voice shaking. "I'm sorry for my unprofessional behavior over the last year. Tonight, I'll try and make it up to both of you."

Louie and Huey put their hands on his shoulders. "We loved Victoria, too," said Louie. "But it's time to move on."

The bell rang for the start of the first round. Mercy danced around the ring, then moved in closer to his opponent and fired three quick jabs. The Alligator moved back and threw a right hook, which Mercy blocked with his forearm. Mercy threw more jabs and a hard left hook to the Alligator's body. Jones retaliated by landing two shots on Mercy's body, then backed away. The two fighters met in the middle ring and fell into a clinch. "Okay, break it up," said the referee as the bell rang to signal the end of the first round.

Mercy returned to his corner. "You're doing great," Huey told him.

Once again, Mercy glanced over to Victoria's seat. Somehow, he could feel her presence, as if she were right there, cheering him on. Louie and Huey followed his gaze and saw a woman, with reddish-brown hair, sitting in the seat. It was Jane.

Louie and Huey looked at each other and smiled. They shook hands. "Thank you, God," said Louie.

The bell rang for the start of the second round. The Alligator charged over to Mercy and landed two hard shots to his body. Mercy stepped back. Using his jab, Mercy worked his way in and punched Jones hard in the body, following up with a swift right hook to his jaw. Jones staggered slightly as the bell rang for the end of the second round.

The next four rounds were even. In the seventh round, Mercy landed several hard punches and Jones was starting to feel them. In the eighth round, Mercy used his jab again and again, then, using a five-shot combination, he hit the Alligator hard. Jones's knees buckled. He hit the canvas with a thud. The fight was over. Mercy had won.

Louie and Huey rushed over and lifted Mercy up in the air. "You did it, kid," cried Louie. "You did it!"

The *Bitches and Beasts* were on their feet, yelling out Mercy's name and waving their sweatbands and American flags. "We love you, Mercy," they screamed. Mercy looked out at the sea of red, white and blue as Huey carried him around the ring on his shoulders. Tears filled his eyes. *All this for me*, he thought, overwhelmed by the outpouring of love and support. He raised his eyes heavenwards and whispered softly, *Thank you for setting me free, Victoria. I will carry you in my heart forever.*

Sports reporters crowded into the ring. Clamoring around Mercy, thrusting their microphones in his face, they bombarded him with questions, eager to hear what the winner had to say. "Is there a chance you'll get your title back, Mercy?" asked one. "Will you go after Johnson?" asked another.

"Time will tell," Mercy told them.

Jane climbed into the ring, notepad and camera in hand. Wading through the sea of reporters, she walked over to Mercy and planted a kiss on his cheek. "I knew you could do it," she said, smiling.

"Looks like you have an edge over the rest of us," muttered one of her fellow reporters.

"You could say that," said Jane coyly.

As Mercy left the ring with Louie and Huey, a priest walked up to him and said, "Some of the people here tonight have a come a long way to receive your blessing."

Mercy felt his face redden. "Father, I will give everyone my blessing, but please believe me, I don't have any special powers. And I'm certainly not a miracle worker."

The priest touched Mercy's arm. "Well, my son, miracles or no miracles, just keep doing what you're doing." He paused and smiled. "And remember, God works in mysterious ways."

About twenty people were waiting the arena, some in wheelchairs, others leaning on crutches. Mercy blessed them all. Then he turned and said, "Have I missed anyone?"

A young boy in a wheelchair cried out, "You missed me."

Mercy walked over to him. "I'm sorry," he apologized. "What's your name?"

"Adam," the boy replied.

Adam's mother, who was standing nearby, introduced herself to Mercy and told him that Adam was suffering from a rare lung disease. "He only has a short time to live," she said quietly, tears filling her eyes.

Mercy patted her gently on the shoulder, then reached out to shake Adam's hand. As he did so, a small drop of blood fell from his nose onto the boy's hand. Kneeling down, Mercy whispered in Adam's ear. "You have to get better, young Adam."

Jane, standing off to one side, had witnessed the whole scene. Scribbling furiously in her notepad, she thought to herself, *This will make one helluva story in this week's sports section.*

And what a story it was! Mercy's fan mail doubled overnight. As for Mercy, he felt happy in one way but sad in another. He wished that he really did have the power to heal people. He decided to keep his promise to Jane, and see Father White.

"You are doing a wonderful thing, my son," Father White explained to Mercy the next day. The two men were sitting in the priest's sunlit study, surrounded by a mountain of books. "Miracles do happen because people have such a deep, spiritual love for God. The people you have helped look upon you as a strong, spiritual being. The combination of God, and the sick and injured, and yourself generates such power that a miracle occurs." The priest paused for a moment and touched Mercy's forehead. "I believe you may have this power. God Bless you, my son."

"Thank you, Father," replied Mercy, somewhat overwhelmed by the priest's words. "I'll see you at Sunday Mass."

Chapter 28

As the months passed, Mercy's winning streak continued. He had won his last seven fights. His record now stood at forty-five wins by knockout, and three losses.

The next fight was scheduled in Youngstown, Ohio. Jane would be covering the fight for her newspaper, flying to Ohio and back on the same day. She had tried to persuade Mercy to fly back to New York with her but he had come up with some flimsy excuse. But Jane knew the truth – Mercy was afraid of flying, just like Louie and Huey.

On fight night Mercy was victorious once again, knocking out his opponent in the eighth round. Louie and Huey were proud of their young protégé. Since his bout with the bottle, he had come back smarter and faster than ever. His punches packed more power, and he could knock out his opponent with either fist.

The two friends would often reminisce about the first time they saw Mercy, at *Your Favorite Place*. He was dancing with Corinne, and they had admired his fancy footwork on the dance floor. "I wonder what would have happened if those two thugs hadn't started a fight?" said Huey.

"Yeah, me too," replied Louie, scratching his head. "And what if we hadn't been there that night, we would have missed Mercy altogether."

It was fate, they mused. *Fate that brought them together.*

After the fight was over, Jane flew back to New York, while the three friends stayed over at a local hotel near the boxing arena. The next day, they rose bright and early and set off for New York, in Louie's brand new Lincoln Town car.

As usual, Louie took the back roads. "Just as the crow flies," he reminded Mercy and Huey.

Around noontime, they started getting hungry. "Let's stop there," said Huey, pointing to a sign emblazoned with the words *The Best Juicy Hamburgers in Ohio – Straight Ahead,* in bright red letters. Louie continued driving down the road for a couple of miles until they reached the restaurant. "Here we are," he said, pulling up near the entrance.

As they walked inside, they noticed that the restaurant was small and clean, and decorated in a quaint, old-fashioned way. It was a Mom and Pop business, with only one waitress. Taking a seat at one of the window tables, they scanned the menu. "I'm starving," said Louie.

"Must be all that driving," chuckled Huey, and they all laughed.

287

The waitress walked over to their table and took their order. She was a tall, slender woman, with dark hair piled up on her head in a bun. "What would you like?" she asked, with a smile.

They all ordered a hamburger with the works. And before they knew it, the waitress had returned with three big, juicy hamburgers. She placed the three platters on the table. "Enjoy," she said, "and don't forget to leave a big tip." They laughed.

"You got it," said Louie, winking at her.

Huey was about to bite into his hamburger, when Louie said, "Hold it, Huey."

"What's wrong?" Huey asked. "Is there something wrong with my hamburger?"

"No," Louie said, "I just want to tell you and Mercy something about hamburgers."

" Well, hurry up. I'm hungry. And my hamburger is getting cold," Huey said, with a hint of annoyance in his voice.

"Well," Louie began, "to really enjoy a big, beautiful juicy hamburger, like this, you have to know when and where to bite into it."

"I don't have time for this bullshit," Huey said, chomping down on his burger, the juice dribbling down his chin.

Louie continued explaining to Mercy. "You have to pick up your hamburger off the plate, look at it, turn it around and it will tell you when and where to bite it for the best taste."

Mercy picked up his hamburger, turned it around and took a bite out of it. "You're right, Louie, the hamburger does tell you when and where to bite it."

"I told you, Mercy," Louie said, "this hamburger wants to be eaten. And if you take your time, it will tell you when and where to take a bite, and it will taste much better."

Meanwhile, Huey had finished eating his hamburger and was watching Louie and Mercy taking turns repeating the phrase: *When and where. When and where.* He shook his head, thinking how ridiculous they looked and sounded.

Louie turned to Huey and said, "Why did you eat your hamburger so fast?"

"Because I was hungry, that's why," Huey said, irritated by Louie's behavior.

"Why don't you order another hamburger?" Louie said.

"Why?" Huey said, "when I got, *When and Where* hamburger, right here." And Huey reached across the table, trying to grab Louie's and Mercy's hamburgers off their plates.

Louie and Mercy quickly pulled their burgers away before Huey could grab them. "And besides, my name's not Huey," said Huey. It's *Why.*"

"Why is *Why* so pissed off?" Louie said to Huey. "Because he don't have nothing to eat. And we're still eating,"

"You're damned right, I'm pissed off," Huey said. "And do you know what *Why* would like to do to *When* and *Where*, right now?"

"No, what would *Why* like to do to *When* and *Where*, right now?" asked Louie.

"*Why* would like to take *When's* and *Where's* heads and smash them together like two watermelons." Then Huey reached over and grabbed Louie's car keys, which were sitting on the table. Jumping to his feet, he dashed out of the restaurant, ran to Louie's car and sped off in a cloud of dust.

Louie and Mercy sat there in stunned silence. Finally, Mercy said, "I've never seen Huey so mad. I can't believe that he would storm off like that and leave us stranded."

Louie wrinkled his brow. "That wasn't Huey," he said, "that was *Why*, and *Why* has a very nasty temper."

The waitress had witnessed the entire scene. She walked over to their table and set down her own hamburger. Taking a seat, she said, "Hi, I'm Sally, and this has got to be the biggest tip I will probably ever get." She surveyed their shocked faces, both men still reeling from Huey's sudden departure. "Now, you boys need a ride?" she continued.

Louie extended his hand. "Hi, Sally, I'm Louie, and this is Mercy," he said, patting Mercy's shoulder. "And we'd sure appreciate a ride to New York. Our buddy has left us high and dry."

Sally smiled. "I noticed," she replied. "Now, how do I get involved in this fun game you two are playing?" she asked.

Louie described the game. "Do you understand the rules now, Sally?" Louie asked.

"My name's not Sally," she said.

"It isn't?" said Louie, puzzled. "Well, what is your name?"

"What," said Sally.

Louie and Mercy, thinking that the waitress was hard-of-hearing, raised their voices and said in unison, "What's your name?"

"What," said Sally.

Louie and Mercy grinned – Sally caught on fast.

The squealing of tires interrupted their conversation. And a few moments later, in strolled Huey. As if nothing had happened, he pulled up a chair and sat down next to Sally. "Hi," he said to her, "what's your name?"

"What," Sally replied.

"What's your name?" repeated Huey, a little louder.

"What," Sally repeated.

Huey was ready to shout louder, but Louie stopped him. "She's playing the game," Louie told him, "and she's having fun."

"You mean to tell me that her name is *What*, my name is *Why*, and you two dummies are *When* and *Where*? Well, that takes the cake," Huey said, scratching his head.

"Well, *Why*, *When*, and *What*, I think it's about time we hit the road," said Louie.

"Don't forget that big tip," said Sally, winking. "And come back soon, y'all hear."

Chapter 29

As a sportswriter and reporter, Jane had been working hard over the last few months to get Mercy a shot at the title. Along with the other sports reporters, she had been putting pressure on Sparkey. Their efforts had paid off. Sparkey had finally caved in to the pressure and agreed to have a championship fight in five months…in Australia!

Sparkey had just called Louie to let him know. He was his usual blunt self. "Okay, asshole," he barked into the phone, "you got yourself a fight with my boy. But, listen, asshole, you're gonna have to travel to the other side of the world. The fight's in Sydney, Australia – no negotiation – it's Australia or nothing." And Sparkey slammed down the phone.

Louie was ecstatic. "We have a title fight, a title fight, a title fight," he sang, dancing around his desk. Huey and Mercy walked over to see what all the fuss was about.

"What's happening, Louie?" said Huey. "Why are you dancing around like a maniac?"

"We got the title fight," he gushed. Mercy and Huey couldn't believe their ears. Now all three of them were dancing around the desk.

Suddenly, Louie stopped dancing and looked over at his friends. "But," he began, "there's just one small problem."

"What's that?" asked Mercy, noting the sober expression on Louie's face.

"The fight's in Australia, and you know what that means?" said Louie. "We have to fly!"

Silence. They all stood there in a daze, worry lines replacing their jubilant smiles. And the same thought drifting through their heads: *We have to fly.*

The phone rang, jolting them back to the present. Louie picked it up. "Hello," he said.

It was Adam's mother, calling to tell them that Adam had made a complete recovery. "I just don't know how to thank Mercy," she said. "This is the greatest moment in my life. Please tell Mercy 'God Bless him.'" She paused. "God Bless all of you."

Louie hung up the phone and turned to Mercy. "Do you remember giving your blessing to a boy named Adam?"

Mercy nodded. "Yes, I remember, he had a rare lung disease – the doctors said he only had a few months to live."

"Well, Mercy, you just performed another miracle. That was Adam's mother on the phone. Adam's lungs are clear – he's gonna make it."

"That's wonderful news," said Mercy, beaming. "But listen, guys, I keep telling you both, I cannot perform miracles."

"Not true, kid," said Louie. You've definitely got the magic touch."

Mercy shook his head and smiled. "I give up," he said.

"Hey, perhaps you can perform another miracle," said Louie.

"Yeah, what's that?"

"Cure us all of our fear of flying," chuckled Louie. And they all burst in laughter.

. . . .

Mercy had five months to prepare for the fight. He took a few days off and then started training in earnest. He knew he had to give his all to bring the title back to the good old U.S.A. And if that meant training from dawn to dusk, then so be it.

Meanwhile, Jane kept trying to explain to the three friends, about the joys of flying. "Beautiful airline stewardesses, delicious food, an assortment of drinks to relax you, non-stop movies," she said, "what more could you ask for?" She scanned their faces for a reaction. Nothing. "And besides," she continued, "you don't even know you're flying."

The three friends looked doubtful – it would take more than glamorous stewardesses and airline cuisine to conquer their fear of flying.

Jane tried again. "I want us all to wear red, white and blue sweatbands," she told them.

"Why is that?" asked Mercy.

"So that if you look at the stewardesses too much, I can pull the sweatband over your eyes." They all chuckled.

The next few months flew by. The big fight was now only two weeks away. An air of excitement pervaded the boxing world. The fans had high hopes for Mercy. If anyone could bring the light heavyweight championship belt back to the United States, he could. And his fans would be there to support him, all the way. The *Bitches and Beasts* were going to Australia!

Jane was covering the fight for *Sports and More Sports*, so she would be accompanying Mercy and Louie and Huey on the flight. Her presence would provide moral support and, hopefully, help to calm their nerves.

The day of the flight arrived. The four friends arose at dawn and headed for JFK International Airport, in a black limousine. A heavy snowstorm overnight had disrupted the flight schedules. Many planes were delayed, including their flight to Sydney, and the airport was crowded with people.

The delay played havoc with the three friends' nerves. Jane tried to calm them, but as the hours ticked by, they became more and more anxious.

"I need a stiff drink," said Louie. "Let's head to the bar."

"Lead the way," said Huey, "we're right behind you."

Two drinks later, they finally heard the announcement: Quantas Flight 237 to Sydney, now boarding at Gate 3.

"Let's go," said Jane, leading the way to Gate 3. Louie, Huey and Mercy followed meekly behind.

As they walked down the gangway to the plane, Louie tried to turn around, but Jane grabbed him by the arm and propelled him forward. "It's okay, Louie, everything's going to be fine," she soothed.

Once on board the plane, they quickly stowed their hand luggage, and took their seats. Louie grabbed the nearest stewardess. "We need some drinks here – double Scotches all around. And please hurry," he said anxiously. Beads of sweat dotted Louie's brow, his whole body trembled. The tough boxing promoter was petrified.

The stewardess was used to dealing with nervous passengers. "Try to stay calm, sir, there's nothing to worry about." She glanced over at Mercy and Huey. They were also terrified but trying hard not to show it. "I'll bring the drinks for you and your friends as soon as we're airborne," she said.

Louie leaned back in his seat, struggling to control his nerves. Glancing out of the window, he spotted a couple of men spraying the wings with fluid. He jerked upright and yelled, "Hey, that's not gasoline, is it?"

Jane touched his shoulder. "Relax, Louie, they're just de-icing the plane. It's de-icer fluid, not gasoline," she said. "They have to clear the wings of ice and snow before we can get airborne."

Louie exhaled. "Talking of air, I could sure use some fresh air right now," he said, loosening his collar. He looked over at Mercy and Huey who were also squirming in their seats.

"Will the three of you just try to relax," said Jane. "Close your eyes and pretend that you're sitting in *Your Favorite Place*, having a drink."

"Easier said than done," replied Mercy. Louie and Huey nodded in agreement.

Moments later, the plane screeched down the runway and soared into the sky. They were finally airborne. As promised, the stewardess brought their round of drinks, and then another and another and soon the nervous travelers were veteran flyers.

"Flying's a piece of cake," said Louie, knocking back his third Scotch. "I don't know what all the fuss is about."

"Yeah," agreed Mercy. "Nothing to it."

"I'll drink to that," said Huey.

"Men!" said Jane, shaking her head.

Mercy knew that Louie and Huey would be having quite a few drinks, but he was surprised to see Jane drinking so much. She seemed nervous and edgy, more so than the three novice flyers. Now on her fourth glass of wine, she suddenly nudged Mercy in the ribs. "Look at that guy," she said, pointing to a swarthy-looking man sitting across the aisle from them. "He looks a little strange. Do you think he might be a terrorist? He could have a bomb."

Hearing the words "terrorist," and "bomb," Louie started humming, and Huey ordered more drinks. But Mercy laughed, thinking that Jane was just trying to scare the crap out of them. And in the case of Louie and Huey, she was succeeding.

"Okay, Jane, enough of the bomb and terrorist crap," admonished Mercy. "You're scaring the hell out of us. You know we don't like to fly. He pointed at Louie and Huey. "Look at Louie and Huey, they're shaking."

Louie and Huey had ordered yet another round of drinks to calm their nerves. They looked at Jane expectantly, waiting for her to tell them that she was kidding.

But Jane seemed to be serious. "Look closely," she said. "He's wearing a disguise. That's definitely a wig. And just look at those eyebrows."

They all looked over at the man, who was talking to his wife. The man's black bushy hair matched his thick bushy eyebrows and scraggly beard. Thick black glasses framed his dark eyes. In contrast his wife was petite and blonde with pale porcelain skin and china blue eyes.

"He looks normal to me," said Louie. "And his hair looks real." Mercy and Huey agreed.

Jane insisted that he was a terrorist. "I just know he has a bomb," she said, taking a gulp of her drink. Now on her fifth glass of wine, her eyes were glazed, her speech slightly slurred. "Look, he's rummaging in his bag now, and he keeps checking his watch and looking up and down the aisle."

Louie, Huey and Mercy just looked at her and chuckled. "He's probably wondering when dinner is gonna be served," said Louie.

"I'm telling you, he has a bomb on this plane. It's probably under somebody's seat," she slurred.

The three friends checked under their seats. Nothing.

"Come on, Jane, cut it out," said Mercy angrily. "You're drunk. A joke's a joke, but you've gone far enough with this terrorist and bomb crap."

But Jane refused to listen. Jumping to her feet, she lunged over and grabbed the so-called *terrorist* by the hair. "Where's the bomb?" she yelled. "Where's the bomb, you terrorist bastard, I know it's on here someplace."

The poor man screamed out in agony. "Let go of me, you crazy bitch," he yelled as he struggled to free himself from Jane's viselike grip. "I don't know what the hell you're talking about. You're crazy, and you're drunk!"

Mercy leapt from his seat and tried to drag Jane off the screaming man, while Louie and Huey looked on, in shock, wondering if maybe Jane was right, and the plane might explode at any second.

Two stewardesses rushed over. And with the help of Mercy and the man's wife, they managed to pry Jane's fingers loose from the man's hair.

The man's wife pressed her face close to Jane's. "You crazy, drunken bitch," she yelled. "You better not grab him by the hair again, or I'll kick your ass."

"Just try it," challenged Jane, thrusting her body forward.

"For God's sake, Jane, be quiet," said Mercy, holding her back. "Why don't you apologize to these people and then we'll go back to our seats."

"Not until they tell us where they've hidden the bomb," she cried.

As the two women continued to stare at each other, the captain walked down the aisle toward them. "What's going on here?" he demanded. "I could hear all the commotion from the cockpit."

Mercy tried to explain. "We're really sorry, sir. Jane had one too many drinks and overreacted. She was convinced that this poor gentleman was a terrorist. She thought he was wearing a wig. That he was in disguise."

The captain looked over at the man, who was rubbing his sore head. "If that's a wig," said the captain, "he must have it nailed on!" He walked over to the man and extended his hand. "Please accept our apologies, sir. The lady was out of control. She won't bother you again. We invite you and your wife to be our guests in first class for the rest of the trip."

The couple thanked the captain, then turned and glared at Jane. "Psycho," spat the man.

"As for you, young lady," said the captain, turning to Jane. "Return to your seat and stay there. If I hear one peep out of you, you'll be restrained and then turned over to the authorities in Australia. Do you understand?"

Jane was still muttering under breath, "Where's the bomb? Where's the bomb?"

"What did you say?" said the captain.

"She said, 'I'll be good, I'll be good,'" said Mercy, stepping in and leading Jane back to her seat. Within seconds she was asleep against his shoulder.

Louie and Huey looked over at her sleeping form. "Well, at least she's not a dull person," Louie chuckled.

"I'll drink to that," said Huey.

301

Chapter 30

After a brief stop in Dubai to refuel, the plane touched down at Sydney International Airport in the early morning. It had been over 24 hours since the four friends had left New York. They were now on the other side of the world, in a different time zone, in a different season. Warm sunshine greeted their arrival. It was summer in Australia – a far cry from the snowbound streets of New York.

As the four friends stepped off the plane wearing their red, white and blue sweatbands, they were surprised to find a crowd of fans waiting for them. The fans, some in wheelchairs, others wearing their trademark sweatbands, greeted them enthusiastically. Mercy blessed the wheelchair bound and signed autographs.

"Good on yer, mate," said a young paraplegic who had been paralyzed in a car accident. "We may live Down Under, but we've heard all about you and your healing powers."

302

Mercy was amazed. *Word travels fast*, he mused, *even to the other side of the world!*

For the next five days Mercy worked out in a gym, close to the arena where the fight was being held. There wasn't much time for sightseeing, but the four friends managed to tour the city, and take a couple of short trips to the surrounding area.

"Sydney is a beautiful city," remarked Jane one day as she and Mercy dined at a restaurant overlooking the Sydney Opera House. "The view of the bay and the opera house is breathtaking, and the people are so warm and friendly."

Mercy agreed. "And I love the Aussie accent. From now on, I'll probably be calling everyone, 'mate.'"

Jane laughed. "Good on yer, mate."

The fight was being televised worldwide, so the city was brimming with reporters and fight fans from all over the world. Although nervous, Mercy felt confident that he could win. *I've traveled all this way*, he thought to himself. *Stepped on a plane and conquered my fear of flying. I'm not going back empty handed. That belt is going home with me.*

The night of the fight arrived. Louie, Huey and Mercy sat the dressing room, waiting for the call to the ring. "Okay, Mercy, this is it," said Huey, grabbing him by the shoulders. "This is the day we've been working towards. Let's bring it home."

Mercy nodded and looked straight ahead. He was struggling to control his nerves.

Louie sensed the nervous tension. "We're one hundred percent behind you, kid. Remember, you're faster, fitter, smarter, and stronger than ever. And you're gonna run circles around that dumb Aussie."

A knock on the door interrupted their conversation.

"Come in," said Huey. The door opened and to everyone's amazement, in walked Percy "Mean" Williams.

"Could you use any help in your corner?" asked Percy, grinning.

"Yes, we sure could," they all replied in unison.

"Damn, it's great to see you, Percy," said Mercy, jumping to his feet.

They all crowded around Percy and shook his hand.

"Welcome to our corner, Percy," said Louie. Percy beamed.

"How's the family?" Mercy asked.

"Oh, they're fine. Rachel has come over with me to watch the fight. And the kids will be watching on television," replied Percy. "They want the belt back in the United States."

"I'll try my best not to disappoint them," said Mercy.

"Attaboy," said Percy, patting Mercy on the back. "We'll all be rooting for you."

A second knock on the door summoned Mercy to the ring. Showtime!

As they marched down the aisle, chants of "Kangaroo, Kangaroo," echoed around the stadium. The place was packed with Australian fans and they were all rooting for their champion.

"At least we have Percy," Louie said to himself.

Once in the ring, Huey gave Mercy a little pep talk. "Listen, kid, Johnson may have the hometown advantage, but you have the advantage of speed. You are faster on your feet, and your punches are quicker."

Mercy nodded. The nerves had taken a hold and he didn't trust himself to speak. He looked over at Jane who was sitting at ringside. Their eyes locked. "You can do it," she mouthed.

Huey continued. "This time, Johnson is fighting against the real Mercy, not the heartbroken one."

As Mercy started to respond, a huge roar went up from the crowd. Johnson had entered the stadium. "Kangaroo, Kangaroo, Kangaroo," yelled the frenzied Aussie fans as the Kangaroo and his entourage made their way down the aisle. Two large kangaroos and their keepers led the way, followed by thirty people waving the Australian flag. Sparkey and the corner men brought up rear, and finally, the Kangaroo.

The crowd erupted when they saw the two kangaroos hopping down the aisle, in full boxing regalia, throwing punches at each other.

The announcer walked to the center of the ring and spoke into the microphone. "Ladies and gentlemen, miracles never seem to cease when it comes to Mercy. You would never guess who's working in Mercy's corner tonight." He paused, building up the suspense, then continued, "They used to be bitter enemies, bitter rivals, but if my eyes are not deceiving me, I could swear I see Percy "Mean" Williams working in Mercy's corner."

All eyes turned to Mercy's corner and there stood Percy, a huge grin creasing his face. He turned to the crowd and waved. They greeted him with cheers and applause. Cries of "Good on yer, mate" echoed around the stadium. As a former world champion, Percy was admired and respected worldwide.

"And now, ladies and gentlemen," continued the announcer, we are proud to announce a Sports Australian Inc. fight, a twelve round fight for the light heavyweight championship of the world." The announcer went on to introduce the two fighters, eliciting boos and catcalls when Mercy's name was called and thunderous applause, and cries of "Kangaroo, Kangaroo," when the hometown boy, Bret "Kangaroo" Johnson was introduced.

The bell rang for the start of the first round. The two fighters danced around the ring, feeling each other out. Mercy's jabs were quick and powerful, keeping the Kangaroo back. The Kangaroo threw a couple of hard shots, driving Mercy back to the ropes. Mercy danced away from the ropes and threw a hard combination.

The fight continued like this through the next seven rounds. So far, both boxers were even. In the ninth round, the pace picked up with both fighters inflicting powerful crushing punches. And by the end of the tenth round, both fighters had sustained severe cuts and bruising. Mercy had a deep cut over his left eye, and the Kangaroo was bleeding profusely from the nose.

Bloody and battered, the two fighters met in the middle of the ring at the start of the eleventh round. The Kangaroo circled Mercy, catching him with a swift right hook. The crowd roared, "No Mercy, No Mercy. Go, Kangaroo, Go." Mercy staggered but managed to stay on his feet. The Kangaroo continued to attack, driving Mercy against the ropes and pounding him with a volley of punches.

Mercy punched and danced his way off the ropes, and started throwing his jab to keep the Kangaroo away from him. The Kangaroo smelled victory. He charged in only to find himself the recipient of one of Mercy's powerful combinations. He staggered. Now Mercy had the Kangaroo on the ropes.

Huey, Louie and Percy cheered from the sidelines. They were hoping that Mercy could finish the Kangaroo off, but the bell rang. The two fighters returned to their respective corners.

As Huey and Percy worked on Mercy, cleaning his cuts and toweling him off, Huey said, "Throw two or three jabs, then step in quick and throw as many combinations as possible." Mercy nodded. "Then step back fast," continued Huey, "then step right back in, before he gets himself set up, and hit him with everything you got."

The bell rang for the last round. With Huey's words ringing in his ears, Mercy started throwing his jabs, then he stepped in quickly and landed five swift punches. The Kangaroo staggered. Mercy stepped back, then stepped right back in, before the Kangaroo could recover from his other punches, and threw two quick combinations. The Kangaroo hit the mat. The crowd gasped.

The referee told Mercy to go to the farthest neutral corner, then he started to count. "One, two, three, four, five, six…" The Kangaroo tried to struggle to his feet, but his legs buckled and he fell back down. …"Seven, eight, nine, ten." The fight was over. The light heavyweight championship belt would be going back to the good old U.S.A.

The crowd cheered wildly. Even though their champion had lost, the Australian fans knew that they had just witnessed one of the best fights ever. Both fighters, winner and loser, deserved their respect and admiration.

At ringside, Huey, Louie and Percy were jumping up and down with excitement. They rushed into the ring and raced over to Mercy.

"You did it, you did it," cried Louie, tears of joy rolling down his face. He glanced over at Sparkey. "The belt is ours again," he shouted. "Now who's the asshole?"

For once Sparkey was at a loss for words. Glowering at Louie, he turned on his heel and stalked out of the stadium.

"You've done us proud, son," said Huey, his voice breaking with emotion. "You brought it home."

Percy stepped in and grabbed Mercy's hand. "You're a true champion, Mercy."

Huey lifted Mercy up on his shoulders and paraded around the ring with him. The fans continued to cheer and yell. Overwhelmed with emotion, Mercy felt as if he were caught up in a dream.

The Kangaroo walked over to Mercy and said, "You're one helluva fighter," he said, giving Mercy a sportsman's hug.

Mercy returned the hug. "You're one hell of a fighter yourself. I just happened to throw a lucky punch."

Reporters and officials crowded into the ring. Jane pushed her way through the melee and planted a sloppy kiss on Mercy's face, smearing his cheek with lipstick.

"I knew you could do it," she said, smiling.

Before Mercy could respond, a reporter came over and said, "I can't believe that Percy "Mean" Williams was in your corner. I thought that you two were bitter enemies?"

"We were never bitter enemies," replied Mercy, "we were just rivals in the ring."

"What about Sparkey?" asked the reporter. "I don't think he likes the fact that Percy is in your corner."

"Sparkey and Percy went their separate ways," said Mercy.

The reporter adjusted his camera. "Could I please have a photo of you and Percy?" he asked.

Mercy called Percy over, and the two friends put their arms around each other's shoulders and posed for the camera. Within seconds, reporters and photographers surrounded them, all clamoring to take a photo of the two fighters.

The reporters bombarded Mercy with questions: *How long before the next fight? Will there be a rematch? Do you plan on changing managers? Do you plan on changing trainers? Who was the reporter who gave you a kiss? Do you have marriage plans? What's your favorite cereal?* He patiently answered them all.

"And now, if you'll excuse me," said Mercy, "I have to go get cleaned up."

Mercy had taken a punishing beating from the Kangaroo. He was still bleeding, and both of his eyes were almost swollen shut. Huey and Percy tended to his injuries, while Louie came over and placed a sweatband on his head. "Way to go, kid," he said, patting Mercy on the back. "Way to go."

The fans were slowly filing out of the stadium. People in wheelchairs surrounded the ring, hoping that Mercy would bless them on his way back to the dressing room. They were not disappointed – Mercy blessed them all. One by one, he asked them their names, then placed his right hand on their foreheads and whispered in their ears. *You have to walk again, Harry. You have to get better, Helen.*

Finally, Mercy came to a beautiful young girl named Vicki, with flowing black hair. Her mother spoke up and told Mercy that Vicki needed a kidney transplant, but none were available. Mercy placed his hand on Vicki's forehead as she looked up at him with sorrowful brown eyes. "Your kidney has to get better, Vicki," he whispered. A few drops of his blood dropped onto her hand.

"Did I miss anyone?" asked Mercy.

There was no answer. He had blessed everyone.

Inside the dressing room, Jane threw her arms around Mercy and kissed him on the lips. Only then, did she notice his discolored face, the swollen eyes and open cuts. Tears flowed down her face. "I love you, Mercy," she whispered as she held him close.

Chapter 31

Mercy, Louie and Huey spent a few more days in Australia, until Mercy regained his strength. Meanwhile, Jane had flown back to New York, to file the story of Mercy's victory for her newspaper. She could not stop thinking about Mercy. After seeing him all battered and bruised, in the dressing room, she knew that she wanted to be his wife. *But how did Mercy feel about her?* she thought. *Did he love her, or was he still in love with Victoria?* Jane made up her mind she was going to find out, one way or another.

When Mercy's plane landed in New York, Jane was there to meet him, and Louie and Huey. She ran to him, grimacing when she saw his black and blue face and the spidery stitches etching his eyebrow. He looked terrible.

Jane hugged him close and kissed his battered face. "I'm so glad you're home," she whispered. "I've missed you."

"I've missed you, too," he said, giving her a long, soft kiss.

"How about us?" Louie said to Jane. "Did you miss us too?"

Jane turned and hugged Louie and Huey. "Of course," she said, smiling. "Welcome home."

"God, it feels good to be on solid ground again. I don't think I'll be flying anywhere for a long, long time," said Louie.

"How was the flight?" asked Jane.

Louie and Huey exchanged glances. "Oh, quite boring really," said Huey. "No sign of your bushy haired terrorist this time."

Jane drove Louie and Huey back to the gym, then took Mercy to her apartment.

"You need some rest after that long flight," she said. "And I can take care of your wounds."

Mercy took a long, hot shower, while Jane prepared dinner. For dessert, she had his favorite: Cherry pie. Mercy smiled when he saw the pie. "Thank you, Jane," he said, kissing her tenderly.

After dinner, Jane told Mercy that one of her co-workers had asked her out to dinner. "He's very handsome, and very rich," she said, looking straight ahead. She was expecting Mercy to protest, but he said nothing.

Jane looked over at Mercy and said, "Hello, I'm talking to you. I'm talking to you, Mercy."

313

Mercy just sat there. Silence. Then Jane noticed that he had fallen asleep. He had not heard a single word she had said. "Oh no," she groaned. "I have to go through this again!" Placing a blanket over Mercy, she sighed, then cuddled up next to him and promptly fell asleep.

The next morning, Jane woke up early and made breakfast. As she busied herself in the kitchen, scrambling eggs and frying bacon, Mercy crept up behind her and pecked her on the neck. "Will you marry me?" he asked.

Jane jumped. The frying pan clattered to the floor, along with a glass dish, scattering bacon and egg everywhere. "What did you say?" she said, scarcely believing her ears.

Mercy repeated the question. "I said, will you marry me?"

Jane flung her arms around him. "You already know the answer, it's yes," she said. "But only on one condition."

"What's that?"

"That you marry me before the next fight."

"That's no problem, but what about this handsome, young man from your office?"

Jane thumped him on the shoulder. "Why, you little stinker!" she cried, "you did hear me last night!"

Mercy laughed, and Jane started chasing him around the kitchen table. He was running in his bare feet when he stepped on a piece of broken glass. "Ouch," he yelled.

"Oh, honey, I'm so sorry," said Jane as she pulled the sliver of glass from his foot. "It's not like you don't have enough cuts and bruises already!"

She bathed Mercy's foot, then kissed it tenderly. As she rose to her feet, he pulled her onto his lap and gently wiped her hair from her eyes. "I love you, Jane," he whispered.

Jane's robe came loose, exposing her luscious breasts. Mercy rubbed his hand across one breast, then leant forward and kissed the other. Jane sighed. Her entire body tingled at his touch. "Don't stop," she whispered breathlessly, running her hands through his hair.

Mercy gathered up Jane in his arms and limped towards the bedroom, leaving small droplets of blood on the floor. He lay Jane on the bed and slid the robe from her body. Then disrobing, he lay down next to her, gently caressing her nipples, her stomach, slowly making his way downwards. His touch was electric. Jane felt as if her entire body were on fire. "Oh, Mercy," she panted, "I want you so much."

Mercy spread her legs and gently kissed her wet mound. Jane quivered. She wanted him, God, how she wanted him. "Now, Mercy, now," she said, grabbing his throbbing cock

"Not yet, my love, I want to taste you first."

Jane groaned as his tongue slid inside, probing her innermost parts. She could bear it no longer. "Now, Mercy, please," she begged. "I want to feel you inside of me."

Mercy did not hesitate. He plunged inside her, thrusting hard. Jane gasped and wrapped her legs tightly around him. Mercy plunged deeper and deeper, Jane meeting his every thrust. They moved together as one, and together toppled over the edge.

It took two months for Mercy's cuts to heal completely. He had been working out at the gym, but not sparring with anyone. Sparkey had called Louie many times, trying to arrange a rematch, in Australia! Louie had refused – no way would they be traveling back to Australia. If Sparkey wanted a rematch, it would have to be in New York. Sparkey was furious. He had called Louie asshole so many times that Louie was beginning to get used to it.

Louie was busy making plans for Mercy to fight an unknown fighter from a small town in Columbia, called Eljo. Although little was known about this fighter, his backers were extremely rich. They believed that their fighter would have no problem taking the title away from Mercy.

When Louie and Huey told Mercy about the next title bout, he was all for it.

"I've asked Jane to marry me," he informed them, "and she has said 'yes.' But she has one condition."

"What's that?" asked Louie.

"That we get married before my next fight."

"No problem, we have plenty of time," said Louie.

"Congratulations, Mercy," said Huey, enveloping him in a bear hug.

"Yeah, congratulations, kid," said Louie, joining in the embrace.

"I've called my family in Michigan, and they want to meet Jane before the wedding," said Mercy. "They also want both of you to come with us. He grinned, then continued, "They're having a pig roast back by the pond, so get yourselves packed. We'll be leaving in two weeks."

"We'll be there," said Huey.

"Wouldn't miss it for the world," deadpanned Louie.

Two weeks later, the four friends arrived in Michigan. Family and friends, wearing the trademark red, white and blue sweatbands, greeted them warmly and welcomed Jane into the family. Once again, the pig roast was a huge success, lasting well into the wee small hours. They stayed a week, then stopped in Ohio to meet Jane's family, before heading back to New York.

On the Sunday after their return, Mercy asked Jane to get in his truck.

"Come on, let's take a drive," he said, opening the passenger door for her.

"Where are we going?" Jane asked.

"Please, Jane, just get in, I want you to come with me."

"Okay…" Jane looked puzzled. *I wonder why he's being so mysterious*, she thought to herself as she climbed into the truck.

They drove in silence until Mercy reached the florist's shop. "I won't be a moment," he said, jumping out of the truck. Jane watched him disappear into the shop.

When he emerged a few moments later, he was carrying a single red rose, with baby's breath. Without saying a word, he started the truck and headed in the direction of the cemetery

"Are we going to Victoria's grave?" asked Jane.

"Yes," said Mercy quietly. "I usually come here by myself, but I want you with me today."

When they arrived at the cemetery, Jane grabbed his hand and followed him to Victoria's grave. Mercy placed the red rose in front of the headstone and bowed his head. Jane put her arms around his waist and lay her head on his shoulder. She felt Mercy's tears on her face, and held him tighter.

A hush seemed to descend over the graveyard as the young couple stood there, each lost in their own thoughts. Then Jane felt a soft breeze caress her cheek, and she knew Victoria was present. *You are a wonderful young woman*, the breeze seemed to whisper. *And you have a wonderful young man. He needs lots of love, and between the two of us, we can give him that love.*

Jane shuddered. "Yes," she whispered softly, "yes, we can."

Mercy slowly raised his hand and stroked Jane's long hair as she held him even closer. Neither spoke. Then hand-in-hand, they turned and walked away in silence.

Back in the truck, Mercy broke the silence. "Thank you for coming with me, Jane." Tears still bubbled in his eyes.

Jane squeezed his hand gently. "I'll come with you anytime you need me," she said. "Victoria loves you, and I love you. You have it made, Mercy."

Mercy turned and looked at her with his piercing blue eyes. And then he smiled that special smile, and Jane felt as if her heart would melt. "I love you, too, Jane.

Chapter 32

The day of the wedding was drawing closer. They had planned to have a simple church service and a big party afterwards. Mercy had plenty of money and he liked to spend it, especially if people were having fun. Invites had been sent to all the *Bitches and Beasts*, and three busloads of family and friends were coming from Michigan. Mercy's uncles were roasting a pig at the party. And Jane's family was flying in from Ohio.

Jane had agreed to invite Mercy's fan club, but she had put her foot down on two things: No blessings, No autographs!

"This is *our day*, and they have to understand that," she told Mercy.

"Okay, you're the boss," he replied.

On a sunny Saturday in August, Mercy and Jane stood before an assembled congregation of family and friends and exchanged vows. Father White conducted the wedding Mass. The bride, stunning in a shimmering white gossamer gown, her hair braided with white daisies, smiled as she looked up into her lover's eyes and whispered, "I do."

"I do," said Mercy, his blue eyes sparkling with happiness. "I most definitely do."

After the service, the party began, and what a party it was! Eat, drink and be merry was the order of the day. The drinks flowed, the band played, and the happy couple glided effortlessly across the dance like two birds in flight. Louie and Huey watched from their table.

"They sure make a handsome couple," said Louie.

"Sure do," agreed Huey. "I wish I could dance like that," he sighed. "They make it look so easy."

"Yeah, they sure do," said Louie. "Me, I have two left feet."

The two friends chuckled and raised their glasses in a toast. "To Mercy and Jane," said Louie.

"I'll drink to that," said Huey. "To Mercy and Jane."

Later, as the bride and groom were getting ready to take their leave, Louie approached them and asked Jane if Mercy could bless him. "And how about an autograph?" he grinned, producing a pen and paper.

Jane grabbed the pen and paper and signed it with a flourish. *Don't make this your last meal. Signed: Jane Aller.*

Louie chuckled. "Is that something like 'The Last Supper'? he asked.

"Exactly," said Jane, struggling to suppress her laughter.

The newly married couple had decided to postpone their honeymoon until after Mercy's next title fight. The fight was coming up soon and it was imperative that Mercy stay in shape. As such, he continued to train rigorously, working out at the gym everyday. During his training sessions, he noticed that Louie was getting more phone calls than usual. He also noticed that Louie and Huey were not as talkative as usual. *What's going on?* he thought to himself. *They are acting so weird.*

Mercy was worried. He decided to mention his friends' strange behavior to Jane.

"They are acting very strange," he told Jane one evening. "They're always huddled together in a corner, whispering, and they never include me in their conversations." Mercy sighed. "In fact," he continued, "they hardly talk to me at all, these days."

Jane shrugged. "Don't worry about it," she said, "they're probably discussing business at the gym." But Jane was worried. Her boss had heard through the grapevine that Mercy's upcoming fight was being heavily backed. "And no one knows where the money's coming from," he had told her.

"Yeah, you're probably right," said Mercy. "I guess I'm just reading too much into it."

Jane decided not to share her fears with Mercy. *No distractions*, she thought to herself. *He must stay focused on his training.* She smiled and squeezed his hand.

"You'll see, they'll be back to their usual selves in no time."

A few days after this conversation, Mercy and Jane were having a sandwich lunch at the gym. It was too chilly to sit outside, so they picked a spot by the window. As they munched on their sandwiches, Jane noticed that a black limousine kept circling the block.

"Did you see that limo," she said, pointing outside, "it's passed by the gym at least three times?"

"Yeah, I noticed," replied Mercy. "And what about the three guys sitting inside it. They're all wearing black hats and dark glasses."

The limousine circled the block one more time, then pulled up in front of the gym. As the three men emerged from the car, hats pulled low over their brows, Louie and Huey walked out to meet them.

"Who are those guys?" said Mercy.

Jane shook her head. "I have no idea, but they obviously know Louie and Huey."

Mercy and Jane continued to observe the group of men. There were no greetings, no handshakes, and the conversation seemed to be mild. Until, suddenly, one of the men, tall and thin, with a small moustache, removed his dark glasses, stepped in close to Louie and prodded him in the chest.

Louie slapped the man's hand away, and Huey stepped forward, shaking his fist angrily. The three men turned on their heels and jumped back in the limo. Tires squealing, they sped off down the street, leaving a trail of smoke in their wake.

Mercy looked at Jane and said, "What the hell was that all about?"

Jane shrugged. "I don't know, but I think we'd better find out."

Finishing their lunch, they walked over to Louie and Huey who were standing near Louie's desk.

"What's going on?" Mercy asked them. "Who were those men?"

Louie and Huey exchanged glances. Neither responded.

"We want some answers," said Jane. "You owe us that."

Still no response.

Garcia had been standing nearby, listening to the conversation. He marched over to Louie and Huey and said, "If you don't tell them, I will."

Louie took a deep breath and finally spoke. "We've been getting these threatening phone calls at the gym. And then they started calling us at our apartments. We had to get our phone numbers changed."

"They want us to throw the fight, otherwise there's going to be a big problem," said Huey. "People could get hurt." He sighed and looked toward the front door. "Those guys you just saw, they're behind the threats, and we just told them to go to hell."

"Who the hell is *they*?" exclaimed Mercy. "We saw you with the three guys, but who exactly are they?"

"They are linked to a drug cartel in Columbia and they want to take the championship belt back to Columbia, at any cost," said Louie.

"They've offered us money to throw the fight, or else," said Huey.

"Did you notice the guy with the little moustache and the mean-looking eyes?" asked Louie. "He seems to be the leader."

"Yeah, I saw him," replied Mercy, "and there's no way I'm going to throw the fight for him, or anyone."

Jane was frightened. She grabbed Mercy's hand. "Why don't you cancel the fight, Louie?" she asked.

"It's too late, we've signed the contract. We'll just have to watch our backs for the next few weeks." He looked at each of them in turn. "Let's be very careful."

Chapter 33

The fight was a month away. Mercy continued to maintain his rigorous training

schedule, and was in the best shape of his life. If the drug cartel wanted the title belt,

they would have to knock him out.

The phone calls had stopped, and since the confrontation outside the gym, they

hadn't seen hide nor hair of the three thugs. They were beginning to breathe a little easier.

Then one night, about two weeks before the fight, Louie received another threatening

phone call. "Throw the fight, and take the money," growled the voice on the other end of

the line. "Otherwise you'll be sorry." *Click.* The man hung up.

When Louie told the others, they were more outraged than scared. And more

determined not to give in to these ominous threats. Mercy became more fired up than

ever. *Come and get me, you assholes, I'm ready for you!*

One evening, Mercy, Garcia, Louie and Huey stayed at the gym later than usual.

Garcia had a fight coming up in one week, and Mercy and Huey were working on

Garcia's uppercut as Louie looked on. The phone rang, interrupting their workout. It was Maria, Garcia's wife. One of the children had a fever, and she wanted him to come home. Grabbing his stuff, Garcia bid everyone goodnight and ran to his car.

Earlier, Louie had noticed a dark colored car pass by the gym several times, but he thought nothing of it. All of a sudden, three quick shots broke through the silent darkness. Mercy and Huey rushed outside to find Garcia lying by his car, in a pool of blood. He had been shot.

"Quick, call an ambulance!" Huey yelled to Louie. "Garcia's been shot."

Mercy cradled Garcia's head in his arms. "He's lost a lot of blood, Huey, we need some towels to help stop the bleeding." Huey raced inside and grabbed some towels, then rushed back to Garcia's side.

Louie joined them moments later. "The ambulance is on its way," he said, looking down at Garcia as Mercy and Huey struggled to staunch the bleeding. "My God, there's blood everywhere," exclaimed Louie. "Is he going to make it?"

Garcia had lost consciousness. He had been shot twice: once in the leg, just above the knee, and once in the chest, close to his heart. The third shot had gone through the side window of his car.

Huey shook his head. "It looks bad. I think the shot in his leg has severed an artery," he said as he tore a piece of his shirt and tied it tightly around Garcia's leg in an attempt to stem the bleeding.

Meanwhile, Mercy was applying pressure to Garcia's chest. "Come on, Garcia," he pleaded, tears filling his eyes. "Stay with us, stay with us."

The sound of sirens blaring filled the street. An ambulance screeched to a stop and out rushed two paramedics carrying a stretcher. "Okay, guys, we'll take over now," said one as they placed Garcia on the stretcher. "You did a great job stopping the bleeding."

Louie, Huey and Mercy just stood there in a daze – they were all in shock.

"We're taking him to City Hospital, if you want to follow," said the other paramedic. And with that they whisked Garcia off to the emergency room.

Louie called Maria and told her what had happened. Then Mercy called Jane and arranged to meet her at the hospital. They were all waiting outside the emergency room when Maria raced down the corridor, tears streaming down her face.

"Oh, my God," she sobbed, "please let him be okay."

Mercy put his arm around her shoulders and pulled her close. He's gonna pull through, Maria," he assured her. "Don't you worry, he's made of tough stuff – I should know, I've sparred with him."

Maria looked up at him, and then over at Louie and Huey. "Why? Why did this happen?" she asked.

Mercy shook his head, while Louie and Huey looked down at their feet. No one had an answer for her. They blamed themselves for what had happened to Garcia. Finally, Louie said, "We're so sorry, Maria, we're so sorry."

Before Maria could respond, the doors to the emergency room opened and out stepped the surgeon dressed in dark green scrubs, his face mask dangling by the side of his chin. "Mrs. Garcia?" he asked, looking over at Jane and Maria.

Maria stepped forward. She nodded silently, then held her breath waiting for the doctor's next words.

The doctor smiled. "Your husband has lost a lot of blood, but he's going to pull through." A collective sigh echoed around the corridor. "The bullet to the chest area missed his heart by a fraction. He's one lucky man," the doctor told her.

Maria sagged with relief. "Thank you, thank you, doctor," she said, grabbing the doctor's hand.

Louie and Huey wiped the perspiration from their brows. "Thank God," muttered Huey.

"I'll second that," said Louie.

Mercy and Jane hugged each other. "I told you he was fighter," said Mercy. No pun intended!"

The police arrived moments later. After informing the doctor that a policeman would be posted outside Garcia's room, until he left the hospital, they turned their attention to Louie and company.

"Now," said the chief detective, a ruddy faced man by the name of Murphy, "can any of you tell us what happened?" His deputy, Detective O'Malley, stood by his side, notepad and pen at the ready.

Louie told them about the dark car circling gym. "I don't know if there's any connection," he said, "but I saw this black sedan drive by the gym when Garcia left. I couldn't see the license number because it was too dark."

Detective O'Malley scribbled a few notes as Murphy continued. "We've searched the area, looking for evidence, shell casings, etc., but we've found nothing." He paused. The only thing we have is the bullet from Garcia's body."

"Tell them about the phone calls, Louie," urged Mercy.

Louie sighed. "I've been getting these threatening phone calls for the last few weeks. I did report it to the police, but nothing was done. They told me to change my number – said it was probably just some crank."

"And just what were these threats about?" asked Murphy.

Louie told him all about Mercy's upcoming fight and the confrontation outside the gym.

"When we refused to throw the fight," continued Louie, "I think they shot Garcia to let us know they were serious."

"Can you describe these men?" asked Murphy. "Do you know their names, do you know anything about them?"

Louie shook his head. "Well, we think they're linked to a drug cartel in Columbia. They were all wearing dark glasses, with broad-brimmed hats, pulled down low over their faces. But one of them did have a moustache, and when he stepped in close, he removed his glasses and I saw his eyes – the meanest-looking eyes you've ever seen. I think I'd be able to recognize him again. Would you, Huey?"

Huey nodded. "Yeah, I'll never forget those eyes. He gave me the creeps."

"Well, it sounds as if there's a connection, but we have no proof. No one saw who shot your friend. If you think of anything else, or if you receive any more threats, let us know," said Detective Murphy, handing Louie his card. "Call me anytime, day or night. In the meantime, we'll leave a guard outside Garcia's room. So far, he's the only witness and as such, his life could still be in danger.

Maria gasped and put her hand to her mouth.

"Don't worry, ma'am, we'll make sure nothing happens to him," Murphy reassured her. "As soon as your husband regains consciousness, we'll talk to him. Maybe he can tell us who shot him. Then we'll put these bad guys away."

He turned to his deputy. "Okay, O'Malley, let's go find the doctor. Find out how long Garcia is going to be out." And with that, the two detectives took their leave and marched off down the corridor in search of the doctor.

Garcia spent the next two weeks in hospital, recovering from his injuries. The police interviewed him, but he couldn't shed any light on his assailants. It was too dark, he told the two detectives. And everything happened so quickly. One minute, he was about jump into his car, and the next he was sprawled on the sidewalk, bleeding profusely from two bullet wounds.

Louie, Huey and Mercy were convinced that the guys from Columbia were responsible for the shooting of Garcia. They just couldn't prove it.

"I've heard through the grapevine that these thugs have a lot of serious money riding on their fighter," said Louie. "Shooting Garcia was a warning. They're trying to scare Mercy into throwing the fight."

"Well, I don't scare easily," said Mercy. "I've always stood up to bullies." But deep down, he was worried. Not so much for himself but for his friends. *We're not talking about a couple of school bullies here*, he thought. *What if they tried to harm Jane or Louie and Huey?*

The next few weeks passed without incident. Garcia, now recuperating at home, continued to regain to strength, and Mercy continued his punishing training regime. The police had drawn a blank on the shooting, turning up no new evidence. Louie and Huey had been down to the police station a couple of times, to tell Detective Murphy of their suspicions regarding the backers in Columbia. But without proof, the police could do nothing.

It was the day of the fight. Mercy, Louie and Huey sat in the dressing room, waiting to be called to the ring. An air of nervous tension pervaded the room. All three men were on edge, wondering if and when the thugs from Columbia would strike again.

Percy was standing outside the dressing room, waiting to catch a glimpse of the Colombian fighter and his entourage as they made their way to the ring. As the light heavyweight champion, Mercy would enter the ring last.

"Hey, guys, listen up," said Percy, bursting into the room. Felipe Cortez has just passed by with his gang of thugs. Leading the way was a little guy with a moustache and mean-looking eyes."

Louie and Huey exchanged glances. "Sounds like our man," said Louie.

Percy agreed. "Yeah, from what you told me, he definitely fits the description. Cortez came next, followed by eighty or so supporters. And get this," Percy paused and looked at each of the men in turn, "they all have moustaches, including Cortez, and they're all wearing black hats, brown shirts and brown ties. Cortez is wearing a long black and brown robe."

"What's that all about?" asked Mercy.

Percy shrugged. "Beats me," he said. "Anyway, they were all waving black and brown flags, and yelling, 'Killa! Killa! Killa! No Mercy! No Mercy! No Mercy!'"

"Sounds like trouble," said Huey.

The others nodded in agreement. "Yeah, definitely trouble," said Louie, "but when, how and where is it going to hit us? That's the 64 million-dollar question."

A knock sounded on the door and the four men jumped. Their nerves were frayed. "Time!" shouted a shrill voice.

Donning their red, white and blue sweatbands, they marched out of the dressing room, heads held high and with the same thought running through their minds: *"We refuse to be intimidated. Bring it on.*

A crowd of *Bitches and Beasts* fans greeted them, all wearing their trademark sweatbands and waving the Stars and Stripes. "Mercy, Mercy, Mercy," they yelled, "we love you, we love you."

Louie, Huey and Percy raised their hands in the air and yelled, "Yes, Yes, Yes."

Mercy jumped into the ring to the sound of thunderous applause. His supporters clearly outnumbered the fans from Eljo, Cortez's hometown in Columbia. Mercy raised his arms in recognition and bowed to his loyal supporters. "Mercy, Mercy, Mercy," they screamed. The stadium rocked.

The announcer grabbed the microphone and waited for the noise to die down. Ladies and gentlemen, Palmer Enterprises are sponsoring this twelve-round title fight. Before we go any further, I'm sorry to announce that the referee, Joe Cucci, has been taken ill, and will be replaced by Jose Cortez.

The fans started yelling, "We want Cucci, we want Cucci."

The noise died down and the announcer continued. "Unfortunately, two of the judges have also been taken ill, and will also be replaced. They all came down with food poisoning. We send them our best, and hope they recover quickly.

The crowd started booing, and the Eljo men yelled out, "Killa! Killa! Killa!"

Louie turned to his three friends and whispered, "Sounds fishy to me. Quite a coincidence that the referee and two of the judges should all come down with food poisoning, eh?"

"Yeah," said Huey, "what are the chances of that?"

"I bet the Eljo guys had a hand in this," said Mercy.

The others nodded in agreement.

"In the red corner," continued the announcer, "hailing all the way from Eljo, Columbia, wearing the black and brown trunks, and weighing in at one hundred and seventy-two pounds, with twenty-five wins by knockout, I give you the challenger, Felipe Cortez."

The Eljo fans screamed "Killa! Killa! Killa! and waved their black and brown flags.

The announcer then went on to introduce Mercy, and a huge roar went up from the crowd, drowning out the yells of the Eljo supporters who shook their fists in anger.

"I don't like this," said Louie, surveying the crowd. "I have a bad feeling about this fight."

"What's the name of the referee, again?" asked Percy. "Didn't the announcer say his name was Cortez? Wonder if he's related to the fighter."

They all looked over at the red corner, where Cortez and his trainers were talking with the referee, Jose Cortez. The referee had his back to them. When he turned around to face them, they all gasped. Jose Cortez looked just like the trainer and the fighter:

Same height, same build, same black hair, same dark eyes, and same little black

moustache.

"I can't believe this!" exclaimed Mercy. "They're obviously related. I bet

they're brothers."

Louie yelled, "Security! Security! Security!"

Huey said, "Dear Lord, the house is on fire."

Percy said, "They all look identical; they must have cloned them."

Louie raced over to the boxing commissioner and asked him if they could have

another referee.

The boxing commissioner shrugged his shoulders. "I'm sorry, we've tried to get

another referee, but no one is available at such short notice," he told Louie. "Jose Cortez

is the only referee available."

"But it's against boxing rules for a relative to referee a fight, and this referee, Jose

Cortez, is obviously related to the fighter." Louie pointed at Jose and Felipe. "They look

like twins!"

"I see the similarity," replied the commissioner, looking over at the two men.

"But Mr. Cortez has assured me that he is not related to the fighter, Felipe Cortez. Cortez

is a very common name in Eljo, like Smith or Jones."

"Bullshit!" cried Louie, shaking his fist. "And you believed him! Any sucker can

see that they're related."

The commissioner's face went a deep shade of red. He started to speak, but Louie

cut him off. "How do you know that he's not lying?" asked Louie.

The commissioner raised himself to his full height and looked down at Louie. "Because, Mr. Costello, we had Mr. Cortez sign a legal document attesting to that fact. Now, I suggest you calm down and return to your corner. It's time for the fight to start."

Louie snorted in disgust. "Thanks for nothing," he sneered as he turned on his heel and walked back to the blue corner. "I knew I had a bad feeling about this fight!"

Chapter 34

The referee called both fighters to the center of the ring. In broken English, he told them to follow his commands. "You don' ave to touch zee gloves if you no want to. Eez up to you."

Mercy was furious. "This is America," he said angrily, "and in America, you have to touch gloves." Jose ignored him.

Felipe Cortez had already walked away, without touching gloves. Mercy stalked after him, to touch gloves, and Felipe spun around and hit him upside the head. Mercy tried to retaliate, but Percy and Huey pulled him back. "Calm down, Mercy," cautioned Huey. "You'll get your chance in the ring."

Mercy and Huey could hear Percy's friend, Henry, yelling at Felipe and Jose from his ringside seat. "You lousy bums," he called, "get your shit together."

Loud booing and jeering echoed around the stadium, and fighting broke out in the stands. Police and security rushed to quell the disturbances.

The boxing commissioner called the referee over and told him to start again. "They have to touch gloves," he told him, "it's the rule."

"We no 'ave zis rule in Columbia," retorted the referee.

The commissioner bristled. "Tell them to touch gloves, otherwise the fight will be stopped and you'll be flying back to your country, pronto," he said sharply, motioning a plane in flight, with his hands.

Cortez called Mercy and Felipe back to the center of the ring and told them to touch gloves. "May zee best man win," he said.

The two fighters touched gloves, then Felipe took another swing at Mercy. This time, Mercy was ready for him. He blocked the blow with his forearm and hit Felipe in the chest.

The referee raced over and gave Mercy a warning. "Go to your corner," he ordered.

Mercy realized that it would be futile to argue with Cortez. *He's obviously biased toward Felipe*, he muttered to himself as he stalked back to his corner.

Huey and Louie were waiting for him. "I don't like this, I don't this one bit," said Louie, clearly agitated.

The bell rang for the start of the first round. Felipe charged over and attacked Mercy, pinning him to the ropes in the blue corner. He was throwing everything he had at Mercy, but Mercy was covering up. Gathering strength, Mercy finally pushed him away and moved quickly to the center of the ring. The two fighters slugged it out, dancing around the ring and dodging each other's blows. The bell rang.

Back in the blue corner, Huey told Mercy to keep jabbing. "You're doing a good job of covering up," he said. "Let Felipe tire himself out." Mercy nodded.

The bell rang for the second round. Both fighters charged to the center, pounding each other back and forth. The round ended.

Huey and Percy toweled off Mercy. "Continue throwing your jab," said Huey.

"And try to throw a few combinations," said Percy.

The bell rang for the third round. Felipe charged again and pushed Mercy to a neutral corner, pinning him against the ropes. Then raising his right knee, he rammed it into Mercy's stomach. Mercy staggered forward but managed to stay on his feet.

Huey, Louie and Percy yelled at the referee, but he paid no attention.

Although winded from the blow to his stomach, Mercy recovered quickly, side-stepping to the left. Now he had Cortez up against the ropes. He pummeled him mercilessly, letting him know that he didn't appreciate the knee to the stomach. Cortez tried to knee him again, but Mercy was ready – he stepped quickly to the side. The round ended.

At the start of the fourth round, the two fighters met in the middle of the ring. Felipe forced Mercy into the red corner. The referee pointed to a towel lying in the corner and signaled to Felipe's trainer to retrieve it. Jumping to his feet, the trainer grabbed the towel, then slyly jabbed Mercy hard in the kidney. Mercy staggered backward, wincing in pain, but once again, he managed to stay upright.

Louie, Huey and Percy sprang to their feet, shaking their fists angrily and screaming at the referee. "What's the matter with you, ref, are you blind?" they yelled.

Once again, Jose ignored them. Louie tried to scramble into the ring, but Huey and Percy held him back.

The punch did not go unnoticed by the television commentators, who were relaying the fight live to their television audience. "I could swear I just saw Cortez's trainer punch Mercy in the back," said one of the sports announcers, "but I must be mistaken, because the referee did nothing."

Jane and Rachel were outraged. Jumping to their feet, they screamed at the referee, from their seats at ringside. And a chorus of "Foul! Foul! Foul!" rang out from the *Bitches and Beasts*. The whole stadium was in an uproar.

But nothing was done. The bell rang, and Mercy returned to his corner. Upset and angry, he plunked down on the stool. "Did you see that?" he bellowed. "Did you see what that guy did?" he repeated, pointing to Cortez's trainer. "I bet he's the guy who put the hit out on Garcia."

"You could be right," agreed Louie. "All the more reason to win this fight."

The bell rang for the fifth round. Cortez tried to push Mercy over to his corner again. But Mercy backed him off with his powerful jabs. Cortez moved in and head butted Mercy, opening up a cut over his left eye. Blood started pouring down Mercy's face. Knowing that Cortez would try to aim for the cut, Mercy started throwing jabs to keep him back; dancing on his toes and moving quickly around the ring, until the bell rang.

During the sixth round Cortez continued aiming for the cut above Mercy's left eye. Mercy staved him off with his quick jabs, rocking Cortez with a powerful combination. Cortez staggered. Regaining his balance, he tried to push Mercy back to the red corner, where the trainer would be waiting to give Mercy another punch to the kidney.

Huey had warned Mercy about this, but Mercy had his own plan. He let Cortez push him back to the corner. The referee yelled, "Towel, towel, towel," and that was Mercy's cue. He felt the movement of the ring, and knew the trainer was going to deliver another punch to his kidney.

Mercy moved quickly, stepping around Cortez and putting him in the corner. There stood the trainer, looking straight into Mercy's eagle eyes. Mercy hit him with a powerful right hand to the jaw. The force of the blow sent him flying through the air, landing him right on top of his comrades.

Shocked and stunned, they started cursing and shaking their fists at Mercy. Mercy bowed to them, and the crowd broke out into rapturous applause. The *Bitches and Beasts* sprang to their feet and cried, "One, two, three, four, five, six, seven, eight, nine ten, you're out!"

The referee stomped over and gave Mercy a warning. "One point will be deducted from your score," he snarled.

Louie and Huey were furious. The crowd started booing, and fighting broke out between the rival fans. Police and security soon restored order, and the crowd quieted down. The bell rang, and Mercy marched back to his corner, grinning.

"What a punch, kid!" said Louie, patting Mercy on the back.

"Yeah, you really showed 'em," laughed Huey.

"Way to go, Mercy. Way to go," said Percy, enveloping him in a bear hug.

"That was for Garcia," Mercy told them.

The bell rang for the seventh round. Cortez charged over to Mercy and their bodies clashed together. Bending, Cortez put his arms between Mercy's leg, picked him up in the air and body slammed Mercy to the canvas. Mercy lay on the floor, dazed and disoriented.

The referee started to count, but Mercy managed to stagger to his feet.

"Okay, enough of the rough stuff," said the referee, wagging his finger in front of Mercy's face. "I'm deducting another point from your score."

Incensed, Louie, Huey, and Percy jumped into the ring and rushed toward the referee. They all wanted a piece of him. Security held them back.

"I'm gonna beat the shit out him," said Louie, struggling to get past the security guard.

"Okay, everybody calm down," said the guard, ushering Louie, Huey and Percy back to their seats.

Meanwhile, pandemonium had broken out in the stands. Police and security had formed a protective ring around the Eljo fans, so no one could get near them. The crowd was thirsting for blood.

The fight resumed. Cortez gave Mercy a low blow; again, the referee said nothing.

"Low blow, low blow," yelled Huey and Percy. The referee ignored them. Before the round ended, Cortez had hit Mercy four times, below the belt.

Mercy returned to his corner, ready to explode. Louie and Huey were so enraged they could barely speak. "I don't like this. I don't like this at all," croaked Louie, his face suffused with anger.

"Look," said Huey, pointing over to the red corner, "the trainer is doing something to Cortez's gloves."

Mercy and Louie turned to look at Cortez and his trainer. "I don't like this," repeated Louie. "I have a bad feeling."

The bell rang for the eighth round. Mercy and Cortez met in the middle of the ring. As they circled each other, Mercy landed a few good punches; Cortez backed away, then hit Mercy with a couple of shots to the face. Mercy staggered backwards, rubbing his eyes. His eyes were burning -- the more he rubbed them, the more they burned.

Cortez continued to punch Mercy – a hard jab to the stomach, a swift upper cut to the face, another punishing jab to the stomach – the blows rained down on his body. Mercy could only cover up, and rub his eyes. They were on fire. He tried to defend himself, but he could hardly see Cortez. Somehow, he managed to make it through the round and stagger back to his corner still rubbing his eyes.

Huey, Louie and Percy huddled around him. "It's my eyes," wailed Mercy, "they're burning up, I can hardly see."

Huey knew what had happened as soon as Mercy told him. He and Louie had both seen the trainer fiddling with Cortez's gloves before the start of the last round. "I'm guessing that they put Bengay on Cortez's gloves," he exclaimed. "That's what's causing the burning."

Louie decided to take matters into his own hands. He called to the referee, but he was busy talking to Cortez. "I told you I had a bad feeling about this," he cried. "I can't take this any more," and with that, he jumped through the ring and attacked the referee.

"You sonofabitch!" yelled Louie, grabbing the referee by the throat and flinging him to the canvas. "What the fuck do you think you're doing? Mercy could have been blinded!"

The referee just lay there stunned as Louie delivered a few swift punches, before security rushed over and pulled him off.

"They got Bengay, they got Bengay!" yelled Louie as the security guards dragged him away. "They put it on Cortez's gloves." Louie kicked and screamed all the way out of the arena.

Fighting broke out between the Eljo fans and Mercy's fans. The entire stadium was in an uproar. A voice over the loudspeaker called for calm, and extra police and security charged into the arena to restore order.

The crowd finally settled down. And now the Eljo fans were completely surrounded by police and security, for their own protection.

Back in the blue corner, Huey was telling Percy to use dry towels to wipe off Mercy's face, chest and arms. "We have to get the Bengay off," he said. "Use the towels only once and then throw them away. And don't use water!" he cautioned.

Percy nodded and proceeded to follow Huey's instructions, gently wiping Mercy's face and body with the towels.

"Now, give me one of those big towels," Huey told Percy.

"What are you going to do?" asked Mercy and Percy in unison.

"I have to get the Bengay off Cortez's gloves," said Huey.

Huey rushed across the ring, pushing the trainer to the canvas. Then he plunked down on Cortez's lap, enveloped the fighter's gloves in the towel and wiped them off. Cortez sat there in astonishment. Then Huey stuck the towel right in Cortez's face.

Cortez snapped out of his daze. "Police, security, police, security," he yelled, pushing Huey off his lap.

The Eljo fans joined in the call for help. "Police, security," they cried.

The trainer scrambled to his feet. Grabbing Huey from behind, he wrestled him to the canvas, and the two men began fighting. Once again, police and security rushed into the ring and pulled the two men apart.

"Kick his ass, Mercy. Kick his ass," yelled Huey as he too was dragged out of the arena.

Jane and Rachel had tried to stop the police from hauling Huey away, by kicking them in the legs. "Sit down, or you'll be next," warned one of the officers.

Percy's friend, Henry, had also tried to intervene, but he too was hauled away.

Anger and emotion continued to build inside Jane. She had watched her beloved husband get kneed in the stomach and kidneys, body slammed to the canvas, hit below the belt, punched from behind, headbutted, and now he'd been Bengayed. It was too much. Jane had reached breaking point; the Bengay was the final straw.

Jumping to her feet, she rushed up to the ring and shoved Cortez's trainer, hard. He landed on top of his comrades, with their black hats, brown shirts and brown ties. Then Jane grabbed Cortez by the hair in a death grip. "Where's the Bengay? Where's the Bengay, you bastard?" she screamed.

Police and security jumped into the ring and dragged Jane out of the arena, to join Huey and Louie in a holding area. Rachel soon followed after she started kicking the police again.

Back in his corner, Mercy was unaware of all the commotion. All he could think about were his burning eyes. Percy was still rubbing them, trying to mop up every trace of Bengay. When Mercy finally opened his eyes, the first thing he saw was Jane and Rachel being hustled out of the arena.

"What the hell's happening, Percy?" he asked. "Where are they taking Jane and Rachel?"

"It's a long story, kid, I'll tell you later," said Percy. "Don't worry about them, they're fine. Just concentrate on the fight." Percy dabbed Mercy's eyes. "How are the eyes? Still burning?"

"Yeah, a little, but I'll survive." Mercy smiled wryly. "At least I can see now!"

The bell rang for the ninth round.

"It's just you and me now, kid. Go get'em!"

Thank God for Percy, thought Mercy, *otherwise I'd be all by myself.* A look of fierce determination crossed his face as he rose to his feet and danced toward his opponent. *I'm going to knock out that cheating bastard, if it's the last thing I do!*

As the two fighters met in the center of the ring, Mercy noticed that Cortez was swinging wildly, and if the referee came over to break them up, he would probably keep right on swinging.

They continued to trade punches, Cortez still swinging wildly, hoping to land that one punch that would put Mercy down. The referee came in to break them up, and sure enough, Cortez took one of his wild punches. Mercy ducked. The punch slammed into the referee's jaw, lifting him off his feet and sending him sprawling to the canvas, spread eagle.

The crowd loved it. "One, two, three, four, five," they chanted, "six seven, eight, nine, ten, you're out!"

The boxing commissioner signaled for the doctor, who rushed into the ring to examine the fallen man. "He's all right, just stunned," said the doctor. "But I think we'd better check him out at the hospital. He may have concussion."

The boxing commissioner nodded. "Okay, let's get him out of here." Then, turning to his assistant, he shrugged his shoulders and said, "Now what are we going to do? We don't have a referee – the fight will have to be stopped." He looked over at the crowd, who were still chanting and stamping their feet. "The fans aren't going to like this. We'll have to give them their money back."

Before his assistant could respond, Joe Cucci, who had been standing nearby, stepped forward and said, "Commissioner, let me referee the fight. I'm feeling much better now."

The commissioner looked startled. "Are you sure, Joe? Do you feel up to it."

"Well, my stomach's still feeling a little queasy, but I can handle it," he said. "And besides," he added, "if you stop the fight now, the crowd will be baying for your blood."

The commissioner gulped. "Okay, let's resume the fight. Make the announcement."

The announcer walked to the center of the ring and called for calm. "Settle down, everybody. The fight will now resume, and Joe Cucci will be the referee for the rest of the rounds."

The crowd cheered. Joe Cucci was one of the most respected referees in the boxing world. His honesty and fairness were beyond repute. The fans were thrilled - now, finally, they would have a fair fight.

"Cucci, Cucci, Cucci," they chanted as Joe stepped into the ring and beckoned Mercy and Cortez to the center.

The Eljo fans started booing and waving their flags. "No Mercy! No Mercy!" they yelled. "Killa! Killa! Killa!"

Ignoring the chants, Joe told the two fighters to follow his commands. "And may the best man win," he added.

Mercy and Cortez returned to their corners, and the bell rang for the tenth round.

Cortez charged out of his corner at lightning speed and came right after Mercy as if it were Mercy's fault that his brother had been knocked out. He forced Mercy into his corner, but this time Mercy wasn't worried. Joe Cucci would make sure that the fight remained fair.

Mercy covered up and remembered Huey's words of advice. *Let him tire himself out*. He could tell that Cortez was tiring because his arms were coming down, and his punches lacked power.

Fighting his way out of the corner, Mercy decided to give Cortez a dose of his own medicine. He put him on the ropes and landed four hard punches to Cortez's stomach and chest area. Then danced away to the middle of the ring.

Cortez came after Mercy, but Mercy fended him off with his hard jabs. Cortez shoved Mercy to the ropes, then kneed him in the stomach. Mercy staggered forward, gasping for breath. The wind had been knocked out of him.

Cucci rushed over and wagged his finger angrily in front of Cortez's face. "I'm warning you," he said. "Any more knees to the stomach and you will lose points."

Cortez nodded, but when the fight resumed he kneed Mercy again, blatantly ignoring the referee's warning.

"Cortez, one-point deduction, foul play," announced Cucci.

A chorus of cheers erupted from Mercy's fans; booing and jeering from the Eljo mob.

The bell rang to signal the end of the round. As Mercy turned in the direction of his corner, Cortez hit him up the side of the head. Cucci was right on it.

"Cortez, second-point deduction, striking his opponent after the bell."

More booing and cheering rang out from the crowd. "Killa! Killa! Killa!" yelled the Eljo fans.

"Mercy! Mercy! Mercy!" screamed the *Bitches and Beasts*. "Knock him out! Knock him out! Knock him out!"

In the blue corner, Percy was busy giving Mercy water, washing him off, and tending to the cut, which had opened up again above his left eye.

"You're doing great, kid," said Percy dabbing at the cut above Mercy's eye with a cotton swab. "He's going to go after that cut, so cover up and try to protect your face."

"Yeah, I'll try," said Mercy. "Half the time I'm busy trying to protect my stomach. I never know when he's going to knee me again."

"I hear you, kid. He's the dirtiest fighter I've ever seen, but at least Cucci is all over him."

Mercy nodded. "I wonder what Jane, Louie, Huey and Rachel are doing? Hope they're all right."

Percy shrugged. "Don't worry about them. I'm sure they're fine. Just concentrate on the fight and knock that sonofabitch out!"

"You got it," replied Mercy.

"Attaboy," said Percy, patting Mercy on the back. "By the way," he added, "how are the eyes?"

"They're still burning a little, but I have no trouble seeing Cortez."

The bell rang for the eleventh round. Percy grabbed Mercy's chair, and hustled out of the ring.

As Mercy circled Cortez, he noticed that the Eljo fighter was running out of steam. *Time to take advantage*, he thought to himself. Jabbing and working his way in, Mercy landed four hard shots to his opponent's body, sending him sprawling to the canvas.

Cucci stepped in and told Mercy to go to the farthest corner. Then he started to count, "One, two, three..."

The crowd started to count with him. "…four, five, six…"

On the count of six, Cortez staggered to his feet. "Are you all right?" asked Cucci, staring into the fighter's eyes, looking for any signs of concussion.

"Yeah, I okay," replied Cortez, glaring at Mercy.

The referee rubbed off Cortez's gloves, and the fight resumed.

Mercy didn't let up. Now was the time to keep the pressure on. *This is it*, he said to himself. *This is the time to strike.*

His emotions bubbling over, Mercy hit Cortez with a rapid combination, followed by another, then another. Cortez hit the canvas. *Got you, you dirty bastard. That was for Jane, Louie, Huey, Percy, Rachel and Henry.*

Once again, Cucci ordered Mercy to the farthest corner, and began his count. And once again, the fans joined in. "…four, five, six," they yelled.

"…eight, nine, ten, you're out," finished Cucci.

Mercy's fans roared with delight. In contrast, a grim silence settled over the Eljo fans. Their fighter had lost. Shocked and dazed, they couldn't even manage a single boo.

Percy rushed to Mercy's side and hugged him. "You did it! You did it!" he cried. "Here, put this on for your fans," he said, thrusting Mercy's red, white and blue sweatband into his hands.

Mercy obliged, and placed the sweatband around his forehead. The *Bitches and Beasts* fans applauded, and waved their sweatbands in appreciation. "Mercy! Mercy!" they shouted. "You're our champion! You're our champion!"

353

Mercy beamed, soaking in the crowd's adulation. *If only Jane, and Louie and Huey were here to share this moment with me,* he thought to himself. *But at least I have Percy.*

Percy tugged on his arm. "Come on, Mercy, let's go and check on Cortez."

The two men strode over to Cortez, who was now standing up, near his corner. As they approached, Percy began to speak, "Hey, Cortez, how are…" Wham! Cortez slammed his fist into Percy's face, cutting him off mid-sentence.

Percy fell back, and Mercy caught him with his left arm. Blood gushed from Percy's nose. "Why, you sonofabitch," yelled Percy, struggling to regain his balance.

"Easy, Percy," cautioned Mercy. "I'll take care of this." And with that, Mercy let Cortez have it with a powerful punch to the jaw. The Eljo fighter hit the canvas with a resounding thud.

Mercy looked at Percy and grinned. "This time he'll stay down for a while."

Broadcasters were telling their television audience that Mercy had put Cortez down for the count, once, in the fight, and then again, after the fight.

Percy thanked Mercy and said, "I never saw a fight like this before, in my whole life."

Mercy laughed. "How are you feeling?"

"Damn, my jaw hurts," he said.

"Not as much as his," said Mercy, pointing to Cortez. And they both started laughing.

Reporters and sportscasters crowded into the ring, all scrambling to get a quote from the champion. Mercy was hit with questions from all sides.

"Where are Louie and Huey?"

"What happened to Jane? Where is she?"

"What's with the Bengay?"

"Did he hit you in the back?"

"Was the referee related to Cortez?"

Mercy tried to answer all their questions the best he could. Then, donning his red, white and blue robe, he jumped out of the ring. Percy followed behind, still rubbing his sore jaw.

Jane, Huey, Louie and Rachel were waiting for them in the dressing room. Rushing forward, Jane enveloped him in a warm embrace. The others gathered around, patting him on shoulder and congratulating him.

"Oh, Mercy, you did it, you did it," she cried. "Despite the kidney punches, the knees to the stomach, the headbutts, the low blows, and the Bengay, you did it!"

Mercy looked around at all his friends, his eyes brimming with tears. "No, Jane, we did it. I couldn't have done it without all of you." He raised his arm in victory. "Garcia, this one was for you."

Chapter 35

A week later, it was back to business as usual. They had expected a backlash from the Eljo mob; after all, their fighter had been heavily backed and he'd lost. But nothing – not a word. No more phone calls, no more threats, no more black limos circling the gym. *Nada.*

"Must have gone back to Eljo with their tail between their legs," said Louie one day. "Good riddance. Let's hope they stay there."

They had celebrated Mercy's victory in style: lavish dinners, a Broadway Show, a trip to Atlantic City. Now it was time to knuckle down and prepare for the next fight.

Mercy arrived at the gym early, to find that Louie and Huey were already there. They called him over to the desk. "We've just received a phone call from Sparkey," said Louie, tapping his fingers on the desk. "He's coming to the city for a rematch."

"I don't believe it," said Mercy. "How long before this happens? And what came over Sparkey?"

"Well, he said he could have everything worked out in about six months," replied Louie. "I think he needs the money."

"So, the Kangaroo is coming to New York, hoping to get the belt back," said Mercy. He exchanged glances with his two friends. "Well, I'll be ready for him."

When Mercy gave Jane the news, they decided that now would be as a good a time as any to go on their honeymoon. If they waited much longer, Mercy would be too busy training for the upcoming fight. They opted for a seven-day cruise in the Caribbean.

"What's wrong, Mercy, you don't like to fly with Jane?" ribbed Louie and Huey when he told them about the cruise.

Mercy just smiled, and said nothing.

The cruise was everything they had ever dreamed about, and more. Seven idyllic days and nights spent swimming, sunning, wining, dining, dancing, and making love. Mercy had never felt so happy.

Now it was back to the gym, back to reality, back to his rigorous training schedule. He had gained a few pounds, which did not go unnoticed by Louie and Huey. Louie strutted around the gym, sticking his stomach out and making fun of Mercy.

"See what happens when you go on a cruise," Louie said, patting his belly.

Mercy winced. "Yeah, but it was worth it," replied Mercy, giving them both a sly wink.

Two weeks later, Mercy was back to his normal fighting weight. His punishing exercise regime had taken care of the extra pounds. Each day, he arrived at the gym at the crack of dawn, and was usually the last to leave. Even Huey, noted for being a hard taskmaster, suggested he ease up a little.

"Take it easy, kid," he told Mercy one day as he watched him pummeling the punching bag. "You're gonna drive yourself into the ground if you keep up this grueling pace."

"If the Kangaroo wants another shot at the belt, I'm gonna be ready for him," said Mercy. "I'm going to hang on to this belt, even if it means training morning, noon and night."

"Well, Thanksgiving is just around the corner, I hope you're gonna take the day off," said Huey, grinning. "We're all coming over to your house, remember?"

Mercy and Jane had moved into a new luxury townhouse close to the gym.

Mercy smiled. "Yeah, I know, but I'll have to train extra hard afterwards. Jane's preparing a huge turkey dinner with all the trimmings, so I know I'll put on a few pounds." He patted his stomach. "We all will."

At Thanksgiving, Mercy was overcome with emotion. Surrounded by his beloved wife and his dear friends, he rose to his feet and looked around the table. "I feel truly blessed," he said, raising his glass in a toast. "I have a lot to be thankful for, but most of all, I give thanks to God for all of you." His eyes brimmed with tears.

Mercy looked over at Garcia, who was seated with his family at the far end of the table. "The first day I walked into that gym, Garcia, you welcomed me with open arms.

You showed me the ropes, sparred with me every day, took me under your wing. Here's to you, my friend," and Mercy raised his glass in salute.

Garcia returned the salute. "Gracias, my friend, I will always be there for you."

"Percy," Mercy continued, turning to Percy and his family who were seated to his left. "We used to be enemies, but look at us now – bosom buddies. You had my back at the bar when that guy almost killed me, and then again at the Cortez fight, you were right there by my side. I'll never forget it. Here's to you, my friend." And once again, he raised his glass in salute.

Struggling to hold back his tears, Percy raised his glass to Mercy. "I'll always have your back, kid," he replied. "You can count on it."

Mercy turned to Jane who was seated by his side. "My beloved Jane, you came along when I needed you the most. If it wasn't for you, I think I'd be on skid row, drinking my life away. You gave me a reason to start living again, to stop feeling sorry for myself. You showed me how to love again." He bent down to kiss her tenderly on the lips. "I love you, Jane."

Jane looked up at him, smiling through her tears. "I love you too, Mercy."

The tears were now flowing freely down Mercy's face. Brushing them away with his hand, he turned to Louie and Huey, sitting across from him. "Louie and Huey, what can I say? Words aren't enough to let you know how I'm feeling right now," he said, blinking back the tears. You took this naïve, young kid from the Upper Peninsula of Michigan and shaped him into the light heavyweight champion of the world. You guys have always been there for me, every step of the way: guiding me, teaching me, training me, advising me, looking out for me.   You've treated me like a son, and I look on you both, not only as my dear friends, but as my fathers." Mercy raised his glass in salute. "Here's to you both, I wouldn't be where I am today, if it weren't for you."

There wasn't a dry eye in the room now. Mercy's emotional speech had touched them all. Even the wisecracking Louie was unable to come up with a joke – he was too choked to speak.

Huey finally spoke up, his voice husky with emotion. "You are the son I never had, Mercy. The son I always wanted. You have given this tired old burnt out boxer a new lease on life, a reason to keep on going." Huey raised his glass in salute. "I'm proud of you, son."

"Aw, the hell with this mushy crap," said Louie, the tears streaming down his face. "My food's getting cold, let's eat."

"Trust Louie to think of his stomach first," said Huey. Everyone laughed.

"Hey, Mercy," said Louie, raising his glass. "Here's looking at you, kid." His eyes met Mercy's. "I love you, son."

Chapter 36

Christmas found Mercy and Jane celebrating the festive season with Mercy's family in Michigan, along with Louie and Huey. Braving a fierce blizzard, the four friends had driven to the Upper Peninsula. If it was a choice between flying and driving, they always opted to drive, Jane being the lone dissenter. None of them had ever forgotten the flight to Sydney.

On the return journey, they stopped off in Ohio and celebrated the New Year with Jane's family. Then it was back to New York in time for Mercy to start training again for his fight against the Kangaroo. He had done a lot of celebrating over the past few weeks – now it was time to knuckle down again and resume his grueling regime. If he wanted to hold on to the belt, he would have to be in tip-top shape. The Kangaroo was waiting in the wings, ready to pounce.

Two weeks before the fight, the Kangaroo and Sparkey had landed at Kennedy Airport, with their entourage of trainers, kangaroos and keepers. A large contingent of reporters, and fans had greeted their arrival.

"How do you feeling about the upcoming fight, Kangaroo?" asked one of the reporters, thrusting a microphone in the Australian boxer's face.

The Kangaroo grabbed the microphone and glared at the reporter. "The belt will be going back to Australia with me," he snarled.

"Yeah," sneered Sparkey, "that Mercy kid don't stand a chance against the Kangaroo. Only reason we lost that belt is because the Kangaroo weren't feeling so good that night. We're taking belt back with us."

The next day, Louie read about the interview in the sports section of the local newspaper. "Says here the Kangaroo will be taking the belt back to Australia," he told Huey and Mercy. "Well, we'll just have to make sure it stays right here." He patted Mercy on the back. "Okay, kid?"

Mercy looked at his two friends. "You got it. I'm ready for him!"

"That's our boy," said Huey, smiling.

The next two weeks passed like lightning and once again, Mercy, Louie, Huey and Percy found themselves sitting in the dressing room, waiting for the call to the ring.

A nervous energy filled the room. It was a tense time for all as they waited for the knock on the door. Louie paced the room, anxiously chewing on an unlit cigar, while Huey kept checking that Mercy's gloves were tied properly. Mercy struggled to clear his mind of random thoughts, trying to focus solely on the fight. And Percy kept looking at his watch and saying, "Isn't it time yet?"

"We have about 10 minutes," said Huey, strapping Mercy's gloves for the fourth time. "Time for Mercy to walk back and forth for a while, to keep limber."

Mercy nodded and proceeded to pace up and down the dressing room, his face now a mask of concentration.

The call came right on cue. "Time," called an official, rapping on the door.

"It's show time! Are you ready, kid?" asked Louie. Let's go get'em."

"I'm ready," said Mercy, and the four friends marched out of the dressing room.

The arena was filled to capacity, standing room only. The Kangaroo and his circus had already made their grand entrance, complete with live kangaroos hopping down the aisle, throwing wild punches at each other.

Louie knew that the Australian fighter would have put on quite a show, so he came up with his own idea. He had hired four couples to dance in front of them as they walked slowly down the aisle. He thought that the dancers would give the crowd a little musical treat.

The male dancers were dressed in black top hats and tails, the women in long slinky dresses, slit down the side. Dancing to a fast, up-tempo song they floated down the aisle as if on air. The music brought the crowd to its feet, and soon the entire stadium was dancing, clapping and cheering.

Mercy, Louie, Huey and Percy walked behind the dancers followed by the *Bitches and Beasts* fan club, wearing their trademark sweatbands and waving American flags.

As the dancers approached the ring, they stopped, and formed two lines on either side of the aisle. And raising their arms to form an arch, they made a path to the ring for Mercy. He loved it! What a grand entrance!

Mercy jumped into the ring, and when the music stopped, the crowd took over, yelling out, "Mercy! Mercy, Mercy!"

Mercy looked over at the red corner where the Kangaroo was shadow boxing under the watchful eye of Sparkey. Sparkey returned Mercy's stare and gave him the thumbs-down sign, as if to say *you're finished, kid.* At ringside, he noticed Joe Cucci talking with the announcer. Joe would be refereeing the fight. *Thank goodness, we have a fair and honest referee,* he thought to himself.

Mercy turned and surveyed the crowd, still yelling out his name. His eye caught Jane who was sitting in her usual seat at ringside. They exchanged glances and she blew him a kiss. He mouthed a silent *I love you,* then proceeded to dance lightly around the ring. *Stay focused,* he told himself. *Stay focused.*

The announcer introduced the two fighters, then Joe Cucci beckoned them to the center of the ring. "Touch gloves," he said. "And may the best man win."

The bell rang. The two boxers circled each other, both throwing jabs. Mercy's jab was fast and hard; it just seemed to snap out there. The Kangaroo landed a couple of hard shots, but Mercy tied him up and put him against the ropes. They fell into a clinch.

"Break it up," said the referee as the bell rang for the end of the round.

Mercy returned to his corner. "The Kangaroo is out of shape," said Huey. "Try to tire him out."

In the second round, the two fighters were still feeling each other out. Mercy stepped in and gave the Kangaroo a two-shot combination. The Kangaroo came right back at Mercy, hitting him with a powerful right hand. The bell rang.

Back in the blue corner, Huey told Mercy to keep throwing his jab. "And circle right, away from the Kangaroo's power," he added. Mercy nodded.

When the bell rang for the third round, Mercy stepped quickly across the ring and slammed the Kangaroo against the ropes. Catching the Kangaroo by surprise, he hit him with three hard punches, then stepped back. Before the Kangaroo could retaliate, Mercy stepped quickly back in and delivered two more bruising punches. The Kangaroo backed Mercy against the ropes, landing three hard shots to his body. The bell rang and the fighters returned to their respective corners.

Huey was waiting with more words of advice. "You're doing fine, kid," he assured. "The Kangaroo seemed to get a little annoyed after being hit by that combination. Keep the pressure on, he might get careless."

The bell rang for the fourth round, and this time the Kangaroo took the initiative. He came right after Mercy, wanting to make a brawl out of the fight. He was swinging wildly, hoping to connect with a big punch. *Huey was right*, thought Mercy. *the Kangaroo is losing his cool, and he might make a mistake.*

The two fighters continued to slug it out in the middle of the ring. Mercy took a quick side step right and the Kangaroo stepped into a left hook and a powerful right hand punch. The Kangaroo went down.

The referee directed Mercy to the farthest corner, then began his count. "One, two…"

The *Bitches and Beasts* joined in. "One, two three…"

At the count of four, the Kangaroo was on his feet again. Ding! Saved by the bell!

"He's definitely tiring now," said Huey as he toweled off Mercy. "Keep the pressure on and try to work your way in."

At the start of the fifth round, the two fighters met in the middle of the ring, both jabbing at each other and trying to work their way in. Mercy circled to the right, away from the Kangaroo's power. He was right in front of the Kangaroo's corner, when he slipped on some water and lost his balance. The Kangaroo seized his opportunity, and hit Mercy with two powerful punches. Mercy went down.

The referee started the count. "One, two, three…"

"Get up, Mercy! Get up, Mercy!" screamed his fans.

"Kangaroo! Kangaroo! Kangaroo!" yelled the rival fans.

"…Four, five, six…" and Mercy was up on his feet.

"Are you all right?" asked the referee. Mercy nodded.

Cucci rubbed off Mercy's gloves, then walked over to the red corner.

"Get the water off the canvas," he told the Kangaroo's trainers.

The two trainers jumped into the ring and mopped up the water. Cucci motioned for the fight to resume. Only a few seconds remained. The Kangaroo charged toward Mercy and slammed him against the ropes just as the bell rang.

The fans started yelling and booing, "Foul! Foul! Foul!"

After Huey had checked to make sure that Mercy was all right, after his fall, he said, "The Kangaroo's temper is worsening – keep trying to take advantage."

In the sixth round, Mercy noticed that the Kangaroo's gloves were not as high as usual. *He's definitely tiring*, he thought as he danced around the ring.

For the next few rounds, the two fighters slugged it out, and the fight was pretty much even. Then, in the tenth round, the Kangaroo's gloves were dropping lower and lower. Angry and tired, he moved sluggishly around the ring.

Mercy started jabbing, and working his way in, but the Kangaroo pushed Mercy to the ropes, forcing him to cover up. Fighting himself off the ropes, Mercy started jabbing again. The Kangaroo took a wild swing, and Mercy countered with a five-punch combination. Once again, the Kangaroo hit the canvas. And this time, he didn't get up.

"…Nine, ten, you're out," cried the referee.

Huey, Louie and Percy rushed to Mercy's side and lifted him up in the air, parading him around the ring, much to the delight of his fans. "Mercy! Mercy! Mercy!" they chanted.

When the referee raised Mercy's arm in victory and pronounced him the champion, the crowd went wild. The entire stadium was a sea of waving red, white and blue sweatbands and American flags. The championship belt was staying in the U.S.A.

Jane leapt into the ring and hugged Mercy so tight he thought he would burst.

"I knew you could do it," she said, squeezing him even tighter.

"Wow, Jane, I didn't realize you were so strong," said Mercy. "You have literally taken my breath away." And they both burst into laughter.

The Kangaroo took them all by surprise. They had fully expected him to be sulking in his corner with Sparkey. But instead, he walked over and enveloped Mercy in a warm sportsman's hug. "Hey, mate, you've still got one helluva punch," he said, grinning. "And I should know." He rubbed his sore jaw. "Good on yer, mate."

"Thanks, Kangaroo," said Mercy, returning the hug. "You're a worthy opponent. We had quite a battle out there."

"Yeah, but the best man won. Guess I'll be going back to Aussie empty-handed." He nodded at Sparkey, who was sitting in the red corner, scowling at them.
"Don't think Sparkey is too pleased with me," he said. "But who knows, I may be back to try again."

Then he turned and shook hands with Louie, Huey and Percy. "Keep up the good work, mates, you've got one helluva fighter there."

After answering a barrage of questions from reporters, Mercy left the ring with Jane and his three dear friends, the championship belt firmly clasped firmly around his waist. People in wheelchairs dotted the aisles, waiting for his blessing. Although bruised and exhausted, Mercy made his way slowly up the aisle, stopping to speak to each person in turn, inquiring as to their ailment and giving them all his blessing.

By the time he reached his dressing room, over two hours had passed. Four people waited by the door: two rosy-cheeked boys, a young lady with long, black hair, and an older man with soft brown eyes and thin, greying hair. They told Mercy that after receiving his blessing, they had all been cured.

Mercy was amazed. "But I didn't do anything."

"Well, whatever you did, it worked," said the young lady, whose name was Mary. "I was told I would never walk again, but after you blessed me, I've been walking ever since." She smiled. "I've thrown my wheelchair away – I don't need it any more."

Mercy stood there dumbfounded. He was at a loss for words. God Bless you all," he said, and walked into the dressing room.

That night, the five of them celebrated at *Your Favorite Place*. Mike was tending bar as usual. "The drinks are on the house," he said, grinning. "After all, this is where it all started."

The others looked puzzled. Finally, Mercy spoke up. "What do you mean, Mike?"

"Well, Mercy, see that spot you're standing on." They all looked down at Mercy's feet. "That's the very spot where you knocked out those two thugs." Mike flashed a broad smile, looking at each of them in turn. "The rest, my friends, is history!"

Epilogue

Mercy continued to fight for three more years. After that, Jane insisted he hang up his gloves. He had taken some punishing beatings, but somehow he always managed to win. At the end of his stellar career, he had a total of sixty-five wins, no draws and three losses.

Over the years, Jane gave birth to three beautiful children: two golden-haired, blue-eyed boys who looked just liked their father, and one little girl, with soft brown eyes, the image of her mother. Mercy's family was now complete.

As for his other family, Louie, Huey, Percy and Garcia, they all became partners in the gym, and Mercy joined them. Eventually, they bought the whole block, opening a new enlarged gym, a restaurant, a barbershop, a beauty salon, a pizza parlor, a swimming pool, and of course, a dancing school. They also changed the name of the gym: it would now be known as Victory Gym.

Sparkey Morrison continued to harass them for a while, determined to regain the title. Then, abruptly, his phone calls stopped and they never heard from him again. Rumor had it he was involved with a shady boxing syndicate in Las Vegas. Years later, they opened the *Sporting Gazette* to find his name plastered across the front page: "*Boxing Promoter Found Dead in Las Vegas Desert. Police Suspect Foul Play.*" Sparkey Morrison, the man determined to win at any cost, had now paid the ultimate price.

As the years passed, the close knit group of friends continued to lead a vibrant and prosperous life. Their business boomed, and the bond that bound them together grew stronger than ever.

Mercy never forgot Victoria. Every week he would take flowers to her grave. She would always be his first love, burned in his heart forevermore.